RETURN TO MASADA

Second Edition

ROBERT G. MAKIN

Editing, book design by Jonni Anderson, Starwatch Creations (Star-
watchCreations.com)

Front cover image courtesy Andreas Zeitler/Shutterstock.com
Back cover image courtesy ArtMari/Shutterstock.com

Books by Robert G. Makin:
Return to Masada
Return to Masada, Second Edition
Strathnaver
The Faces of Inanna
Aleister through the Looking Glass
Where the Clouds Sleep
Dirt McGirtt

Sons of Aaron Publishing

sonsofaaronpublishing.com

ACKNOWLEDGMENTS

It would have been impossible to author such a story without the help of my Hebrew teacher Max Jaffe, 32° or Richard Rebeck, 32°, the teacher who shared some of the beautiful mysticism of Judaism. The slide show concerning archeological digs at Masada, mentioned in the Prologue, and which I viewed at the Lancaster Theological seminary of the United Church of Christ, was a major force behind the story. Albert Pike's 17th Degree of the Scottish Rite certainly played an important role because of its content and the thrust of its teachings.

I think there are none to whom I am more grateful or indebted for their help in producing this book than the late Tam Mossman who provided "expeditious condensing," as he put it, and very able editing; and Kathleen Landers who found the manuscript gathering dust in my study and whose enthusiasm for it motivated me to keep trying to find a publisher, as a first time author.

I would especially like to thank my treasured friends Christy Saenz, Elaine Crutchfield, Joyce Bunch and Sandra Rodriques for their pats on the back and words of kindness and encouragement. I also thank the late Max Kaplan 33°, and the late Eugene Sayers 33°, for the insights and understanding that they were willing to share.

The list goes on and on, filled with warm memories and fun anecdotes. But then, what can we ever be or accomplish without the love of our friends?

CONTENTS

Acknowledgments iii

Prologue 1

1   The Eternal Fire...13

2   The Escape 25

3   Taken by Ruse 31

4   Flight 48

5   David and Soo-ooni 56

6   Raised from Profanity 65

7   A Little Prestidigitation 72

8   Concealment 77

9   Opening the Day 81

10 Scorpions 86

11 The Order of Malchesidek..95

12 The Ankh of Therapeute 102

13 Six...110

14 Reinventing the Wheel 171

15 The Ark..125

16 The Hammer...131

17 The Divine Spark 139

18 First Blood 146

19 Bad Dreams 154

20 Power's Corruption 162

21 The Prophecy 173

22 Zayin 180

Glossary of Names 191

About the Author 197

RETURN TO MASADA

Second Edition

ROBERT G. MAKIN

PROLOGUE

The employees' Christmas party had been a blast. "Or maybe a bash," Johnny B. Lewis cackled to himself as he made a third attempt to walk up a flight of stairs to the exit. "Or merely a debauch?"

Stumbling again, he sat down on the first step, laughing at himself. Very drunk, Johnny lit a cigarette, took a deep puff, and coughed. With one hand on the wall for support, he hoisted himself to his feet and renewed his attempt.

"How th' hell 'm I gonna get back to the dorm?" he mumbled. He *had* to be back and awake and in class by 10:30 tomorrow morning, in time for Professor Prill's slide show on ancient Judean archeology. But one problem lay in the way: the Pennsylvania State Police barracks that Johnny had to pass on the road to his dormitory. He lost his balance and sat down on the second step. *I'll just snooze a little in the car,* he thought, repressing his awareness that the outside temperature was down around 15 degrees.

Fahrenheit!

Plastered as he was, Johnny knew that if he fell asleep in the car, he could easily freeze to death before morning. In the car, he closed the door, didn't start the engine, but leaned his head against the back of the seat.

"Screw it," he muttered. "If I die, I die."

He fell asleep immediately and woke only half an hour later. Very cold, he looked around. There was no one in sight to watch him back out of his parking space. He glanced at his watch. 3:15 A.M. What were the possibilities of his being spotted, weaving, when he passed the police barracks? *Can't stay here any longer.* He started the 1968 Dodge Charger.

As he crept out of the parking lot, Johnny carefully watched his speed—not so fast as to draw attention, nor slow enough to signal his condition. *Can't get busted and risk missing classes. How embarrassing it would be for a seminarian to get a DUI!!* Lest he meander, he kept intense watch on the white line in the middle of the road. Making a very careful left turn, he drove at exactly 35 miles per hour, westbound on Lincoln Highway, Route 30, in Lancaster, Pennsylvania.

Back at the seminary dormitory, there was one parking space left in back, and he had to parallel park. He pulled up beside the car in front, put the Charger in reverse, and inched the big car back into its spot on his first try. Getting out, he discovered that both inner tires were exactly 10 inches from the curb. He had no recall of the trip from the party and wondered what had happened to his missing right rear hubcap.

The "B" in Johnny B. Lewis stood for Bertram, a traditional name on his father's side of the family. A tall man of 27 years with thin dark hair and a reddish beard, Johnny was divorced, with one child. He had been a stable boy, bartender, truck driver, gasoline jockey, preacher, short-order cook, insurance salesman, and rehabilitation counselor. He was now a general entrepreneur, and half-master of at least half a dozen other professions. His teaching degree didn't help much, because his college grades hadn't been high enough to get a job. *And that's okay,* he thought as he staggered up the back stairs, *'cuz otherwise I'd be stuck in one of those stinking bureaucracies they call high schools.*

All his working life, he'd had to start at the very bottom. Never satisfied with beginning positions, he kept trying for better.

Sitting on the seventh—or was it the eighth?—step from the top, he remembered the singing voice of his old friend Rick:

And who's gonna be the one
T' say it was no good what we done?
Dare a man t' say I'm too young,
For I'm gonna try for the sun . . .

But he didn't sit there very long, because the freezing concrete was draining the heat out of his butt.

"Hey, Johnny!" someone shouted. Squinting in the faint light from a street lamp, he saw Larry H. leaning out of his window. "Johnny, is that you? Pretty good parking job for a man who can't walk!" followed by laughter.

That was embarrassment enough. Johnny pulled himself together and staggered the rest of the way to his room in the dormitory, where restless thoughts of his ex-wife and three-year-old son kept him from sound sleep. In less than an hour, dreams of guilt and anguish brought him awake. He stumbled down the hall to the bathroom.

Running a stable that boarded twenty horses, Johnny's parents had taught him the work ethic, but not the patience it required. The seminary was a retreat—a place where he could escape the mainstream work-a-day world, into academic constructs: Beginning Greek. Hebrew. Christian mythology. Mysticism 101. But to Johnny, the world looked pretty bleak. And mysticism didn't address the questions he wanted answered.

"Why did God create man? Only to suffer and die? There must have been some reason for it," Johnny insisted to one of his professors.

"God created man to love Him and worship Him forever," was the canned answer. But Johnny couldn't accept that God's ego was quite that needy. What he was really asking was,

Should I kill myself or not?

If God gives a shit either way, why doesn't He say so?

Why doesn't He help a little bit? Why does my life have to be so hard?

But those merchants of masses, supposedly in the know, said only, "Love Him forever."

Johnny stormed at them in his thoughts. Their lives were very successful, and their wives and husbands loved them, and their children were there when they got home at night. And they didn't have to pay 40% of their income in child support, or go to jail when they lost their jobs and couldn't pay it. He'd only been jailed for four days that time, before his first unemployment check arrived. It was emotionally disrupting for an already emotionally disrupted young man.

His classes were fun, even a breeze, except for Greek, but he had a running "A" in it until he went to jail for losing his job. All his grades were much higher now because he had finally learned that most tests are written by idiots. In college, he had been too analytical, and in high school, too exacting. He dissected test questions in too much depth, but never took the opportunity to support his answers. *A confidence problem, maybe.*

The seminary professors were more fun than the ones he'd listened to in college. Dr. Paul S. Prill was in his sixties and taught Ministry to the Bereaved. Johnny thought that was pretty ironic, since Professor Prill looked just like Vincent Price—tall, thin, graying, and always dressed in a gray suit. Because of it, some students made gentle fun of his taste in clothing. Dr. Prill's lone affectation was wearing a gold ring whose insignia—of a pelican feeding her four young from a wound in her breast—matched the one carved into the cloister wall outside.

Prill's teaching was not especially inspirational, but he got his message across, and his occasional sidetracks made the classes fun. The field trip to the funeral parlor included lunch at Dr. Prill's expense. Not until the actual practice of counseling began did Johnny start to see the serious side of things.

His first field assignment was Mrs. Henry, whose son had just died. The whole time Johnny was with her, counseling techniques were far from his mind. Mrs. Henry was the same age as Johnny's own mother, her eyes were the same color as hers, and the whole experience was very disturbing. After that, he requested younger clients.

Sitting in Prill's classroom now, Johnny's head pounded like a kettledrum every time his heart was cruel enough to beat. His stomach was acidic and he felt that he was going to be sick at any moment. For breakfast at the refectory, he took only a cup of coffee and a small glass of tomato juice. That helped his stomach a little, but it would take a while for the headache to pass.

The summer before, Dr. Prill had returned from Israel with slides of archaeological digs in the Holy Land that he'd scheduled to show at 10:30, half an hour before class. Despite his hangover, Johnny made it a point to be there. Brownie points from Prill were worth it—and needed.

Moments after Johnny settled into his seat, the lights were darkened and paper blinds were pulled down to cover the tall windows. Johnny could hear the hardwood floor creak as Prill walked toward the projector. Each creak from the 130-year-old wood felt like a nail being driven into Johnny's brain. Someone pushed the heavy wooden door shut. It sounded to him like the blast of a goose gun, close up, 10-gauge, 6-foot barrel.

Prill's slides were disappointing—close-ups of pottery shards, the occasional Roman coin or corroded shekel, clothing fragments and bones. The focus of the dig was Masada, a site Johnny had never heard of. Thanks to its inaccessible location, it had been virtually ignored for centuries. But what had transpired there motivated twentieth century Israeli archaeologists to perform thorough—and ongoing—excavations.

****

Masada is a high plateau somewhat south of Jericho, near the Dead Sea's northwestern shore. Half a century before Christ, during the days of Mark Antony, one of Israel's kings had constructed a fortress and two palaces atop Masada. As Dr. Prill explained it, King Herod (The Son of Antipater), known as Herod the Great, feared that the Roman Mark

Antony, was about to give all of Judea to Cleopatra of Egypt. Many wondered that this never happened, since, according to Josephus Flavius, Mark Antony was "such a miserable slave to his lust for her." If that had happened, Herod's life might have been in grave danger.

"Thanks to its remote location, he believed his fortress at Masada was invulnerable—and Herod made sure that it was very well supplied with food, weapons and water," Dr. Prill went on. "The plateau stands to this day, 850 feet above the plain at one end, and 650 feet at the other. Herod built his summer palace on the northern lip, in the shade of Masada's cliffs. He spent much of his time there during Israel's sweltering summers.

"Over the following centuries, the fortress at Masada was maintained by Israel's later kings who, as in Cleopatra's time, were still puppets of Rome. In 70 AD, roughly a generation after Jesus' crucifixion, Judea rose against Rome. Judea lost. During this insurrection, according to the historian Josephus, a handful of Jewish zealots took Masada by ruse. And defended it until all but a chosen few of them were dead.

"Thereafter, for nearly 2000 years, Judea—Israel—did not exist as a nation. And so, today, Masada is Israel's Bunker Hill, her Gettysburg, her Dunkirk. Before the great Dispersion, Masada was the last spot where Jewish men and women stood free and independent, on their own soil."

By this time, Johnny was lost in his own thoughts. About his son, his former wife, his employment situation—all the things that had driven him back here. His first stay at the seminary had ended with his marriage, just as his current stay began with his divorce.

The next three slides depicted an ancient pair of sandals, a comb, and two braids woven from black hair.

Johnny froze.

He stared at the close-up of the sandals, the worn soles, the way they turned up at the corners . . . He stared at the way they were there on the screen, and then gone, vanishing into the next slide of scattered bones, skeletons found in a cave . . . vanishing into the back of his mind, and again, a close-up . . . too close. He was suffocating. It was hot, very hot, and damp. His head was throbbing and he broke out in a sweat. *What was it? Something too familiar—but what?*

Spinning, his head was spinning, and it was so high he didn't dare look down. Dizzying heights, and images of stone walls, but not on the screen, in his head, *not there in front of him, but THERE, in his mind, somewhere in the past* . . . his feet hurt, those sandals were cutting into them, his feet were bleeding from the rough thong between his toes. His mouth filled with a bitter taste, a taste from the past, from drinking water that had been standing too long in those stones.

"The taste of granite is no match for the spring at Ayin Feshka," he muttered. *Where did that thought come from? What was happening to him?*

"These bones," Dr. Prill was saying, "belonged to a young man, a young woman and a child of about three years of age."

Johnny struggled to his feet, dizzy with the onrush of more thoughts, more visions. *Dammit, was he hallucinating? This wasn't alcohol. What was this all about?* His eyes locked with the professor's. "They're too close," Johnny warned loudly, his voice rising to a shrill. This was urgent; why was Prill just standing there, staring at him? "They're too close," he shouted, staggering toward the professor. "Where is Zayin, now?"

Zayin!?

As if struck by a bolt of lightning, Prill's hand fell away from the slide projector. The two men locked into each other's eyes. Johnny gripped the lectern to steady himself as more images whirled before him. The room filled with men clad in white robes, reciting a language that Johnny didn't understand. *And he was standing among them, with Prill at his side!*

"*Haeeychan Zayin?*" (Where is Zayin?) Johnny's Aramaic was flawless. The rasping glottal fricative of the "ch" was drawn out for emphasis. The fully voiced "een" at the end of "Zayin" lifted in a tone of desperate command.

As if in a daze, Prill moved out from behind the projector, reaching for Johnny. *So he's finally come to me!* marveled Prill. *After all these years, he's finally come!*

****

Johnny opened his eyes. He had passed out and Prill had caught him before he'd landed on the floor. "So where did you learn Aramaic?" Prill was bending over him and offering him a glass of water. Gratefully, Johnny took a few sips and tried to remember what had happened. The two men were alone in the classroom. Where were the rest of the students?

"I ordered them to leave," said Prill, as if reading his mind.

Yes, slides. Masada. Prill's slide presentation of a place called Masada.

"What's Aramaic?" Johnny asked.

"You spoke to me in Aramaic. Don't you remember?"

"Remember!? You wouldn't believe what I remember! Dr. Prill, tell me—more about this place—Masada."

"Not now, Lewis. Not now. You need to go home and get some sleep. Rest. Come and see me tonight. Rest and come to my place at seven tonight."

Prill watched Johnny from the window as he crossed the walks in front of the building and headed toward the library. "No, he won't go and lie down." Prill shook his head, smiling to himself. It was going to be quite an evening. They would sit for hours and talk . . . get caught up on things . . .

Johnny knew his head was spinning from more than a hangover. It was like a door had opened somewhere inside, to another world, another lifetime.

Masada had become as real to him as a recent memory, as familiar to him as the house where he grew up. *The Complete Works of Josephus*—that was the book he needed. Quickly he pulled it down from the shelf and started reading. There it was, the whole story which he already knew by heart, stone by stone, with every fissure, every crack . . . it was all there, just as he'd remembered. There was the cart path on the west side of the mesa; and the serpentine path, on the east side . . .

He found more recent writings about Masada on the same library shelf. Some of these had aerial photographs which fascinated and amazed him. The thirty-eight towers that once existed on Masada were now gone. The buildings were all in ruins. It was a shock to him, like returning home after a tornado and finding everything suddenly gone. Even the synagogues were rubble. There had been two. The summer palace which had been so magnificent, rubble and ruin.

After five hours of reading Josephus' *War Books* and *Antiquities,* Johnny needed to speak more with the man who'd opened the gate to these thoughts and feelings. *How can I go to Prill after making such an ass of myself in his class? He must think I'm a total shithead. And what was it I said before I completely lost it? I can't even remember the words. I wonder if he even understood what I said. He probably did. I hope it wasn't some inane insult or something.*

****

Paul S. Prill's apartment was on the top floor of a four-story building at the corner of School Street and Mulberry. He'd chosen the address for its seclusion. His front door opened on a bedroom to the left and a kitchen and dinette at the far end. It was furnished comfortably, if inexpensively. For a grad school professor of more than 30 years, a very humble apartment.

Dr. Prill was Marge Kauffman's favorite topic of conversation. Like him, she was in her sixties. Marge had been working in the seminary's offices ever since she graduated from high school. "A Lifer," she had begun to call herself.

"When Paul came here in 1950," she told Denise, the new secretary, "he didn't even have his first doctorate. But he was driving a nice new Chevy, at least. Now he doesn't even own a car."

For Marge, Paul S. Prill had been a crushing disappointment. The first time they met, his deep brown gaze had weakened her knees, and she had set out to make him her own.

"In the Fifties," she told Denise, "there wasn't much a girl could do. If I was too forward, he'd think I wasn't a nice girl. But if I didn't make any moves, he'd never notice me."

"Today we just trip and jump on 'em," Denise replied with a giggle. "Well. Maybe it's not quite like that." Laughing.

Marge had invited Paul Prill to come to her church. The following Sunday, she was delighted to see him in one of the rear pews, but disappointed when he declined to sit with her.

"And so it went. How could I know he'd never marry? Hell, he never even dated anybody that I know of. Bet you that old fool's still a virgin."

****

Dr. Prill never told anyone that in the final days of the war he had lost his French wife in Normandy. He'd never revealed to anyone his role in the war, smuggling many of France's art treasures to hidden safekeeping. But then, Paul Prill seldom talked privately with anyone.

He sat at his small dinner table with a bowl of sprouts, nuts, and raw broccoli as he did every night. He debated whether he should have taken a more active, visible role in the life of the seminary.

As always, his conclusion was the same:

No! That is not why I came here!

****

"It's not like he's been a hermit, exactly. But he's *like* a hermit," Marge told Denise. "He helped . . . naaw, that's wrong! On his own, he secured *and managed* the funding for that halfway house down on South Duke. After that, he started this Endowment—whatever that is. Before it goes anywhere, we'll all be dead and buried.

"I think Paul's working at some orphanage. He's been odd, ever since his first trip to the Middle East in 1957, right after he came to work here. Now he goes back to Israel every two or three years. Matter of fact, he just returned from there."

****

Dr. Prill had saved enough money to purchase a two-family rental property. Once he'd paid off the mortgage—in less than five years—he placed the duplex in an endowment. The rent money could be used to buy more rental properties all over the United States, and the rents they generated would buy even more.

The Endowment provided that when the total rents coming from this project were enough, that half of the income would be used to create and support a very special school. Marge was frustrated by Dr. Prill's comment, "We'll have no more Einsteins struggling to pay tuition to go to inferior schools. We'll find the best that we have and give them the best education available."

****

Seated at his table, Dr. Prill closed his eyes to pray.

"Father! God Almighty. *El Shadai* of the deserts and mountains. God of my fathers and theirs. Forgive my conceits about my work. Help me recognize my mortal condition and forgive my hopes for my fellow man. And my belief that, through my effort, I can make a difference. How kind you are, Great God, to provide me with the nourishment I am about to eat. I beg you, Lord, to bless these creatures of yours, whose lives I must consume to nourish my own life."

Dr. Prill opened his eyes and took the first bite of his heavy salad. Chewing slowly, he could feel the joy in the life of his food bursting in his mouth. Eating for him was a form of meditation. He was a true Essene, believing that it was not the vitamins, minerals and carbohydrates but the life his food contained, that nourished him. The knock at his door startled him. He jumped, dropping his fork. *It's him. He's early.*

"It's young Mr. Lewis, of course!" Prill said. "Come in. Make yourself comfortable."

The professor's smile was enough to relax a sheepish Johnny Lewis—for the moment. Dr. Prill went to the table, covered the bowl he'd been eating from, and put it in the refrigerator. Then he put a kettle on for tea.

When was the last time he'd had to use this stove? Ah, yes, when Marge dropped in several years ago. She sure was full of herself that day, telling him to start an IRA or some kind of retirement fund, instead of spending all his money on charities like the Endowment. He was disappointed that she even found out about it—a slip of the tongue in his attorney's office . . . Prill would love to see the expression on her face if ever she ever found out about the other ones!

Back in the front room, he announced that tea would be ready in a few minutes and sat down in his favorite reading chair.

Johnny was uncomfortable. Dr. Prill's presence dominated the room. There was an almost palpable energy around him that Johnny thought he could just about see. Johnny's face was still tear-stained and his eyes were red, not only from the remnants of his hangover.

"Mr. Lewis? You look like hell. I hope you're feeling better."

"I've had a hell of a day."

"I'm acquainted with part of that day. You were partying last night? Hope you don't do that too often. It's not healthy."

"Guess I do. It seems to pass the time." Johnny winced as a wave of discomfort swept over him. He hadn't realized that the faculty knew about his nightly carousing. He had convinced himself that it was easier to sleep with a few drinks in him. *Easier to pass out than go to sleep, sometimes.*

"You're here about Masada, I suppose?"

"Dr. Prill, I don't think I can even describe what happened to me in your class today. It was very intense."

Johnny had spent the day reflecting on his experience. Masada was much on his mind but he had come to understand that the woman and child were probably not his in some past life. His rush of guilt was a result of his own present-life experience, losing his wife and child to divorce, not to death. It was easy to suddenly associate his own experiences with that poor young man on Masada who had had to do even worse to his family than Johnny had done with a divorce. But that understanding didn't explain the new memories he thought he had of a past life ending at Masada.

"I was expecting you, but not so soon. In a couple of days, maybe," from Prill.

"Expecting me? I don't understand."

"It'll be a long time before you do. Fully." Dr. Prill took a deep breath. "I'll tell you what I know, or what I can. First, what about your experiences? This morning."

"This is a bit strange, Dr. Prill."

"It will get stranger! You can trust me on that."

"Okay." Johnny B. was getting uneasy again. "I was watching your slide show."

Dr. Prill waited quietly, his insignia ring glistening under the lamp.

"I had a hangover from the Christmas party last night, so I wasn't really with it, just watching and listening. I mean, it kept my attention; it was an interesting show. Thanks for bringing us those slides."

Dr. Prill, uncharacteristically direct, replied, "In what way did you find them interesting?" *I have to make him say it,* Prill thought.

Growing steadily more uneasy, Johnny could feel the power of the man. How could he flee from this place without being rude? "Dr. Prill, do you believe in reincarnation?"

Prill smiled a long slow "Yes."

"The Church doesn't teach that."

"Ah, but it used to, before the first Vatican Council. That was so long ago the only ones who remember are theologians and historians. But the Church did teach what it used to call Transmigration of the Soul. This is a version of it. The New Testament is thick with references to it. Now it's called reincarnation. Remember John 3:3, '. . . Unless one is born again he cannot see the Kingdom of God'; and John 3:13, 'No one has ascended into heaven but he who has descended from heaven . . .' Others acknowledge the experience, but refer to it as genetic remembrance. You know, the idea that your ancestors' memories are carried in your DNA?" He smiled. "Go on. Did you have a genetic remembrance this morning or a past life memory?"

"I responded to the slide show like most others. It was interesting, but I wasn't exactly enthralled. Then came your pictures of the sandals and the braids and skeletons."

"Mr. Lewis, may I interrupt you for a moment? You're telling me exactly what I expected. To prove it, let me finish for you. You think they were your sandals, don't you? That you were there on Masada when all that took place?"

Johnny was astonished. "How did you know that? Well, maybe the sandals . . ." His voice drifted off as he was caught up in thought. *I could have had sandals like that.* His feet began to annoy him again at the thought. It seemed that a piece of sand or grit of some sort was caught between his toe and the leather thong. He crossed his legs and rubbed his foot through the shoe. "They weren't very comfortable sandals. My feet hurt at the very thought of them."

Dr. Prill smiled. The kettle on the stove started to shrill and he rose, heading for the kitchen.

While Prill was gone, Johnny's eye wandered to the couch where a magazine lay open to the first page of an article and an aerial photograph of Masada. Under the photo was the article's title, "Dr. Jacob Levi to Dig for Sacred Ark at Masada."

Prill reappeared with a plate of cookies, a teapot and cups. "Do you take milk?"

"No thanks. Just sugar."

Johnny dropped two lumps into his cup, reached for a cookie and munched thoughtfully.

"I thought at first that the skeletons had belonged to me and my family. If that were true, then I would have been their killer. The people of Masada died by mass suicide with the women and children being slaughtered by the men in the family."

"The rationale was to prevent them from falling into slavery under Rome. But there's so much more. Do you remember the role you played?"

"Vaguely," Johnny replied. "No, I guess not. But you seem to readily accept that I can remember a past life involving Masada. This is as strange to me as my acceptance of it. I do wonder if you're involved somehow?"

"Somehow? Yes. *Somehow.* Are you ready to begin your education?" Dr. Prill's eyes twinkled. "We've so much to do. I've been looking for you for a long time. I knew you'd come, but I didn't know when, or who you would be. First let me tell you that the bodies found at Masada were not your family, exactly, but your role was much more comprehensive than that of an innocent bystander."

Prill clasped both hands behind his head and leaned back in his chair, smiling. "Maybe I should begin by telling you the story. Hopefully that will stimulate more of your own memories. I have memories of my own, you see. I was at Masada too, during those years. Your involvement at that time was peripheral, but intense enough that I'm not surprised that you remember it, after all this time. Your real involvement is only about to begin, as you will see. It will be necessary, of course, that we go to Masada. And we should leave soon. Maybe over the next few weeks your memories will return in full."

1

The Eternal Fire

And one of the Elders said unto me: "Who are these who are arrayed in white robes and whence came they?"

And I said unto to him: "Venerable, thou knowest."

And he unto me: "These are they who have been purified by sorrow and suffering, and by the intercession and blood of the redeemer. Therefor stand they before the throne of El Shadai and serve him day and night in His temple. And He who sits upon the throne shall dwell among them and sustain them, and they shall not hunger any more; neither thirst, anymore. The sun shall not scorch them, nor fire again torture them; for the Lamb who sits upon the throne shall lead them unto the living springs of truth, and God shall wipe away all tears from their eyes."

Masada; 1st Century C.E.

An old man was seated on the edge of Masada's western casement wall, muttering.

"Does he often mumble like that?" whispered the girl to the young man beside her.

"Only when he meditates, Soo-ooni. Did you hear what he said?"

"I think he said *'Be-re-shit.'*"

"It did sound like that, I wonder what he means. Is he quoting Torah?"

In memory, the old man remembered himself as a very small boy, on the steps leading up to the great temple in Jerusalem, his earliest memory.

Jerusalem; 0006 C.E.+

The half-naked seven-year-old got up from where he had been sitting. His tawny skin and matted black hair were filthy from sleeping on the ground, with animals for warmth. Every day, the boy would come to the steps of the temple where all sorts of merchants of every kind had stands and booths. They sold marvels and goods from as far away as Persia, from the headwaters of the River Nile, from the icy mountains north of Rome.

Most of the merchants called the boy "little thief," but he knew that was not really a name and did not answer to it.

"Insolent robber!" a voice shouted.

"Never call me a thief, you fat villain," cried a woman. "It's you who asks too much for bread." The boy turned to look. He saw a woman of about 35, her brown hair streaked with gray. "This city's full of thieves!" she shrieked, "and you're the worst of them."

The bread seller was growing angry. "Get out of here, hag, before you draw soldiers to carry you away."

The merchant had a name, and the boy wished that he had one too, not the street name, Pele, he called himself, but a real name. People would call out "Itzchak," and the bread seller would always look, because Itzchak was the name that belonged to him—although some people called him other things. The woman had called the bread seller "robber," but some called him "Sadducee." The bread seller didn't like that name for some reason, although he would answer to it.

"My name," said the little boy, "must be Heyyu, since that is what most people call me."

"No," Itzchak the bread seller told him. "Your name is what your father gave you, or what others give you and you accept. Heyyu is not a name."

"I never had a father to name me."

"Of course you had a father. Here, have a crust of this loaf."

Some days, like on this one, one or two of the men who were there made the boy feel uneasy. They were not garbed in two or more pieces of clothing of different colors. These men wore only one piece of clothing: usually a white robe if the weather was chilly, or a loincloth and shirt on hot days. They wore no head covers. Their hair was long and wild-looking, always braided into a single strand and thrown forward over one shoulder.

People called beggars also wore loincloths, but these men didn't beg. When they were in the market, the boy noticed that people spoke more softly, and sometimes he would hear the word *wizard* or *watcher.*

"They are the pious ones," Leah had told him. The boy didn't know the word *wife,* but he knew the word *property,* and he knew that Leah was Itzchak's. Itzchak would tell her to fetch this, or carry that, and Leah always did.

"What are *pious ones?*" the boy asked that day.

Leah looked down at the boy. She put a bundle of grain back on Itzchak's stand, spit over her shoulder as she sometimes did, and sat down on the ground beside the boy.

"Some call them Watchers. They come, and they look around, then they go back to their farm and their stone walls at the oasis near the Sea of Salt."

"Like that one is watching me?" the boy asked.

"Yes," she said. "Some say they are looking for the Messiah, who is yet to come. Others say they are evil and to be feared. Yet others say they are good and to be welcomed. No one really knows for sure. But you know, no one has ever seen them eat!"

Itzchak stopped haggling over the price of a loaf of bread. "Leah! What are you doing? Go grind the wheat as I told you to do."

Leah got to her feet.

"Wait," the boy said. "Tell me about the light I see around them. What is it?"

Her expression changed, and she looked hard at the boy. She brushed some hair out of her face with a wave of her hand. "What light?"

"The light around them is brighter than around others. Can't you see it?"

"No," Leah replied harshly. She picked up the grain, glanced again at the Watchers, and hurried off.

The boy turned his gaze on the Watchers. They looked very thin. Of course they were, if they didn't eat, he thought. He marveled at how the white light seemed to play around their bodies. The men seemed to become aware of him and returned his gaze. As they did so, the boy saw their light change color, becoming pale blue, and then magenta.

The Watchers turned away from the temple area, walking in the direction of the south gate. The boy seemed to feel them calling to him, *Come with us, come with us.*

The boy followed them with his eyes. *I can't go,* he thought. He had to eat, and the Watchers don't eat. His food was what Itzchak and Leah gave him, and what he could steal.

The Watchers turned the corner of a building and disappeared from sight. The boy's big black eyes turned to where Itzchak had been, but the bread seller wasn't there any more, and his stand had been carried away.

Other merchants were packing their stands and leaving. "Best hurry," he heard one say to another. "The sun is almost down. The *Shabbat* is upon us."

The boy knew the word: *Shabbat* was the day when he couldn't eat. Now, all the vendors would go home for *Shabbat*, and he would have no one to steal food from.

With the sun going down, it was cooling off rapidly, but the boy knew where to keep warm for the night: The smoldering garbage dump at the edge of the city. *Gehenna* it was called, and he would at least be warm enough there.

****

In the first light of Shabbat, the boy could see the outline of the hills in the distance, with a small tree here and there. He could hear the song of morning birds, but closer to him was an intermittent rustling—the sound of a rat scavenging in the rubbish. Looking down, he found a date that was overripe, but not yet rotten.

"Who are you and what do you think you're doing?"

The boy turned, startled. Three boys, all older, were glaring back at him. All were deeply tanned from constant outdoor living. Their hair was matted and black like his, and only one of them had any teeth. Their bodies were nearly covered with dirt. So it was with these children of Gehenna.

The biggest boy of the group had spoken. "I said, 'Who are you?'" His tone was quieter but menacing. "You know, Trespasser, that date in your hand belongs to me."

"I found it here on the ground," the boy said.

"Hear that?" the boy with teeth said to the other two. "This puny little urchin is not only stealing my food, but is arrogant as well!" Now just out of reach from the boy, he swung the large stick in his hand, catching the boy on the chin. The end of the stick had been sharpened on a rock for just such a purpose, and the point tore a ragged cut.

The boy dropped the fruit, let out a shriek and fell back, one hand on his chin, his eyes round in fear. His attacker jumped forward swinging the stick again. This time the boy dodged, and the stick missed its mark.

"Sapas, you missed!" one of the others called.

"Yes, Sapas, try again," said the other.

HaSapas glared back at them. "Watch your mouth, shitface. It'll be you next time." He popped the date in his mouth and began chewing.

"So, little trespasser," he said through his chewing, "I'm going to call you Tzaleket, because today I have given you a scar. Maybe it'll remind you who owns Gehenna."

The boy had been exposed to many languages in this center-of-the-universe city, Jerusalem. While he didn't know any of the languages well, he knew that HaSapas meant 'the Greek,' and that Tzaleket meant scar. He also knew that the Greek boy did not own the dump; no one did. But if he wanted to think he owned it, that was no concern of the boy's.

"There are others here who claim the food," he said to himself fearfully, realizing he would have to compete with them for food if he stayed there.

Every evening a man would come to the dump with a cart of refuse—usually broken furniture, rotted cloth which had once been clothing, or ashes from someone's fire. But this time, the man brought a small basket of rotting olives, covered with mold. Another child, younger than the boy, who was half crazed with hunger grabbed one of them before waiting for HaSapas to eat his fill. HaSapas attacked him with hysterical fury and beat him nearly to death with his stick.

Around the boy's seventh day at Gehenna, his second Shabbat, he dreamed of a tall, slender man with nearly white hair. The man seemed very old, yet not suffering from the infirmities of age. He had dark piercing eyes that seemed to see right through him. The hair had a natural curl to it and was tied at the back of his head in a tightly braided coil that came down over one shoulder. *A Watcher*, thought the boy fearfully.

"Who are you?" the boy asked in his dream.

"You may call me Simon," the man said. "I am your mentor."

"What is a mentor?" the boy asked.

"One who teaches or helps."

"Why are you in my dream? I dream only of food and shelter. Why are you here?"

"When people are in great need, sometimes help finds them," Simon told him.

"If you are my help, give me food. Give me a name!" In the dream, the boy began crying quietly. He glanced around and saw stone walls, and a window overlooking a ravine. "Simon, where is this place?"

"You already know. Soon you will come here, when you are ready."

"I think I'll starve first."

Simon walked to the window and looked out thoughtfully. "But you already know how to draw to yourself the food you need."

"You mock me," the boy said bitterly. "How can I eat stones and rotted cloth? Am I a god? How can I create anything but more hunger?"

"Step over here." Simon spoke with kindness, not with the stern tone of authority underlined with anger that Itzchak the bread seller sometimes used.

In his dream, the boy saw himself walk to where Simon was standing.

"Now, hold your hand straight out in front of you." Simon held his own hands in front of him, the palm turned upward. "Like this."

The boy saw himself do the same thing.

"Now look at the palm of your hand. In your palm, picture in your mind's eye, the food you would like to be there."

The boy looked at Simon. The man's face radiated peace. The deeply etched lines in his face were accented by the sharp curve of his nose and heavy white beard. His whole body was encased in white light. At the edges of the light, pastels changed colors from pale blue to magenta and back to blue.

"You're one of them, aren't you? A Watcher."

Simon brushed his hand against his thigh, straightening his white robe. "I am what I am. You will know more when it is time. Now hold out your hands, boy, if you want to eat."

The boy looked at his own empty palms. In the daytime his hand was dirty. Now, in the dream, it was perfectly clean. He visualized dates—whole, ripe, sweet dates.

"Not so many," Simon warned him. "Don't create more than you can eat."

The boy smiled and visualized only three dates, but bigger ones.

"That's better," Simon told him, amused. "Now lower your hand and don't drop them. With dirt they aren't as tasty."

The first light of dawn was coloring the eastern sky with rosy brightness when the boy awoke, shivering and aching with hunger. Immediately he began foraging for a scrap he may have missed the evening before. In his frustration, he kicked a clump of rotted cloth, and it fell away to reveal three plump dates.

He looked around to see if HaSapas and any of the others were nearby. No, all was quiet. The boy sat down and began wolfing down the fruit.

Where had they come from? he wondered. Dreams weren't real. Things like this couldn't happen!

A rat had smelled the dates and was creeping nearer. "Don't come any closer," he warned it. "I'll call my friend Simon."

He'd never had a friend before. It was a new and warm feeling. Itzchak was like a friend, but not really. He didn't always give the boy bread, and he called him a beggar. No, he thought bitterly. He wasn't a beggar, just a thief and a starving orphan. HaSapas called him Tzaleket, but he didn't like that.

"I am not Tzaleket. I am *Me!*" He thumped himself on the chest proudly, saying it again. "I am a thief and a starving orphan with a friend named Simon." Still smiling, he drifted back to sleep.

Hearing footsteps, he opened his eyes to see HaSapas coming toward him. He stood and quickly backed away. All of the other children living in Gehenna feared the cruelty of HaSapas, and none would willingly allow him within ten cubits. "Tzaleket!" HaSapas was shouting. The boy tried to put more distance between them. "Tzaleket! Stop backing away!" The boy stopped and let HaSapas get a little closer, but not so near as to be able to use his stick.

HaSapas looked angry, as usual. He was picking out small stones on the ground and striking them with his stick as he walked along.

"You little whore's son. Someone saw you eating dates. Where are they?"

In my belly, the boy thought. "There are no dates."

"Don't lie to me. I'll twist your head off and eat your ears!" HaSapas was in a half crouch, as though getting ready to spring. He held his stick by the end and swung it slowly about his head.

"There are no dates, Sapas. See for yourself." He held his palms outward so HaSapas could see them. "Look around. Do you see any dates there? Any kind of food?"

HaSapas leaped, swinging his stick to catch the boy on the side of the head. But the boy ducked the blow and ran as fast as his small legs could carry him. HaSapas stood scowling after him, then began digging around in the refuse.

For the next few days, the boy stayed far out of HaSapas's sight. HaSapas ignored him, but to the other children, he seemed even crueler than before.

The dreams came again.

Two nights later, near dawn, Simon appeared to him.

"Hello, friend Simon," said the boy's dreaming self.

Simon seemed tired. His face was peaceful, but drawn. "Little one, you need to learn to defend against the beast. Do you know what a lion is?"

"No."

"Then look out the window."

The boy saw the night sky, a deep wadi or dry ravine with scattered rocks, and the occasional bush or small tree. As he was looking up at the twinkling stars, the scene changed and the wash faded into a blur.

Slowly, a new scene formed outside the window: Gehenna!

He saw a small dirty child, fitfully sleeping, who had half-buried himself in the filth in order to keep warm. A large beast was sneaking around the pile of trash, stalking him.

"Boy!" directed Simon, "take this from my hand."

It was a long piece of leather, very heavy and thick at one end, but it tapered along its length until it was very thin. It was a whip, much like the ones he had seen in the hands of Roman soldiers.

"Will you whip the beast?" the boy asked.

"No. I cannot. It exists only in your dream. Here, take it." He held out the handle; the boy took it and felt the leather. This was a truly strange dream!

"Now," Simon told him, "come to the window so that you are within reach."

Whip in hand, the boy crossed to the window and watched as the beast stalked his sleeping body. The creature was crouched down, ready to spring.

"Hurry," Simon urged. "Strike before it pounces." The beast's hind legs twitched, much like a cat's before the pounce. The boy raised the whip, which suddenly felt very light, and lashed the lion across the neck.

The dream ended.

"Simon," he called out. The sound of his own voice woke him, and he saw the glow of first light brightening over the eastern hill. Half awake, he fell silent and listened fearfully for the beast. There were no sounds apart from the crackle of eternal fires, the scavenging of rats, the far-off voice of another child of Gehenna crying or talking in his sleep.

He opened his eyes. The city wall was in sight, beyond the edge of the dump, with a flock of birds sitting on it, chirping. One of the children of the dump stood nearby, trying vainly to figure out how to catch one of them for breakfast.

Standing up, he saw HaSapas's two companions, dragging HaSapas through the rubbish, away from him.

"There he is," said one in a hushed voice.

"I see him," the other replied, just above a whisper. "Let's get out of here. What did he do to you?" he asked HaSapas, eyeing the welt and swelling at the back of the boy's neck.

"Nothing. I fell. Get him for me."

The two stood and turned toward the boy they called Tzaleket, evil in their eyes. "Come here," one called out.

The boy began to back away more quickly, then turned and ran for the city gates. If he could make it into the city, perhaps he could lose them in the tangled streets. And Itzchak would protect him.

But the older boys were too fast for him. Overtaking him, one knocked him to the ground and held his legs.

The other boy sat on his chest. "What did you do to HaSapas, Tzaleket?" Down his left arm ran a long scar that looked like a sword slash. It was so deep, his bicep seemed to have no muscle in it. Another scar had cleft a part in his right eyebrow, giving the impression that he had three eyebrows. He had no teeth, except one rotted stump on the right side of his upper jaw.

He squinted slightly. With his good right arm, he suddenly slapped the boy's face, hard. "I asked you a question, Tzaleket. What did you do to HaSapas?"

"Nothing," the boy gasped. "Nothing."

"You lie." His breath was fast, and he was working his face muscles as though in pain. The older boy delivered another slap, and another, gloating in his victim's weakness. He drew back his arm and made a tight fist.

"Tell what you did to HaSapas, or I'm going to crush your face like the shell of an egg."

"Stop!" a man's voice demanded.

Amazement crept over the older boy's face. His fist froze in mid-air. A gnarled old hand, the skin wrinkled from many hours in the sun and many years of labor, was grasping his wrist.

The older boy holding his legs had let go and run away. Three Eyebrows stopped struggling, and the hand released him.

"Get up, both of you." With his attacker off his chest, the boy lifted his head. The stranger, wearing a dusty white robe, was tall and very slender, of great age, with snowy white hair drawn back into a single braid behind his head. His eyes were deeply lined, and his nose leaned slightly to the left, as though he had been punched there, hard.

Had the boy been rescued? He wasn't sure, so great was his astonishment.

"Simon?" he whispered.

"Why trouble yourself with this urchin?" the older boy sneered. "So poor he even lacks a name. *We* named him—Tzaleket, for the scar HaSapas gave him. He belongs to us."

"But he already has a name—Hjarai. And Hjarai he has always been."

Friend Simon had come to give him a name! The boy's fear began to melt away and he began to cry. The other boy seemed not to notice. He was watching only for a chance to run.

Hjarai, ['Hj' containing the glottal fricative—like clearing one's throat] the boy thought, savoring the name. It sounded like *Hara*, meaning *mountain*.

"Yes," said Simon. "It does sound like 'Hara'. It is because you are like a mountain, but not the same as one. And a mountain is where you will find the end of your task."

He hears my thoughts! Hjarai realized.

"Yes, I do. Now, where is the beast of last night?"

"What is my task?"

"Take me to the beast," Simon said. "Ah, there he is! Come."

Simon started into the dump, walking deliberately among the refuse and ashes, to where the boys had left HaSapas, who wore a huge, angry welt across his neck. At the top of his spine, a large swelling was turning black. Beneath the dirt and tanned skin, HaSapas's face was green and sickly. As Simon drew near him, his eyes opened in fear.

Kneeling beside him, Simon placed a hand over HaSapas's head. Hjarai saw the white light encasing Simon shrink back into his body and seem to bloom out around his hand.

"I feel hot," said HaSapas.

"It will pass."

Now Simon moved to the lump on HaSapas's neck. Simon's hand glowed brighter. As it did, the darkness around the lump faded. Almost imperceptibly, the swelling began to diminish. When Simon pulled back his hand, the lump was gone. The welt had disappeared.

"Remember this, Yacob: Never underestimate the powers of those unknown to you. Never harm or injure others." His face was still stern, yet his voice was kind and soft. "And perhaps Hjarai can remember to protect himself more gently. Yacob, I may not be here to help you again. Give love—whatever love you have—to others around you. It can only return to you, and you can only be the happier, bathed in your own love. Each injury you cause others brings you only pain. The love you give others, brings you joy."

Simon removed his hand, and his light returned to normal.

"Hjarai, we will go now."

****

Masada

The old man sitting on the wall, who had once been called Hjarai, turned away from his memories. This was not a time for daydreaming and remembering, but for meditation—and very serious meditation it would have to be.

"How can I do it?" he asked himself again. "How can I succeed in the end when I am so unworthy?" He opened his eyes to view the plain below and wondered when they would come. For come they must, and he knew it. He was just an old man living in fear.

And it's your fear that will hold you back, muttered the voice in his mind.

"Yes, Simon. That is what you always tell me," he replied to his old teacher's memory. "But how can I let go of these fears when they are so close to coming true?"

You still cling to the temporal, Harai. The temporal is illusion. All men cling to their illusions. What makes you different is that you can recognize them for what they are. When will you begin to recognize them?

"I do recognize them. But I have tried to join you without success."

It is not yet time for you to do so. The prophecy and the end of your task are still ahead of you.

"I have no prophecy to give," Harai muttered half aloud.

Harai, said the memory in that intimate voice of command. *Listen to yourself. What is a prophet?*

"A spokesman for *El Shadai,* God Almighty."

Yes, Harai. And from whence come the words which the prophet speaks?

"A true prophecy comes out of a human's mouth, spoken by his lips but with the Voice of God."

Do you not know that when Adonai is ready, your lips will move as though they are His? You will have no need for concern as to what they say because their words will be spoken by El Shadai.

"But what good is prophecy to dead people? We know that none will survive this place."

Harai, you know that the future is not written on God's Tablets. He has given us the freedom to choose our own paths. These people can yet be saved. And even though they may die here, the words of God will be written in their souls and they will benefit in their lives to come.

Harai rose from his seat on the wall, shook his head to try to clear it of the imagined conversation and headed for the small shelter where it was his custom to sleep. The people of Masada camped, some in the huts and barracks where the soldiers had stayed, and some in pretended luxury in the summer palace that Herod the Great had constructed on the north lip of the plateau. Soo-ooni and her parents were in one of the tents. Soo-ooni, cleaning a cooking pot, looked up as Harai walked past.

He was a thin and withered man whom they often called Abbi Yashan, or old father. He was not the only Essene at Masada, but as the only one from the inner circle, he commanded much respect. Some still feared him, as they had feared Essenes in Jerusalem when Harai was a boy. Others came to him for advice and prayer and asked him to teach in one of the several synagogues they had built on Masada.

He agreed, but they didn't much like his teachings, because as a true Essene, he held no hate for Israel's enemies. He taught only of peace, the Golden Rule, and return to God. His only remaining student was Soo-ooni's friend David.

"Greetings, Abbi Yashan," Soo-ooni called out.

"Hello again, Soo-ooni."

2

The Escape

Jerusalem

In Jerusalem, much of the rioting had quieted, but people were still milling around the streets. When people are angry and fearful, extreme hunger tends to calm them. Since Flavius Silva had besieged Jerusalem four weeks before, no food had entered the city. Everyone was hungry. Rumors had it that Yoseph Ben Matatyahu, the General of Galilee, had turned traitor.

Was that how Flavius got here so quickly? Jonathan wondered. *What will become of Jerusalem now? Surely it cannot resist much longer.*

Judea had been a rumbling sea of discontent for generations under the constant occupation of Rome. In the past year, the high priests of the temple had passed a ruling that no foreigner would be permitted to make sacrifices at the temple. Since it had been the custom of Rome to make an annual sacrifice out of respect to Judaism, this was taken as a direct insult. Rome insisted on making the sacrifice, adding insult to injury by placing the Roman banner in front of the temple. The people of Judea called this the "abomination which defiles" [the temple]. Judea rose in protest. Nero sent in the Tenth Legion under Flavius Silva to put down the rebellion. Yoseph Ben Matatyahu had been appointed by the Romans to be the governor of Galilee and therefore was the head of the Jewish forces to first meet the invasion by the Tenth Legion. In the view of Yoseph (a.k.a. Josephus in the Latin format) surrender was the only logical option with its object of saving Jewish lives. Josephus accompanied Flavius Silva and the Tenth Legion to Jerusalem. The city, now under siege, refused to surrender, with Josephus negotiating on Rome's behalf.

The darkness was thick and smoky, the night filled with screams and angry swearing. Grey stone and stucco walls framed streets through which flowed the hungry, the sick and the frightened.

"I suppose Jerusalem has seen worse times," declared Jair, barely audible above the noise of the crowd.

"But none that anyone can remember," snapped Jonathan.

"I think this is the entrance. Hurry, and maybe we can bypass some of this mob."

The two men, wearing Jerusalem sandals and coarsely spun loose-fitting robes to ward off the night air, ducked into a low opening off the dirt street. Through a low arch, the two men entered a large courtyard. The stone paving and neatly laid mosaics under their feet had been part of the property of a wealthy family who had abandoned their home in the face of the terror at hand, the Tenth Legion of Rome.

"This way, Jonathan!" Near the far side of the courtyard, they turned and paused before a heavy wooden door. "This leads under the temple and to the valley floor beneath. From there, we can get out of Jerusalem."

"Jair, do you think we can get away with it?"

"Before you gentlemen hurry off," came a voice from the darkness, "would you care for a little food?"

The two froze. Lips close to Jair's ear, Jonathan whispered, "What's that?"

"I thought this courtyard was empty," Jair whispered in reply.

"He offered us food! I haven't had a bite in at least two days."

"Do you think he's from the temple?"

"I don't know." Jonathan shook his head. "They don't have any food either."

"I haven't eaten in days myself," Jair had forced his body to forget how hungry he was.

"Maybe it's a trap."

"Gentlemen, I am called Itzchak Ben Itzchak by my brothers. My offer is sincere. Were I trying to trap you, I would have done well, since the passage you seek is through a locked door."

Indeed, it would not open. Both men turned as the stranger stepped out of the shadows, suddenly visible in the moonlight. "A Pious One!" Jonathan whispered hoarsely.

"We prefer some of your other nicknames for us."

"No one knows what you call yourselves."

"I have told you, I am called Itzchak. Let that suffice. Here is bread and dried figs." He extended a cloth bag. "Take, eat and give to others." His other hand held a skin full of wine. "Take, drink, and give to the thirsty."

After taking some of what was in the bag, Jonathan handed it to Jair. Both ate ravenously as Itzchak silently watched. When Jair and Jonathan were finished, they thanked him.

"Take these also," offered Itzchak, handing them four unlighted torches. "They will help you find the end of this passage you have chosen. Now go through the door. I have opened it. Let your feet hurry you to Masada. My brother Harai is there, with some others. When you arrive there, give him this jewel." In his hand lay an ankh of coin silver, about the width of his palm. "Your delivering this item to Harai will repay my kindness in part. Meanwhile, share what food you do not eat with others who are hungry. That is the other part of my repayment."

Itzchak rose to his full height, his white outer garment practically radiating in the moonlight. Jonathan thought Itzchak's eyes glowed, and when Itzchak raised his hand, Jair swore he could see a white light around it. "I bless your journey. I see that you are protected in your passing and that your names will be remembered."

The door opened easily, although they had not seen Itzchak touch it. When they turned to take a last look at him, he was nowhere to be seen. Inside, they lit the first torch. The sound of the flint striking in this empty cavern echoed in the darkness. Even in this dry climate, the walls of the passageway were damp.

"Jonathan, where exactly does this passage come out?"

"It descends to the bottom of the valley—the original valley under the Temple that was filled by King Solomon's workers. No one has been there for many generations, but you remember what the holy writings say—that a valley of 40 cubits (60 feet) deep was filled in to make a foundation for the Temple. That foundation is full of passageways and crypts that our ancestors put there."

"Maybe we could hide it here?" Jair suggested.

"I think we should do as the Essene suggested. Take it completely out of Jerusalem and hide it where there is no possibility of it being found until some future day when it will be safe."

The aged stone stairs were rough, broken in places. The smell of ancient dust filled the still air. A sound below them on the stairs caused them to stop and listen. Then it came again.

Jair whispered, barely audible: "Could there be someone in here?"

Jonathan lowered the torch he was carrying, trying to see farther down the stairs. He took another cautious step down. A rat scurried out from the shadows cast by the torch.

They both gasped with relief.

"A *hjooldah*!" laughed Jair. "There is one more frightened than we are." Other vermin lived in the tunnel.

At the bottom of the stairs, the passage led off to the right. As the two approached the end of the passage, they saw shafts of dim moonlight around the edges of a large boulder that blocked the entrance, hiding it from view from the outside.

"Do you think there's an encampment nearby?" asked Jonathan.

"There could be. Those filthy Romans are everywhere. Let's try moving the boulder as quietly as we can."

The torch extinguished, both men approached the rock, but it was very heavy and hardly budged at all.

"I wonder if we can even budge it," said Jair. "Perhaps we should get some help with this."

"Let me brace my feet a little better and give it another try. For now, we only have to move it enough for one of us to look outside," said Jonathan.

Both men leaned into the rock again, with much grunting and groaning. It seemed to loosen a little but did not move. This time they attempted to rotate it, and the rock moved so that they could at least see outside. As the rock moved, they were both dismayed to hear a voice outside say to them in Latin, "What have we here? Come, I'll lend a hand. Come, heave."

Grimly, both men put their shoulders to the rock. With the help of the Roman soldier outside, they opened a passage wide enough for Jonathan to squeeze through sideways. The Roman soldier was a bit taken aback, but accepted Jonathan's extended right hand. With his left hand, Jonathan plunged his Sicarii knife into the Roman's stomach, at an upward angle intended to penetrate the heart.

As Jonathan eased the man quietly to the ground, Jair came out of the passage. "A shame he had to be there," he whispered. "Are there any others?"

Jonathan, his head in his hands, was sitting on the ground beside the man he had killed. The memories afflicting him were of his boyhood in Jericho.

****

"I don't want to kill it."

"You must," his father said. "Take the knife."

"Father, I raised it from a lamb."

"You raised it for the sacrifice. Now cut its throat so we can drain the blood. Then I will bless it. Do it now."

****

Jonathan sat beside the dead soldier now, much as he had sat beside his dead lamb then. "Come on," urged Jair. "Drag him back inside the passage before anyone else comes. With the rock moved aside, anyone passing will see the entrance. We have to get away from the city before dawn. The siege could break at any time."

Hearing voices in the distance, the two men disposed of the body and crept silently out of the opening and away from the passage, up the side of the rise west of the city. Not 25 cubits away was an encampment of soldiers.

"Let's get back," whispered Jair.

Having returned to the top of the passage, they eased the door open and peeked out to see that the courtyard was again empty. While Jair waited behind, Jonathan slipped through the door and moved quietly across the mosaic to the archway opening onto the street. A man sat against the wall, seemingly half asleep.

"By whose door do you lean, my friend?" Jonathan asked.

"By the door to the Temple built to house the Name of God," the man answered, identifying himself as the one designated to wait for their return. "I am Dan."

"Is all in readiness?" asked Jonathan.

"The Pleiades are at their zenith. Orion follows." With that, Dan moved quickly away and Jonathan took his place sitting at the doorway.

In the distance, a baby began crying, and a young mother began cooing to it.

"Is the baby all right, Akbar Sheli?" a young man called out softly. "If only we had some little food to give him."

"There is none," she replied, "and I have no more milk."

Other sounds distracted Jonathan now. More men were coming through the street.

Two men rounded the last turn and came into Jonathan's sight. The one called Dan and another were carrying a large box, big enough to be a coffin, covered with a blanket supported by two long poles.

"What are you carrying?" a voice shrieked at them. "Food?"

"Have some respect for the dead, old woman."

Other voices now made themselves heard. "Are they hoarding food?"

"This is the body of the old priest. A little respect, please."

"Did that old windbag finally die?" It was the old woman's voice. "I bet it wasn't from starvation."

Each man held the end of the two poles in their hands. As they came closer to Jonathan, Dan leaned over to him and whispered, "Be careful not to touch it."

Jonathan turned into the archway and crossed the mosaic courtyard, following Dan and the other man. As they approached the wooden door with their burden, Jair pushed it open, letting them enter the doorway. Suddenly they heard loud voices.

"Where is it? I want to see the body! I know of no priest who died! And that box is the wrong shape for a coffin!"

"I think they're hoarding food," another spoke up. "Let's get them."

Jair looked out through the jamb of the partly closed door. Itzchak Ben Itzchak, the Essene, was blocking the door while others in the street shouted and argued.

Feeling Jair's gaze, Itzchak turned to him. "Peace I give to you, my friends. Go in safety now. I will lock the door."

Jonathan and Jair headed back down the dark passage to freedom.

3

Taken by Ruse

Masada

The old man opened his eyes, smiling in fond remembrance of his teacher, Simon. At a great distance, he saw a small group approaching on the plain below. How many? He could not tell.

"Soo-ooni!" Adameh called out to her daughter. "Wake up."

"Yes, mother, I am awake. What do you wish?"

"I am preparing bread and need some water from the cistern. Go now, please."

The old man watched Soo-ooni taking the path from her parents' dwelling. The young girl approaching him was dark-complexioned. Her homespun cotton skirt revealed slim, delicate ankles, and her long hair, almost straight, swung with the rhythm of her stride. Her intense dark gaze glanced about the compound. *Looking for David,* the old man thought.

She shifted the heavy clay jar under her left arm, and, with one foot, gently eased a chicken out of her path. There were many such birds in the camp, together with a few goats for milk and cheese, and a few dogs. Water pots, like the one Soo-ooni was carrying, were rare and hard to replace, since the top of Masada afforded little of the proper kind of clay.

"*Yom Tov,* Harai," she said to the old man.

"Good day to you also, Soo-ooni. The jar you carry is nicely formed.

Did you shape it yourself?"

"I did. My father carried clay from the banks of the Jordan near Jericho. I had it fired in the Kiln of the Shamarine, outside the East Gate. What do you see on the plain today?" she asked, making idle conversation.

"A group approaches. Since they are yet too far away to see well, I judge that they will not arrive until the end of the day after tomorrow."

"Are they Romans?" she asked, shivering.

"I do not think so. When the Romans come, they will be greater in number."

"David tells me that Masada cannot be taken, that we are safe here. So even when they do come, we need not fear."

"The enemy will recognize our lack of respect for his power as our weakness. And when he does so, the top of this mountain will be no different for us than the bottom of a pit. For there is nowhere to flee, but down into our enemy's hands."

"Some say your prophecies are empty. Masada has stood undefeated for many centuries."

"And never assaulted. Remember how easily we took it? The Roman guardians were assured of the impregnability of Masada, yet we hold it now."

"Soo-ooni!" Adameh called. "The water, please?"

"*Shalom,* Soo-ooni," Harai said.

"*Shalom*, Old Father."

The old man turned to watch the visitors approaching on the plain below and remembered his own approach to the mountain with David and the Sicarii. In memory, he could hear the tune David played on the chalil sweetening the night air around a campfire in the plain, not far from where the approaching visitors were now.

****

That had been a chilly night when David and the Sicarii took Masada. Their fire was too small to be seen from the mountaintop; it didn't provide much warmth, but was adequate for a little cooking before sleep. Twenty miles distant, a large plateau rose from the horizon, blotting out some of the stars, but the light of the others clearly outlined the tableland. Masada was a large pedestal rising out of the plain—a giant semi-circle of rock with its face uplifted to the sky, 433 cubits on the north lip, and 567 cubits on the other end. It was a mighty stone giant, standing guard over plains grazed by only the hardiest of wild goats and camels.

"They are like us," David had remarked.

On all sides, the walls of Masada were nearly sheer. No one had ever tried to climb them. Many brave warriors had fallen from the battlements, or met their deaths fighting their way up either the serpentine path on the east side, or the cart path up the western face.

"You will go there today," Eleazar told David. "You have found your way into places where the bravest of us could not enter. See what is there, and if you think our plan too dangerous, you know what to do."

Jair had argued that David was too valuable to risk: "He can speak and understand all of the languages of Judea. His memory is like the pages of a scroll. I have seen fifty men walk past him, and he could tell which one had passed him twice. He is the best spy the Sicarii has ever seen. David it was who gained us access to Herod's palace the night we murdered Salome.

"He has been remembered for that, by others beside the Sicarii. And if he is recognized," Jair concluded, "we lose him."

"That was two years ago. None of the soldiers stationed here then are still in Judea. They'll be back in Rome making *maga-maga* with their whores and their wives." As he said it, he made the usual hand gesture, a closed fist with the thumb and little finger held straight out, wrist rotating back and forth slightly.

That night they slept restlessly, if at all. Eleazar had insisted that Masada should be the first of the Roman strongholds to be taken, and every man understood his reason. But ever since the decision, most of the Sicarii had had misgivings, second thoughts. Could they win Masada? Rome had held Judea, and the children of Israel, captive for so long no living man or woman could remember being free. Bondage to Rome was a long-accustomed lifestyle.

"Since Masada is the strongest of the Roman fortresses, it will be the hardest for them to take back. Its provisions and cisterns can provide for more than a thousand of us for many a year's siege. There is enough land to raise crops and graze a few animals, if necessary."

"Harai," said Eleazar to the old man sitting just beyond the light of the cooking-fire, "you have been to Masada. What have you seen? Tell us."

"First," Abbi Yashan replied. "You will understand that with all my brothers, I deplore any violence done to anyone. I assist in this effort of yours for reasons of my own.

"Further, I remind you of your earlier promise that this will be accomplished without bloodshed. No one is to be hurt. Is that still true?"

"True, Old Father. We agree to try to accomplish this without anyone coming to harm. Abbi Yashan, please tell us about the mountain!"

"Masada?" Harai breathed thoughtfully.

****

Harai recalled the Council of the twenty-four Elders, who had all agreed: *Masada should be the hiding place.*

"But how are we to keep this secret?"

"The secret will be kept," Simon spoke softly, watching Harai.

****

"Masada?" Harai repeated thoughtfully. "I visited as a young man, in connection with other duties. I with twenty-one of my brothers visited Masada on our way to Therapeutae in Egypt. Therapeutae is the place where we were trained in spiritual healing. It is one of our most ancient communities.

"We found two approaches, both carefully guarded at all times, as they have been since the days of Herod the Great. Up the west side wends Caesar's Highway—a path barely wide enough to admit an oxcart with one man walking alongside the beast. The ascent on the east is like a long snake—narrow, with one twist and curve after another. Wide enough for one man—or two—in some places, to pass, carrying a burden. But it is steep and arduous. Strewn with small stones, annoying if not treacherous. The stones roll and slide underfoot. If those two men are bearing anything of value, you dare not ask them to hurry."

"This serpentine path is guarded by only two soldiers. One is stationed half way up the track, the other at the very brink of Masada.

"The so-called highway"—Harai chuckled—"is guarded by two men in a tower, gazing down on it. But two others are stationed at the bottom of the path."

"That few!" Eleazar exulted.

"Wait." Harai lifted his hand. "There are two more. One lookout to the north, at the perimeter wall of Herod's Summer Palace, watching east, west and north. The other guard watches at the south end of the plateau. He watches east, west and south. Their high vantage point is good enough that no one can approach Masada unseen. Unless he is very careful."

That night, the Sicarii approached under cover of darkness. Waiting for the next day to pass, they hid behind the rocks in the plain. During that long day of waiting, David approached—in the clear view of the guards.

"For weeks," said Eleazar to his companions, seeking to avoid the hot sun, "this victory has commandeered my thoughts by day, and my dreams by night. It may come to pass that all Israel will continue to bow to the yoke of Rome. But Eleazar, son-of-Jair, son-of-Caleb, son-of-

Ashar, will not submit. And certainly not meekly!"

Menehem, leader of Jerusalem's Sicarii, and Joshua with him, favored Masada as their first target. Many wanted to wait until after Herodium and Machaerus had fallen. Those fortresses would likely be easier.

"Taking Herodium and Machaerus will alert the Romans," Eleazar argued. "Taking the others first will make Masada all the harder to take—when Masada is the one we want most."

They could see birds flitting around the high cliff walls. "How tiny they look," one said.

"If only we had wings!"

Through the day they waited, while David began climbing the serpentine path. Along the way, he stooped occasionally and threw handfuls of dirt over himself, until he was streaked with dust from head to foot. He then tore one of his sleeves.

The long climb to the top circled back and forth on the mountain, winding its slow way ever upward. In a few rare places, the path was so broad two men could safely walk beside each other. Overall, it was barely wide enough for one with breath-taking drops to threaten any misstep.

The evening sun was just grazing the horizon when David, halfway up the path, encountered the first guard, who spoke to him in Hebrew! Heavily accented, but Hebrew nonetheless:

"Stop where you are. What is your name?"

"David, son of Amos the fisherman."

"And, David-ben-Amos, why are you here?"

"I am traveling into the south and wish to entertain you for my supper," he said, holding up his chalil.

"By the looks of you, you're a beggar who stole a flute. Why do you look so unkempt?"

"I was taken by a band of brigands," David replied, in perfect Latin. He ignored the guard's look of surprise. "They carried long knives. They cursed Rome, and her Emperor Nero, and the three emperors before him. They stole what few denarii and shekels I had. By their talk, they must have been Sicarii."

"*Vade*," the soldier ordered. "Walk ahead of me."

He followed David all the way to the top, where they were met by a second guard.

This one did not speak Hebrew. "*Currite, currite!* Hurry it up! Get along there, Jew!" He prodded David with the butt of his spear.

Even in its attempted glory, the palace had never been lavish. Some two centuries before, Herod the Great had built it in a hurry (32 B.C.E).

Later kings of the Herodian line had made improvements upon it, but without any sense of planning or taste. And worse, with no enthusiasm. The structure resembled the summer home of a prince, not the palace of a king.

Since leaving the top of the serpentine path, David had counted seventeen Romans. Now a soldier shoved him into a room near the western rear of the palace. "Wait here."

The room was not large, but featured a high ceiling. Niches in the wall harbored tiny figures sculpted in stone or cast of metal, mostly of Roman gods or military symbols. In the far corner was a tiny shrine to Mithras. Over the door was a huge eagle, garishly decorated with gilt and bright paint.

After only a few minutes, another soldier entered the room and seated himself with a mug of mulled wine. *"Adrianus sum,"* he stated. Then—in a dazzling tactic meant to intimidate—he switched to Hebrew: "I am Adrian. For you, I have questions."

The room's only window looked over the plain below. The winding path was in sight, almost 100 cubits straight down.

"Primus: Where are you from?"

In most of what he told the Roman, David had no reason to lie: "I was born in Tarichaea. I lived with my father, who earned his bread as a fisherman until he died of a fever. Then my mother brought me to Jerusalem. There I learned to play the chalil."

"Where are you traveling?"

"Into the south, to learn more about the world there, and earn my way by entertaining those more fortunate than myself."

"A musician! Can you play me a tune if I request it?"

"Yes," in Hebrew.

"You know songs? Is that why you understand Latin?"

"Yes," again in Hebrew.

Why else, I wonder? Adrianus thought.

Abruptly, Adrianus went back to Latin, searching David's features for any reaction. "Why else would you, mongrel offspring of Abraham and Isaac and the patriarchs, bother to learn a tongue spoken only throughout the civilized world?"

Any answer, however awkward, was better than silence. But David was careful to reply in Hebrew: "Simple curiosity!"

"Be curious! You might survive long enough to learn something, one of these days!" Adrianus laughed, coughed, and continued in Latin. "Every king of Israel lies dead in his grave. Rome's emperors rule as immortal gods! They are worshiped, in the sacred tongue of Romulus and Remus . . ."

He lifted his pitcher again. Seeing that it was empty, he switched back to Hebrew.

"Da-veed? Why have you come to Masada?"

"I've been to Masada before, and played for the soldiers, only three months ago. Ask your men; surely some of them will remember. I lacked the good fortune of meeting you at that time. You were in Jerusalem, they said. Hunting out Jonathan or some other Leader the Sicarii?"

Adrianus nodded. "We found the bastard, too, and left his innards spread over half the city. Now, I'm told that you bear news of Sicarii, those of the long knives in this very neighborhood. Near Masada? Tell me."

"Yesterday, I was traveling south, with the idea of returning to Masada, hoping to play the flute again. Men with little else to do make good listeners. Last time I was here, they fed me and paid me well . . .'"

Seeing that Adrianus was drunk, bored and not paying strict attention, David made his move. "This time, I was anticipating a good evening again. Some seven leagues north of here, I came to a camp of men . . . perhaps fifty in number."

Adrianus was shocked! *Ne Romani erant?*" Quickly, he echoed himself in Hebrew: "Were they Romans, or weren't they?"

"I cannot believe it. They boasted no chariots, no armor, no Roman advantages. They were garbed like the street-rabble of Jerusalem and bore fearfully long knives with no scabbards."

"Did they speak the tongue of the Caesars?

"No, lord."

"Then what?"

"To my ears, it sounded like Aramaic. I approached their camp, intending to play for them and perhaps earn a healthy supper. But upon seeing me, they fell upon me and seized what little money I had. They questioned me closely about who I might have seen along the road, and forced me to run a gauntlet where I was slapped and struck with bladders. Finally, when they tired of me, I lay quietly until they had moved away. None knew how to play the flute, so I did not lose my chalil."

Adrianus went to the door, where he spoke softly with another soldier waiting outside. "Let two men be sent to the plain below and search for any sign of Sicarii in the area."

Slouching back in his seat, he poured himself a drink from a second flagon of wine.

Adrianus had been immediately suspicious of any Jew warning him against the Sicarii, Judea's underground army, Zealots. Yet David was dressed as a Sadducee, too much color in his torn clothing. That, by itself, lent him some credence, since Sadducees preferred to cooperate and collaborate with Rome.

"Why, Jew, should I believe you? Why should I accept this wild story of yours?"

"I don't care if you believe me or not. You asked me what happened to me, and I answered. I have no reason to lie. As I said, I have come to play for the soldiers, and hope to receive supper and maybe a few copper coins, if they like my music well enough."

"I have not yet decided what to do with you. When my spies return, I will learn if what you have spoken is the truth. Until then, you will remain on Masada, and you will play for us at dinner and after. If my men cannot verify your story, I must assume you have other motives for your visit. And for you, that will be very bad indeed.

"Now," Adrianus continued, "while you are up here on the mountain with us, I grant you freedom to move about, as you wish. But you are forbidden to leave without my permission. If my men do not return within two days, I may change my mind as to your fate. Or even before then! Meanwhile, you will begin your entertainment very soon, because the men are about to dine."

David was led to a main hall furnished with benches and low tables. Hebrew slave girls were carrying trays of food and pouring wine. Watching, he counted twelve more soldiers whom he had not yet seen.

If there are seventeen men elsewhere, he calculated, *and four more on guard, more than thirty men must be stationed here.* But when the twelve had finished eating and were drifting out of the hall, even more men entered. As the soldiers came and went, David totaled slightly more than forty. And, he knew, only 25 Sicarii waited at the bottom of the mountain.

The *chalil*—an exotic instrument on which David was very accomplished—was well received. The soldiers stationed on Masada never heard music except for the trumpet that called them to assemble. Nor did they hear much news of the rest of the world. Sometimes there were couriers from Jerusalem, and rare letters from wives and families at home in Spain, Germany, North Africa, and throughout the Empire. The news was sketchy and, by the time it reached Masada, often months out of date. The soldiers were easily lulled into nostalgic daydreams of home. Often, while commiserating with one another they drank too much. And so it was tonight.

David was quietly delighted as he overheard the men's complaints: "Can't see why they need so many of us. All we have to do is eat, sleep, and sweat like mules."

"True," said another, "the way this mountain is protected. Have you ever seen the rock falls tested?"

"Don't want to be fighting my way up when one of those lets loose!"

"Ten soldiers could hold this place against ten thousand."

"For years!" another joined in.

"Rome wants to keep its fortress well protected," said Adrianus, who had just entered the hall. "That is why you are here. The Assassins are everywhere in Judea."

"There aren't any up here," said one soldier, gesturing around the room.

"How do you know?" asked Adrianus, with a glance at David. "According to our musician here, there are about fifty of them, right below us.

Seated alone farthest from the door was a swarthy soldier. That he was lighter skinned than the others caught David's attention. Stringy black hair hung in his eyes. As he ate, David noticed that he habitually pushed it out of his eyes.

He was Svery of Malschbach, one of the unfortunates taken eight years before in that part of northern Europe the Romans called Saxony. Instead of execution or slavery, he had agreed to fight for Rome, a decision he had long since regretted. This desert heat was a miserable exchange for the plush forests of home; the stale water of Herod's cisterns, a disgusting substitute for the sweet mountain springs that fed *Die Geraldsau Wasserfall* and supplied water for his home in the tiny hamlet of Malschbach. But the location of Malschbach with its neighboring hot springs had been his downfall and that of many of his kinsmen. The Romans' love for hot bathing had drawn them to the area where they built luxurious baths. It became a place for vacationing Roman dignitaries, in the exotic Schwarzwald (The Black Forest).

Svery's first duties had been attending the baths, but his strength and bravery had brought him to military service. Since then he had been taken to Rome and trained. He had seen action in Pisidia, Egypt, and was now stationed in *Die Hoehle der Hoelle* (Hell hole). *Warum koenne Ich nicht nach Hause fahren?* he muttered constantly (Why can't I go home?). His discontent had led him to too much wine too often, of which he liked to say with curled lip, "*Ist vergleichend mit Baerens' Pisse,*" comparing it to the liquid excretions of bears.

Svery of Malschbach had been very fortunate in his military experience. He had one lone injury resulting in a scar on the left side of his mouth and the loss of two front teeth. His remark about the wine had been repeated once too often and in the presence of a German-speaking wine maker.

Svery felt David looking at him and glanced up from his meal. Their eyes met briefly. David broke the contact. The intense hatred in

Svery's gaze had shocked him. *For the warring and impudent Juden who brought me to this hateful land,* David could almost hear Svery's thought.

Adrianus had only begun to savor his meal when a guard rushed into the refectory and spoke to him, in a loud whisper: "At the base of the south wall, there are four cooking fires. From the top of the wall, we've counted some thirty men down there. They're so bold with their knives that you can see them glinting in the firelight."

Adrianus rose quickly and left the hall. A few minutes later, three soldiers entered, carrying a badly wounded man—one of the spies whom Adrianus had dispatched earlier that day. He had been caught at the bottom of the path, but left alive so that he might return and tell his story.

"There must have been twenty," he groaned, "at the bottom of the path. In hiding. While they beat me, they were talking among themselves, assuming I couldn't understand them. They seem to think there are only a dozen of us up here. They laughed to think of Rome leaving such a prize unguarded."

When Adrianus returned, the men in the hall had stopped eating to watch him.

"Let's go," one shouted, "and show them how Romans fight."

Und Scharzwalder Manner (And men of the Black Forest), thought Svery, leaping up.

"Look what they did to Julian here! Let's have at 'em, Adrianus!"

The shout was taken up by all the men present, and others began filtering back into the hall. But Adrianus raised both hands over his head. The shouting stopped.

"Call the north and south guards," he said. "Let them join the two at the bottom of Caesar's Highway. The rest of you, gather your swords. We're going for a march."

With that, David nodded at one of the slave girls clearing the tables. When she left, bearing away platters and scraps of food, another came to replace her, and the first girl in the dark blue tunic did not return.

The two soldiers ordered to join the Caesar's Highway guards to the west were accompanied by twenty more. Yet another twenty carefully picked their way down the serpentine pathway to the east in single file.

Svery was among the twenty marching down the cart path, or Ceasar's Highway as they sarcastically called it. The march was long and treacherous. Too much wine at dinner did not help him. He dreaded the march back up and feared the march down. It was steep with uneven footing. With each step he cursed the day he tried to steal a sheep from the Roman camp at the *Bader* (baths). He almost got away with it, but almost doesn't count in sheep stealing. He never thought he would come to a day when he hated the very smell of mutton.

Adrianus' group descended the east wall, along the snake path. The more treacherous descent was done in single file at a half trot, Adrianus in the lead, calling encouragement to his men.

Adrianus had been recruited from a patrician family in Naples. His father, Genova, was a trader of moderate means who specialized in rare cloth and jewelry. It had been his hope that his son would follow in his footsteps, but Adrianus had other ideas. Adrianus wanted to see the world. He wanted the glory of conquest and recognition. After many years of arguing over it, Genova decided to guide Adrianus' younger rother into the business, and in frustration acquired a position for Adrianus under Flavius Silva in the Tenth Roman Legion.

Adrianus had been in Judea for almost two years, having been stationed there prior to the insurrection at Jerusalem. He expected to be called home at any time for his regular furlough, but then came the uprising. Now he didn't know when he would get home. This madness with the Sicarii frustrated him. *Who do they think they are, to try to stand up to trained Roman soldiers? We are skilled in the use of the best weapons on Earth. They have only their knives and their passions. We have the best armor. They have wool shirts and cotton. Before we arrived, they didn't even have the wheel, and they expect to drive us out of Judea?? Ignorant fools!!*

He had forgotten how dangerous the snake path was. At one narrow point he actually slipped and would have fallen if the man behind had not grabbed his arm. The closeness of death left Adrianus shaken. He was not ready for what he found at the bottom.

Fear of the Sicarii was a second thought only to Svery. It was hidden in his anger at Rome and Judea. He had killed *Juden* (Jews) before and he'd do it again if he had the chance. *Now will be a good chance,* he thought.

At the bottom, they found the guard still at his post, but hardly awake and alert—for at the foot of Ceasar's Highway, Ceasar's guard had been beheaded!

It wasn't a clean job, either. It looked as if the head had been hacked off with many blows from one of their long "sicarii" knives. These weapons were lethal enough to deliver their name to the Sicariis.

To drive home the point, the Sicarii had mounted the head on the guard's pike and left it facing the path, blood dripping down the wooden stake.

The soldiers were furious. This handful of insane Jewish rabble would be slaughtered, they vowed, and any captured alive would be crucified. No available cruelties would be spared. And when they were finally dead, their corpses would be cast from the highest wall of Masada.

Svery was a bit sick from the spectacle. He threw his head back, shaking the hair out of his eyes. He gazed up into the night sky and drew a deep breath. He had known the guard, Epidimo the Iberian. They had been friends since the days in Pisidia at Antioch. They had gambled together, whored together, plotted their escape from Roman service together. *Epidimo has escaped Rome forever,* thought Svery. *Now I will send those who helped him into the oblivion and they shall escape Rome too.*

On Adrianus' side of the mountain, the east side, the scene was slightly different. Here, the Sicarii had stripped the soldier before removing his head and had placed the clothing in a fire they had built at the end of the path, using the guard's breast plate as a hearth.

Adrianus was shocked at the brutality of the murder. He had seen death before. He had even taken part in ending men's lives, but never in so bloody a scene. Adrianus did not think of crucifixion as unnaturally brutal. It was a common method of execution from his perspective. And, after all, criminals deserved what they got. *But this? This is fiendish,* he thought.

Adrianus' strategy was to surround the party of Sicarii between them, so that not a one might escape. From the cooking fires that had been spotted from the top of the mesa, it was thought that the Sicarii camp was at the south end of the plateau. Both groups of Roman soldiers had orders to head that way after reaching the bottom of the two paths.

Their trek was arduous, since no path or road had been cleared to the southern foot of the mountain. The soldiers took almost an hour of climbing over rocks and through ravines to reach the south wall. And when they did reach it, they found themselves facing each other with no adversary between them. The cooking fires they had seen from up top were smoldering ashes, abandoned.

****

The woman in the blue tunic, whom David had signaled in the dining hall, left her platters in the kitchen and went immediately to her quarters. There, four other slaves were waiting. "It is time," she announced.

None spoke. Each knew what must be done, according to the plans laid down when David had first delighted the Roman soldiers with music.

That night, Naomi had been chosen to bring the evening meal to the sentries overlooking Caesar's Highway. They carried hot roasted mutton and wine to the foot of the tower. At the bottom of the tower, Naomi called out, kicking the heavy wooden door a few times.

A sleepy reply drifted down from the window at the top. A few minutes later, the door creaked open to reveal a heavy-set middle-aged Roman in partial armor.

This was Mesalla, called the Sleeper because his right eyelid drooped. Mesalla was slow of speech, but quick with a sword or trident. He had been a professional gladiator, and his promotion to the Roman army—by the Emperor's command—had doubtless preserved his life.

"Ahh!" he breathed. "Two of you tonight? Come in, come in. Platamus," he hollered up the stairs, "Food on its way! And something else to eat, besides."

Rather than return to the kitchen, the slaves waited while the soldiers devoured the mutton. "Could there really be anyone down there?" Platamus asked. "Could the Sicarii be so foolish?"

"If they are *Sicarii*," said Mesalla, "they'll wish they weren't. From the number of their fires, we have them outnumbered. Better than two to one."

"Why did it have to be my turn at the watch?" Platamus groaned.

The Romans had not quite finished eating their platters of mutton, dried figs and dates, when Platamus set his dish aside and grabbed Naomi's wrist.

"After that meat and drink, I feel sleepy," Mesalla drawled. "I think I'll just lean against the wall and watch."

When Platamus moved to kiss her, only to yawn in her face, Naomi wasn't surprised. The lethal powder—which David had given her weeks before and tonight she had mixed into their wine—was working its dark magic. Soon, both soldiers would be asleep—and soon thereafter, relieved of their posts for all eternity.

With a knife used to cut mutton, Naomi made sure that neither soldier's heart was beating. Then the women descended to where huge rope nets held back massive assortments of loose rock, ready to cascade onto the pathway below.

There they waited.

Lifting the hem of her tunic, Naomi wiped the Roman blood off her knife.

By this time, the soldiers in the plain below had discovered four campfires, now little more than ashes. There was no one in sight. *Where could they have gone?* wondered Adrianus.

"Separate in pairs!" shouted Adrianus. "The first man who sees anything, cry out."

Two by two, the soldiers began searching. "Kill anything that moves," Adrianus shouted at their backs, "as long as it's a Jew!"

Silence. No soldier cried out. The last embers of the fires were beginning to wink out.

For the first time that day, Adrianus felt fear. "Something, is wrong," he said to his aide. "Men cannot vanish like ghosts. And ghosts do not leave fires."

Adrianus realized with a shock what had just happened. "We've been tricked," he shouted. "Back to the top, quickly!! Forced march. Double time. Hurry. We've left Masada unguarded. Both paths. Those who came down the snake path go back that way. Those who descended Caesar's Highway, return that way. Keep a sharp eye out for trouble!" The two groups of soldiers headed out at a trot.

In the dining hall, David, finding himself almost completely alone, finally stopped playing. Three soldiers remained.

In the palace there would be only a few men left. And only two more guarding the supplies. Herod had made sure that Masada would be a fortress safe and sure, should he ever need it. David's tour of Masada at his last visit had astonished him with the fortifications and supplies. There were supplies beyond belief, food enough to last for years, dried figs and dates, corn, dried mutton, weapons enough to outfit thousands of soldiers. The cisterns Herod had cut into the rock were adequate to keep the baths he built in the southern palace supplied with fresh water for a long time to come, and the aqueducts he built brought in more from springs on neighboring hills. For drinking, the cisterns had water to last a man's lifetime and more.

David walked to the door of the dining hall.

"Where do you think you're going?" a soldier asked.

"To view the stars and the new moon."

"You will stay right here," the soldier said. "Inside, where we can see you."

Although Adrianus had given him leave to wander the mesa's top, David felt it would be best to not argue with the soldier.

As time passed, David sat waiting, tense, not hearing a sound from outside. One soldier, his legs outstretched, was snoring loudly. The other two were throwing dice.

Again David began playing the chalil. Suddenly, shouts echoed from the palace entrance. A soldier entered, carrying another man over his shoulder.

"Cretos is near death," he called breathlessly. "Here, stretch him out on the table."

"Tell us the rest," one of the guards demanded.

"We were guarding the snake path when two slaves brought us our evening meal. While we ate, they made themselves agreeable. They also brought wine, which I seldom drink when on duty. But Cretos finished all of his. Soon he was stretched out on the ground holding his stomach. And the women were gone!"

David's tension was growing. *One guard from the eastern tower did not drink on duty. How strange,* David thought. Already, the poisoning had been discovered. These two were from the eastern tower. He wondered how it went in the tower overlooking Caesar's Highway.

After a quick conversation, his three guards ran to the slave quarters, where they found no one. Turning to leave, they were astonished to find nine men, Eleazar, Menehem, and seven others blocking the way, brandishing Sicarii knives. The soldiers barely had time to draw their swords before they were cut down.

****

Since David's first visit three months ago, the slaves at Masada—mostly native Judeans, abducted from their families—had put aside lengths of rope, even the smallest scraps, storing them in hidden places around the mountain. Since then, they had assembled the ropes. Piece by piece, they braided and tied the brittle fragments together into four long, impressive lengths.

After igniting the fires on Masada's south face, all the Sicarii had rushed to the foot of the north wall, leaving a handful of men to brandish swords, moving around the fires so they could be easily seen from above.

As soon as Romans started down the twin paths to the plain below, some slaves secured the ropes to the pretentious columns Herod the Great had placed in his terrace overlooking the north plain. Others ran to the south wall to signal the remaining Sicarii that the soldiers were now descending to the plain. From the top of the north wall, the ropes lowered them to the valley floor.

They were hoping that the Romans would be fooled into assembling at the south side of the plateau. For the soldiers to descend that distance along the paths would take several hours. To reach the southern end of the plateau would take at least another hour. If they thought of sending soldiers to circle the plateau looking for the Sicarii, it would take at least another hour, maybe two hours for them to reach the northern side, climbing through the rough terrain.

Even with all that time, if the plan worked the way they hoped, the climb up a rope of over 400 cubits was nothing to be taken lightly. All 25 Sicarii were young and in good condition, except for Harai, who would wait till the deed was done before joining them. The men climbed the ropes, leaving nearly all the Romans on the plain below.

At one horrid moment, near the end of their climb, two of Adrianus' men rounded the corner of the north wall. There they discovered the ropes. Craning their necks upward, they saw the last of the Sicarii clambering over the edge of their fortress. Stunned, they watched as the ropes were pulled up.

****

When Svery got to the foot of the cart path known as Caesar's Highway, the column of marching men came to a stop. They balked at the idea of marching up underneath their own rock falls.

Adrianus' group began to climb the snake path. The guard stationed at the halfway point reported a quiet watch. Three-quarters of the way up, the lead soldier halted and shouted, "Listen!"

For a second nothing could be heard, but then came the rumbling of a great landslide. The soldiers turned to run back down, but it was too late.

When the slide hit, Svery could hear the screams up ahead of him. He remembered helping to prepare the very slide that had just struck. It gave him chills of fear. The rocks were no ordinary pebbles but large enough that a strong man could barely carry one without help. Svery knew that most of the soldiers at the front of the group had been killed, either crushed under the flying rocks or knocked over the cliff's edge. Romans near the center of the line were gravely injured.

Far above, on the plain of Masada, Eleazar turned to Caleb, standing beside him. "Every surviving soldier down there knows that there are four more slides prepared on that side of the hill. If they've found those first rocks a convincing deterrent, I don't believe that they'll disturb us again."

Harai was furious with the Sicarii for the bloodshed, but Eleazar's response was simply a shrug. "It's a war, Harai. Do you expect us to instruct and inspire them off the mountain?"

****

Masada

Now, seated on the casement wall, Harai's attention was focused on waiting and listening to the sounds of the camp on the high tableland. He cringed at the memory and was at the same time thrilled that their victory had been so complete. *How can I take pleasure in this?* he asked himself yet again. *There is no point in killing.* But as a native son of the Promised Land, Harai's own nationalism was working against him. *If I can't overcome these feelings, I'll be trapped here to die!!*

"Soo-ooni!" her mother called. "What is taking so long with the water?" The girl was approaching from the opposite direction, cradling the heavy clay pot in both hands. From the direction of the cisterns, Harai could hear the distant tones of David's chalil. Its sweetness was a bitter contrast with what Harai knew was yet to come.

4

Flight

Jerusalem

The door at the top of the stair closed behind them. In pitch darkness, the two men felt their way, carefully easing their burden down the long flight of stairs. Dan, in front, called out in a loud whisper each time he knew his next step was secure. Behind him, his partner did the same. They did not light a torch immediately for fear that its light could be seen through cracks in the door above. The darkness added to their fear, not knowing if soldiers had crept up the stairs below them.

At the top of the stairs, Jonathan and Jair checked the door. It was securely locked.

"How did the Essene do that?"

"I don't know," Jonathan replied. "He was at the entrance to the courtyard arguing with those people, and nowhere near the door."

"He locked it and unlocked it like that, before," said Jair, "when we first came here tonight."

"You still have the strange-looking amulet he gave you?"

"Yes," said Jair. "And I'm sure he knows what we have here."

"I agree," replied Jonathan. "That must be why he suggested Masada. No one would ever look for it there."

"This very passageway is an excellent place."

"Will you two please quit gossiping and give us some light!" grunted Dan, from down below.

Jair struck the flint, lighting the torch, and moved to squeeze past the two men and their sacred burden.

"Be careful not to touch it," Dan reminded him.

"I won't touch it if I can help it. You be careful too—Kohen or not, you may do something wrong."

The air in the narrow passage was as still and dusty as before. Farther down, they could hear the hjooldah scampering off.

"Jonathan is also a Kohen, Yerod," said Dan. "If necessary, he and I can move it by touching it directly." Strong and youthful like himself, Yerod was a heavy-chinned young man, with broad shoulders and thickly muscled arms and legs.

Just then, Dan slipped and stumbled on the shadowy steps while Yerod tried to keep his footing. The burden between them teetered and barely remained balanced on the two poles. *What a horrendous mistake it would be to drop the Ark of the Covenant,* thought Dan. *Would I live through the experience? Would I want to? The men of old who touched it were incinerated on the spot—just for touching it. If I dropped it—what then??*

Dan had a curse on his lips, then thought better of it. "These stairs are badly worn," he panted. "Nearly broke my ankle."

"Careful not to step on any of the rats," from Yerod.

"Hush," Jair whispered harshly. "Listen! They're trying to get the door open."

Above, they could hear voices. The words were unclear. Those whom Itzchak the Essene had delayed were trying to break down the door in search of the two men with the covered box.

The voices fell silent. Then they heard a pounding, something hard being struck against the door.

Then an angry shout: "You, in there. Open up!"

"Let's hurry," whispered Jonathan, "before they succeed. We can't possibly outrun anyone with this load."

"Fools!" laughed Jonathan. "While Romans are trying to break down the gates of the city, Jews are hoping to break down its back door."

Jair tried to angle the torch so that Dan and Yerod could see well enough not to slip again. A heavy, regular pounding came from above, each one louder than the last.

The passage now slanted sharply to the left, and the right-hand pole was too long to round the curve. The two carriers were forced to pitch it steeply upward. But the poles were already ancient, and when they did this, there was an ominous cracking sound.

"Careful," Yerod cried out in a frightened whisper.

"It's all right," said Dan. "I told you, I am Kohen. I will not be harmed."

"I think we should be more concerned about damaging the Ark than about our individual safety. Let me trade places with you for awhile," said Jonathan. "Jair, take Yerod's place for a while. Give him a rest."

Jair squeezed past the two carrying the box and took the upper ends of the poles from Yerod, while Jonathan took their lower ends from Dan. Yerod was now in the rear of the party. Dan took the lead with the torch.

"Ahead," Dan warned, "Be careful. The passageway has no steps but still slopes downward. And there is loose gravel—"

Even as he spoke, Jonathan's foot slipped on the loose stones. "I nearly dropped it. Careful back there."

They heard a splintering crash from above and yelling, then screaming.

"Someone has fallen on the stone stairs," from Yerod. "That should slow them down a bit. Maybe we should put out the torch."

"They are still at the entrance," said Jair. "Even if they venture down, they won't be able to see the light from this torch. Keep moving!"

Now, at the bottom of the passageway, the path lay almost straight ahead of them.

"Put the torch out now," said Jonathan.

"Are you insane?" barked Yerod. "It'll be totally dark in here."

"A torch can be seen from outside, through the other end of the passage," Jair said. "There's an encampment of Romans nearby who, doubtless, have already found the body of one of their comrades here in this very passage."

With a frightened sigh, Dan extinguished the torch by burying its head in the dirt floor. "Only the Lord knows what we will stumble over next! Walk slowly."

"Quiet," Jair snapped. "Get moving!"

Dan took the lead. After each step forward, he moved his foot from left to right, warning aloud of any irregularities in the ground. Behind him, carrying the poles of the blanketed box, Jonathan and Jair shuffled forward in unison. Yerod brought up the rear.

Nearing the other end of the passageway, Dan could see dim light from the moon illuminating the cave entrance. To his dismay, he saw that the boulder had been rolled completely aside. This secret passageway was no longer a secret! Worse, just as Jair had feared and foretold, they heard voices ahead of them, speaking Latin.

"Hear that?" a man asked.

"Jair," Jonathan whispered, "put this down. We may have to fight."

"Forward," whispered Dan. "Draw your knives."

"What's that cave?" a voice asked, of an unseen companion.

"Not a cave, more like a tunnel."

"Can you see inside?"

"Too dark in there. Let's get some torches and the others to help us. Could this be the servants' entry into Jerusalem?" followed by snickering.

"Might it be so! Flavius would reward us."

The voices receded, seemingly away from the entrance to the cave. Jair and Jonathan picked up the poles supporting the covered box and started off quickly.

They could hear the mob coming down the passageway behind them.

"Quickly," said Jonathan, "let's go."

"*Adonai*," Yerod whimpered in a childlike voice.

Jonathan found him huddled on the floor of the passageway and yanked him sternly to his feet.

Yerod began weeping fearfully, oblivious of Jonathan and the others. From behind them, the voices and shouting grew louder.

"Yerod, we'll be caught by the mob if we don't go." Jonathan grasped Yerod by the hair and slapped his face, hard. "Now move!"

Yerod stumbled forward. With the others, Jonathan crept toward the end of the passageway, watching for soldiers. At the entrance of the passage, Jair paused to look for Yerod, a few paces behind.

Jonathan turned his attention to the night outside, but could see little in the darkness. Over the rise to the west, light was playing to the sky from some unseen campfire, and he heard voices.

At the Roman encampment, a Centurion was glaring into the darkness while the two soldiers were running from tent to tent. "A back door to Jerusalem," they shouted. "Let us seal it off, before they overwhelm us!"

Other soldiers, half-asleep, were buckling on swords and armor, preparing for a fight.

"No one in sight that way" Jonathan whispered, pointing southeast. "Let's get out of here, and quickly!"

The four set off as fast as their burden would allow. The terrain was uneven—soft dirt in places, rocks waiting to trip the unwary in the dark. The soldiers, ready for battle, rushed up the low hill to the cave opening. At the top, they paused.

"I see nothing," one said.

"The cave is down there. In that ravine at the base of the hill."

The four men with their burden between them were nearly fifty cubits from the entrance to the passageway when the first three of the mob broke through. The younger of the three spotted the four men with the box.

"There they—" he pointed to the fleeing men, but was interrupted by the force of soldiers who had burst over the hill.

"What's this?" one of the soldiers cried out. "On them, men!"

The Roman soldiers saw only the noisy crowd at the entrance to the passage, and they fell upon them as the four made their way into the darkness.

Later that night, four leagues from Jerusalem, the four sat to rest. "A short distance south of here is the Jericho Road, where the Romans patrol from time to time. We should avoid it," said Dan.

Jair and Jonathan agreed.

"Where can we take it?" Jair looked first at Dan, then at Jair.

"Maybe we could bury it here," offered Yerod, who had been silent since exiting the cave. "The four of us will never reveal its spot. It will not be found until some future generation discovers it, and then by accident."

"But here it is not easily protected," said Jonathan, "I think we should take it to Masada, as the Essene suggested. There, it could at least be defended."

"But Masada is held by the Romans," objected Yerod.

"Not if Eleazar and David were successful," replied Jonathan with grim certainty. "We have not yet heard, but I will tell you this—I was with David when we put to death that aging whore of the Herods, Salome. Eleazar told me they would do this, and I believe it's done."

Dan said, "It will be light in a few hours. Let's rest during the day, in a low place where no one will see us by chance. I'm exhausted."

"Me too," said Yerod.

They found a spot sheltered from view from the south and west, but they were not sure how far the road to Jericho might be.

The moon had set, and the stars gave a little light. Dan lay watching them move slowly across the sky. Sleep did not come to him, and after a time he sat up.

"I will go south a little and see what is there," said Dan.

"Be careful," Jair whispered.

Dan disappeared into the night. An occasional bush caught at his feet in passing. Some wild mice scampered away, startling him. He hoped he didn't run into any vipers or scorpions. His thoughts wandered back to a time when Israel was more peaceful; when he, his father, and brother Abraham had traveled to Jericho from their home in Be'er Sheba.

****

It had been a long walk of many days. The weather was cold and wet for that time of year. The three of them had set up a simple camp. A low cooking fire was hard to keep burning because the wood they collected was damp. The three of them had huddled shivering around the fire when Abraham leaped up, shouting with pain. A scorpion had stung his ankle; and after that, he had been sick for a long time.

****

There was a sudden loud rustling and a high-pitched shriek as a ground bird, frightened out of its roost, climbed into the night sky with the pounding of wings. Dan's eyes followed the bird's flight and noticed a thin thread of smoke filtering into the nearly cloudless sky, trailing off to the west.

He altered his course to the east, and worked his way toward the smoke. As he approached, he could see that there were many trees clustered around the spot. It must be the very same spring where he and Abraham had camped with their friends so long ago.

Dan crept into the trees, carefully looking ahead. Most likely there was someone on watch. He kept low and moved silently closer to the fire. By its light, he could see a circle of forms covered with thin cotton blankets. A tent was erected on the south side of the circle, facing north. Beside its entrance was a lance planted in the ground, a banner with the image of an eagle hanging from its top. His senses were alert. He could hear every sound of the night—the horses breathing, one of the soldiers snoring. The Roman beside him rolled the snorer onto his side with a punch to the shoulder: "Stop snoring, Agrico. Do you always have to do this?"

By the fire sat two men, talking in low tones. Dan edged a little closer. *Careful of the scorpions,* he reminded himself, his fear growing. There was a slight noise beside him, to his left. He jerked in such panic that he feared he had revealed his presence.

The two by the fire began talking again, this time slightly louder. A big man, who had been lying on the ground almost in front of the tent, tossed his blankets aside and rose to his feet. "Will you two shut your obscene faces! Some of us are trying to sleep."

"Yes, Claudius," one replied with exaggerated tolerance.

Half asleep, the one named Claudius staggered toward Dan. He stopped at the edge of the firelight and began relieving his bladder into a bush to Dan's right.

Baruch Atta Adonai . . . Dan began the prayer in his head for comfort.

"I can see dawn," Claudius told the men by the fire. "Adrianus said to wake him at first light, and then raise the camp. You better wake him. He's been in a fit since we lost Masada. I've never seen him take anything so hard."

"He's afraid he's going to lose rank," one of the men said.

"He'll be lucky if he doesn't lose his head," said another.

"We'll all suffer for Masada," said Claudius, a tall husky man.

"Alexander, see if you can catch another scorpion, it was fun watching him dance in the fire."

"We'll all be lucky if we don't lose our heads, much less rank," the other said softly. "Adrianus may even be executed for doing something so stupid."

Dan began edging his way back out of the oasis. If he didn't get away under cover of darkness, he might not get away at all. Now, with a faint light growing in the east, he knew he would soon be visible to anyone who lifted his eyes.

His foot brushed a fallen limb. Claudius noticed the rustling sound and turned to look in that direction. "What was that?"

"A cursed lizard's been rustling around in the leaves all night. Leave him. He eats the insects. Maybe by the time we have to come back he'll have eaten them all."

"If he's big enough," said Claudius, "we could have his tail for breakfast."

"Just what I want for breakfast," groaned another soldier. "Claudius, don't make us all sick."

Dan made it to the edge of the oasis, crawling on his belly. If he could make it around the corner of the low rift, he could get away.

"Wake up, Adrianus! It's almost dawn," loudly from Claudius.

Just as he rounded the corner of the low hill and was out of sight, Dan heard a voice in the distance call, "Did you see that? A wild goat just dipped behind that hill. Let's see if we can catch it."

"Yes," another cried out. "Goat stew will make a fine meal."

If they picked up his footprints, he was a dead man. Dan rose to his feet and, ducking his head, sprinted toward the northeast, away from his party with their burden from the temple. After about 50 cubits, he curved off to the east for a short distance, then south again. Finally he stopped in a cleft between two low hillocks, panting through his teeth, and listened.

He could hear soldiers, but could barely make out their words. On his belly again, he climbed to the top of one hillock. The sky was still too dim to see very well, but he could see shapes moving behind the low hill where he had disappeared. As he watched, the soldiers started back toward the oasis.

Too close, Dan thought. Slowly he slid back down the hill and lay on his back with his eyes closed, breathing in relief.

Returning to where he had left his companions, he slowed his approach out of caution. But as the camp came into view in the distance, he realized no one was there. As he grew nearer, he saw a form on the ground—a Roman soldier—sprawled awkwardly on his back, with one leg curled unnaturally beneath him. The man was dead.

Dan halted, sick with renewed fear. He buried his face in his arms and sat still for a time. After recovering his courage, he inched forward again. Satisfied there was no one around, he quietly rose and approached the corpse. The soldier had a wide gash his throat and had bled heavily. Sickened again, Dan saw a human hand lying in the dust a few feet away. It had been cut off cleanly, just above the wrist, and did not belong to the Roman.

"Where the hell have you been?" demanded a loud voice behind him.

Heart pounding, Dan snapped his knife out of his belt and whirled around to find a big man in homespuns, with a wild beard and thick black hair smiling back at him.

"I'm sorry I startled you," Jair said.

Dan sat on the ground and cradled his head. Jair sat down beside him. "We were worried. You've been gone for hours."

"What happened here?" Dan asked.

"Two soldiers, apparently sent to hunt for us. We heard them coming and made short work of them. The other is behind that rock. But if there are those two, then there must be others."

"There are," Dan said. "I saw them."

"Even before we left Jerusalem apparently, there were rumors that a certain important item had been taken from the temple. Flavius thinks he knows what it is, and he's right. He sent a party to find us and recover the ark. It must never fall into the hands of our enemies, ever," Jair told him.

"Jerusalem?" asked Dan.

"It has not yet fallen. If we can get this safely to Masada, we must go back and try for the great Menorah that stands before the Kadosh K'doshim."

"Where are the others?"

"Headed southward. Jonathan knows of an oasis in that direction, and we need water," Jair replied.

"We must stop them!" Dan leaped to his feet. "There is a Roman garrison at the oasis, of fifty men at least."

5

David and Soo-ooni

Masada

Soo-ooni walked with her empty clay jar toward the cisterns, Harai behind her. Harai returned his gaze to the visitors approaching on the plain below. Soo-ooni continued on the well-worn path to the top of the stair, and began the descent.

If only she were still living in her father's house in Bethlehem! Masada had beautiful views of the Salt Sea, and she loved watching the birds play on the rocky mountainside; but they were refugees here, and might have to live here a long time.

She continued down the stairs. During the time of Antony and Cleopatra, when the Romans constructed the palace on Masada's north lip, they had taken care to create excellent drainage from the roofs. When the rains came, none of the water was lost, but drained into the vast system of cisterns.

Now Soo-ooni came in sight of the water. "Why is there so much of it?" she'd asked her mother, on seeing it for the first time.

"There are great pools for swimming in the palace, and the Romans must have their baths. Would you believe, under the baths are great furnaces for heating the water!" Her mother had laughed. "Not only must those pigs bathe daily, the water must be hot and perfumed. How could our fighting men lose in a war against such pampered soldiers?"

The light was dimmer in this damp enclosure, but Soo-ooni could see a person seated quietly by the water's edge. Stepping closer, she saw the chalil resting at David's feet and felt his gaze on her. Again she thought of the days in Bethlehem and of David's first visit to her father.

****

Jerusalem

Flies buzzed in the hot sun, attracted by sweaty bodies working in the heat. A merchant was leading a mule loaded high with carpets and sleeping mats, on his way to the market where he would set up his booth with many others.

Soo-ooni's mother was grinding in the front of the house. "There goes Housami the Syrian," she said of the rug seller. "His sleeping mats are from Judea, but he always says they are from Syria. I guess if he made them, then the rugs must be Syrian."

"They are not Syrian rugs," her father had said. "They are made with wool from Judean sheep, woven by hands fed with Judean food, and the mats' straw is softened with water from Judean wells."

"But the knowledge of how to make them came from Syria," her mother answered.

"What does a woman know?" her father demanded. "If I say they are not Syrian rugs, why do you argue with me?"

"Bah!" her mother retorted. "Because you have that silly thing between your legs, you think you have brains too!" Soo-ooni understood and looked back out the window so her father would not see the laughter in her eyes.

Three boys were coming down the street. They were neatly dressed because they were coming to see her father, Saul. He was often sought out to teach young boys their letters, for all boys had to be able to read the Holy Torah before they could become men.

Soo-ooni always laughed when these three came. For fun, she called them Shadrach, Meshach, and Abednego, because they always looked so holy when they came to study. But she knew that Abednego had another name, and she liked to think of it when he wasn't there. It was David.

During their lessons, she kept close enough to overhear so that she too could learn.

"'Aleph' means 'ox,'" her father stated. "It is the first letter and also means 'one.' When Aleph stood before the Lord to receive his duties, he was disappointed that he could not also be the first letter in the Torah, but Adonai said to him, 'Aleph, don't be crestfallen. You will be the first letter in the name most people use to pray to me. You will be the first letter in *Adonai*. And Aleph was satisfied.

"Aleph," Saul continued, "represents the stability and strength of the Earth, for upon it rests all the other letters. Since it means the number one, it also represents the one God and symbolizes the highest spiritual values, goals, and progressions. Of the elements, it is the sign of air."

"Soo-ooni," her mother chided, "he would be angry if he knew you were listening."

"But my mother, my Eema, it's such fun. Have you heard the stories he tells about each letter?"

"Yes, Soo-ooni, I have eavesdropped too. But it annoys him deeply, so I try not to let him know. Go to the market now. Here is a silver coin that one of the boys gave your father for his teaching. It should be enough to fill this pot with olive oil."

"But Mother, can't I listen some more first?"

"Go. I need the oil for my bread. Then you may listen some more."

When Soo-ooni returned, she headed straight for Ha Cheder, the name the boys gave the room where they learned Hebrew.

"Dalet is the fourth letter," her father was saying.

"Soo-ooni," her mother whispered. "If he catches you, you may never be able to listen again."

Soo-ooni nodded with a grin, her finger in front of her lips.

"Adonai made Dalet to look like a door frame, so Dalet means 'door.' It stands for the door to the temple—not in Jerusalem, but the one Adonai will build in heaven. Dalet is the door to the House of God, and through that door pass those who would go to Him."

Soo-ooni's attention quickly wandered from her father's teaching; she was more interested in watching Abednego. The fuzz on his upper lip was most amusing to her. She wanted to touch it some day, but never dared get too close to him, because she would have to giggle. *He knows I'm watching,* she told herself. *I think he likes me.*

Her father stood, holding up a scroll and pointing at a letter. "What is this letter?" he asked Shadrach.

"Gimel, Robbi?"

"Very good, Nathan," said Saul. "A very important letter, though some lend it even more significance than it deserves."

A man appeared at the front door and stood reverently waiting for Soo-ooni's mother, Adameh, to notice him. Adameh continued grinding for a moment, to let the strange man know that his reverence was welcome and appreciated. After a proper wait, she went to her husband, who was still lecturing the boys, and there she stood, as reverent as the stranger at the door.

Saul saw Adameh standing there, and gave her the same treatment she had given the stranger—mostly as an example for the boys. Saul loved Adameh and always answered her promptly, when his pride permitted him to do so.

"Zayin," he continued to his students, "is the seventh letter, thus the number seven. When Zayin stood before the Lord, he said to Adonai, 'I stand for remembrance, for by remembrance comes wisdom. Wisdom produces power. When power is wielded by wisdom, it produces harmony. I, Zayin, am the cudgel that protects the orderliness of society, and guards the path which man must use to return to God.' This is why Zayin means 'a weapon.'"

After he felt the proper time of waiting had been completed, Saul said, "Yes, My woman?"

"A stranger waits at the door."

He already knew this, but had to go through the proper social sequence. Telling the boys to wait, he went to the door, bowed slightly to the stranger and invited him in.

In truth he was no stranger, but Katchum the sheep farmer from the hills south of Bethlehem. They always saw him at worship on Friday night and had known him for many years. He and Saul had studied their letters together as boys. Saul's seemingly aloof treatment was merely social etiquette for the occasion.

"I greet you in love and humility," Katchum said.

"I welcome you to my house," replied Saul, and clapped his hands twice. Adameh had been expecting this signal, and had cakes and wine ready to bring in on her husband's command. "I offer you refreshment."

"I am most grateful, Rebbi. My throat is dry and my hunger delights at such cakes."

Soo-ooni and her mother retired to the other end of the room and sewed, listening carefully to the conversation. The series of pleasantries seemed endless, but such social ceremonies were always attended to when a guest came calling. After the cakes were eaten and the wine drunk, Saul moved for Katchum to state his business.

"Such a nice thing for you to visit me," Saul said. "And such pleasure to eat cakes and drink wine with you, my friend Katchum. What fortunate event has brought you to my door?"

"I will tell you, my friend. I have long carried this thought in my heart and it has given me great joy to think of it."

"What thought is that?"

"As boys, we studied together. We climbed the hills of Judea together. We had Bar Mitzvah in the same month, and were fast friends almost from birth."

"This is true," said Saul, beginning to worry about what favor Katchum wanted to ask. "Our friendship has been long and greatly rewarding."

"You will remember, then, the time we went to Solomon's Pools in the hills south of Bethlehem, and the agreement we made as boys."

"Of course," said Saul, growing even more concerned, because he did not remember, "and I am happy that you now remind me of it."

"Tell me, my old friend," said Katchum, knowing that Saul did not remember, "when shall we plan the betrothal ceremony?"

Soo-ooni dropped her sewing and reached for it, her face rising in color. She knew that Katchum was David's father—but Katchum had two other sons, whom she did not like so well.

"The first Sabbath after Purim. Will that be a good time?"

Soo-ooni heard nothing more that day except David's name mentioned several times. And now, in front of the cisterns of Masada, she was alone with her betrothed for the first time.

He spoke softly. "*Shalom*, my wife-to-be."

"*Yom tov*," she replied shyly, eyes lowered. "Good day."

For a moment she stood silent, waiting for him to speak, holding the water pot closely in front of her.

"Soo-ooni, you are very beautiful."

Briefly she met his eyes before quickly lowering them again.

He said, "I am glad you will soon be my wife." He could see the exposed flesh around her throat darkening. "Let me help you with the water," he added, rising to take the pot from her hands.

****

David also had fond memories of the first time he had seen Soo-ooni, but those of the events surrounding it were not so fond.

It was mid-spring of the year before he began studying with Saul. His father and mother took David and his two brothers to the Holy City to celebrate the Passover, accompanied by many others journeying from Bethlehem. Among them was an Essene who taught as they walked along. His name, David remembered, was Shasha. His long hair was tied to one side, and his eyes flashed with excitement and love of the knowledge he imparted.

"When a thing of great import happens, we remember it for longer than a single lifetime, since the knowledge is passed from parent to child for many generations. Finally the knowledge becomes so old that no one really believes it anymore, and men begin to call it legend. In that form it lives on, until it finally fades from the memories of those who live on the Earth.

"How the center of the world came to be chosen is one of those things. Many seek it now, where Adonai placed Eternity into man's mind, the City of God. Long before the earliest writings of man, the children of God lived in that City, but wandered from it and were lost in the wilderness, until they forgot where they came from, and who they were. But Adonai led them back when the time was right."

The Essene gazed at those walking with him to see that he had their attention. David half listened as he watched the flowers waking to the spring season.

"The City has been known by many names since its birth," Shasha continued. "It has been called Shalem, Salem, and Beth Shalem. Earlier, before the days of Abram, it was called Moriah. But the first names it bore have faded and vanished, even as its streets and houses, gardens and palaces."

Shasha lowered his voice even more, so that only those close could hear him, almost as though he were speaking to himself alone. "Possibly there may exist a shade, lurking in the darkness of early morning, whose heart would be stirred to hear *Ayeedenayee'ah*"—The Essene looked directly at David—"for this was the first name upon its gates."

If Shasha had said that for his hearing only, David did not understand why.

The Essene again raised his voice to a conversational level. "But things will change, and men's hearts grow hardened by constant beauty. The name passed out of knowing, and for thousands of years, the city was not known by many, until the children of God returned. Chastened by centuries of slavery under the Pharaohs, and burned by the sun and the winds of the desert, they renamed it for what it was, and continues to be: the Cornerstone of Peace, the Holy City, *Yerushalayim*."

"Father," David asked Katchum later in the day, "what's a cornerstone?"

"The first stone the builder lays. It is always placed in the northeast corner of the building and bears the builder's signature. It carries the weight of the entire structure, upon which all else is based, just as the letter Aleph is the cornerstone of our Aleph-Bet and precedes all the other letters."

"Why is Jerusalem the 'Cornerstone of Peace'?"

"Just as the cornerstone bears the weight of the building, our cornerstone of peace will bear all the hate of the world, the brunt of all the evil, all the sin, before the building of the great Shalom is finished. But cornerstone it is, and the Cornerstone of Peace it shall be called, until the pillars that hold up the Earth are crumbled and forgotten."

David was frightened. "But father, those pillars will never fall. Will they?"

Katchum laughed, as they walked along a hill overlooking the city. "The old scrolls say they will. 'For everything there is a season, and a time for every purpose under heaven.' Everything gets old. . . ."

"But how could the hills fall? And the city wall? Nothing could bring them down."

"I hope not," Katchum said through a chuckle. "Then the Romans would have no more people to rob and steal from."

To David, the Romans had fair-complected skin and shiny armor. He could hear them coming from quite a distance, because of their rattling shields and swords. He liked to watch them pass by, all walking in step. "They seem brave and strong to me," he once told his father, but was immediately silenced.

"When you are a man, David, you will understand the evil they do to us. They are not brave or good. They are defilers of our land. They steal our goods and our people. They make us slaves. They are to be hated."

David never again defended Romans to his father, but he continued to admire their appearance and apparent strength. Alone, from time to time, he imitated their stride and played with make-believe swords and shields. Fortunately, David spent most of his childhood outside of Jerusalem, and until this trip, had never seen the reasons for his father's hatred.

After the Passover meal, Saul took him to the secret meeting of the Sicarii, and for the first time, he heard the ancient words from other lips than his father's. At the beginning of the meeting, they all cried in unison, *"Shema Yisroel! Adonai Elohenu—Adonai, Echod!"* Hear O Israel! The Lord, our God—the Lord is One!" The reciting of this prayer, David learned, was the opening ritual for the Order.

"We have learned the idea and value of association," they intoned, "the necessity of a union of the oppressed with each other, and of a secret bond of affiliation, to enable us to regain our liberty."

Most of the meetings were little more than an outlet where the men could shout their hatred for Rome. At the third meeting David attended, the men had settled down enough to organize a raid. Afterward, David did not go home with his father, but went walking in the hills to think. He did not know that so many agreed with his father so completely.

He had heard his father accuse the Romans of all sorts and manners of crimes, but never a specific crime, never a specific place. Now, for the first time, he had learned of priests of Jerusalem, murdered for preaching against the placement of the Roman Eagle before the Temple, and captured Sicarii who were executed, without trial, by crucifixion.

David walked all night in the hills, facing the question of death for the first time. "What is death?" he asked aloud. If he or his father were killed by the Romans, what would happen to them? Where would they go? Who was God, who would allow such things to happen? And then he prayed.

Most of the night he spent watching the stars and the setting moon, and still he demanded of himself, *what is death?*

The first light of dawn found him stretched on a large rock beside a stream, crying bitterly that his world was to be soiled with blood. What troubled him most was that the blood might be his own or his father's. As he lifted his face to the eastern horizon, he listened to the song of birds, which he was so afraid he would miss when he was dead.

A new sound was in the air, not so welcome on his ear: women's voices. He was on his feet and out of sight behind a rock.

The women had stopped at the side of the stream. Peeking around the rock, David saw they were carrying laundry. He was about to draw his head back again and wait for them to finish, when one of the women caught his eye. Had she seen him? If so, she made no sign and said nothing to the others. A certain faraway look in her eyes caught his attention. For the second time in twelve hours, he was experiencing intense emotions completely new to him.

There was grace in her movements, strength in the way she handled her work. As she scrubbed the clothing against the rocks, her forehead began to perspire, and he wanted to go and dry it for her. He almost started when she pushed her hair back from her face and sneezed.

"It was really very strange," he told his father that afternoon. "Inside, I began to feel a strange longing, but I didn't know what for." He scratched his head. "It felt like I was hungry, but not for food."

"And still two years to your Bar-Mitzvah!" Katchum wailed in mock agitation.

"This is the way of it with men and women, David. For a few years, you live as children. You eat and sleep, and learn the legends of your fathers and their fathers. You do the chores you must, you grow, then one day your whole world changes, and never again can it be the same. There comes a day when a young man looks at a woman, and knows for the first time, that he is a man. It seems the whole world is filled by only you and that woman.

"This is what is meant in the old scrolls you have learned to read," he continued, "where it says 'She filled his eye.' You once asked me what that meant. Remember?"

****

In the dampness of the cisterns, David smelled the sweetness of the cool air. His first awareness of Soo-ooni lay far in the past; and again he marveled at how different his life had become since his sheltered boyhood. Soo-ooni! He watched her easy grace, the sweep of her hair over her shoulders as she bent the clay pot to the water's edge; and he recalled that first time he saw her at the stream.

His voice broke the silence of the cisterns. "When I look at you, it seems my eyes are filled."

6

Raised from Profanity

Masada

Eleazar was standing before the northwest lip of Masada's plateau, overlooking the palace. He gazed at the silver sickle hanging in the east. "A new moon," he said softly.

Harai, who had not budged from his seat on the edge of the wall, was still gazing silently into the distance. Now he lowered his head slightly, as though considering some important question, and turned to meet Eleazar's gaze.

"The beauty of its light fills my heart."

"You Essenes have such a peculiar way of saying the simplest things. Even so, it is a peaceful sight."

"It calls to the peace you have within; your inner peace answers its call. This is what you feel."

Eleazar considered Harai's wizened silhouette: a man of undeterminable age, his hair neither dark nor white, but silverish. Eleazar felt the great power in him.

During Eleazar's youth, there had been two Essenes at the Jordan River, one baptizing the other. He'd felt the same sense of power emanating from them both.

"Harai, may I ask you a question?"

"Ask."

"When I was a boy, there was a man, Yashua Ben Yoseph, a Nazarite, whom some called a Messiah. The Romans killed him. Do you remember?"

Again gazing at the moon, Harai nodded.

"Was he Essene?"

"He is *Gimel*. My brother." Eleazar did not see the emotions crossing the old man's face. "And my beloved friend."

Eleazar pressed on. "But the Messiah? Of course not! Had he been, every Roman now quartered in Jerusalem's Antonia Fortress would be back in Rome. The Herodian dynasty would have been pruned with a sickle knife, like the rotten branch on a healthy fig tree. Israel would be free."

"The consciousness of the Messiah is in all men," Harai stated. "What man needs to be freed of, men still do not understand. What Yashua accomplished, men do not yet understand."

"What, exactly, did he accomplish? To preach against Rome, and get himself executed. To what end?"

"Yashua is Gimel."

"You meant the past tense: He *was* Gimel."

Harai turned to face Eleazar. "I mean the present tense. Yashua *is* Gimel."

"You Essenes always talk in riddles. Didn't Yashua do the same?"

"Can you read?"

Hajai's question shocked Eleazar. It was the nasty, age-old sneer that almost every 12-year-old boy had to endure, at least once. If he could not read, he could not recite the Torah, therefore could not complete his Bar Mizvah. He could not become a man.

Was Harai smiling? At the least, he was staring at Eleazar with the same expression he had worn earlier, while admiring the sickle moon.

"Tell me about the letter *Gimel*."

Unsure of himself, Eleazar fought to quiet his emotions. "In Ha Cheder, every boy is taught what the letter Gimel means. Surely you needn't hear it all again?"

"Say the words to me," Harai requested, "so that *you* may hear them again."

Instinctively, Eleazar stood. Reluctant, he began to recite: "When Gimel stood before Adonai, the Lord said, 'Tell me your duties.'

"Gimel replied, 'I am the camel, the third of three. Upon me, man rides across the great abyss between the material and spiritual worlds. I carry man to visit the seven palaces, on the spiritual path by which man returns to God, the final home of every mortal being."

Harai merely smiled.

Once again, Eleazar fought his impatience with this baffling Essene, so opaque and yet so transparent . . . "I don't understand your meaning. How could Yashua—how *can* he be the letter Gimel?"

"By sunlight," Harai said, "you have seen a lone ant travel a great distance. To him, each rock is taller than a mountain. Each gap between floor tiles is deeper than the Valley of Shadows. Despite all, he finds his way back home. How can a simple ant accomplish that?"

Hiding his annoyance, Eleazar shrugged.

"The ant can smell where he put his feet along the way. He uses these footprints to find his way home. But without those reference points, he is lost. If you or I rub our fingers across the ant's path, the scent is erased and the insect cannot find his way home. But also, this is true of men."

"Harai," said Eleazar, eager to change the subject, "I invite you to attend our meeting after the supper hour. The party who arrived from Jerusalem today brings tidings, and we crave your reaction to what they say."

"I will come to you," Harai replied. *And I am Zayin,* he thought. Again he turned to watch the setting crescent, remembering his initiation as Zayin.

****

Qumran

They were sitting before the steps to the monastery at Ayin Feshkha, the Essene center in Judea. Simon was with him.

"Will this truly be this enclave's only meeting? Ever?"

"Yes, Hjarai. As you know, each enclave comes here individually, and by choice. Its goal—its task—is agreed upon in advance, and honored throughout time."

"But what task have *I* chosen? I know of none."

"That," said Simon, "is the purpose of the initiation. Afterward, you will know."

Harai was then blindfolded, stripped of all clothing. Then they conducted him, naked, to a door where he made the appropriate four knocks, followed by three.

The door opened. From within, a voice inquired, "Who dares disturb the deliberations of this holy place?"

"Hjarai, the profane," Simon answered for him, drawing out the sound of the 'Hj,' "who desires the enlightenment and self-knowledge of his quest, by which he chooses to serve."

"Hjarai," rasped the voice within. "Are you willing? Are you capable?

Are you wise enough to receive the gift of Ascension, to return to God, who is our Home?"

Obvious euphemisms for death! thought Hjarai. "I am," Hjarai answered.

"To attain this goal, are you willing? Are you capable? Are you wise enough to surrender yourself? Renounce distractions of the flesh? Together with all hopes of acquisition, family, and comfort?"

"I am! God help me!"

"Wait until Aleph, in the northeast, learns of your request and returns his answer."

He heard the door close.

After his initiation, an Essene got to his feet and called out, "Bayt!"

A man seated at the west end of the hall arose and replied: "Master Aleph."

"Your duties?" from Master Aleph.

"To house the ineffable Name of God. To keep its sacred pronunciation in solemn secrecy."

"How do you intend to do this?" Aleph demanded.

"By never speaking it, nor thinking it. So that no one with ears to hear, can hear."

"When will you dispose of the Name?"

"When the three are reunited," Bayt answered. "As was agreed."

Aleph spoke again: "Gee-mel. What is *your* duty?"

Hjarai's classmate arose. "To encourage the meek, to discourage the bold. To remind souls that who does not love will wither and die—for only by giving love are we granted strength in return. My duty? Imparting the knowledge of the Gimel's path."

When it came Hjarai's turn, the Aleph—whose office was held by Simon—called, "Zay-een?"

Hjarai arose.

"What are your duties?" demanded the Aleph.

"I," said Hjarai, "stand for remembrance. By remembrance comes wisdom. Which produces power. Which, wielded by wisdom, creates harmony. I, Zayin, am the cudgel that will protect that which is holy."

"How will you do this?"

"By remembering," replied the Zayin.

"Heretofore," said the Aleph, "you have been named with a profanity: *Hjarai*, which refers to the offal of the streets. From this date, the other side of man's nature will hold sway in your heart, and henceforth you will be called *Harai*, Mountain of Holiness.

"What is the sign of this assembly of Guardians of Holiness?"

Zayin answered, "It is the pelican, rending its own breast to give sustenance with its own life to its young, four in number."

"What truths does this image suggest?"

"The young represent the four letters in the ineffable name of God: *Yod, Hey, Vov* and *Hey,* unpronounceable except by the Bayt, in the presence of the Three. The mother pelican represents the singularity of the one God, and the young collectively represent man. Together they symbolize the King of the Universe, giving of His own Essence to nourish and redeem the spirit of man . . ."

****

Masada

"Harai," called Eleazar. "Come now to the meeting."

The meeting was lit dimly by a low fire atop the north wall. The three men—Abram, Caleb, and Amos—had come in today, their families with them.

"We lived just south of Jerusalem," Caleb began. "By the time we fled, Vespasian's army had besieged Jerusalem for three weeks. The troops took all of our sheep."

"They'd have taken your daughter, too," Abram cut in, "had they been able to catch her."

"Jerusalem must have fallen by now," Caleb mused. "The Sadducees were arguing for surrender, including that traitorous Josephus, the Galilean. He was with the Romans, trying to negotiate for Vespasian."

"Everyone will be slaughtered," moaned Amos. "My father and mother still live there, and my two aunts . . ."

"All of us have loved ones in Jerusalem," said Abram. "All of us will lose them."

"Latest rumors say that Nero has committed suicide," said Amos, "that Vespasian will be called home. But no one believes it."

"Let us pray that it be so," said Adameh, Soo-ooni's mother.

Eleazar cut in: "We have an Essene with us.

Awe and curiosity swept the room.

"They are prophets," said Abram.

"Even Herod consulted them," Eleazar added. "But did they ever grant him a direct answer?"

Harai stepped forward, his white robe glimmering in the lamplight. He stopped before Eleazar, gave him a token bow, and seated himself on the ground across from the three.

"I answer directly," he said. "The problem, Eleazar, arises when you and I lack common points of reference. My answers reflect more than you ask, and as much as you *should* ask."

"Why is there an Essene here?" demanded Amos. "They are opposed to war! Their community at Ayin Feshkha has moved to Damascus, and abandoned Israel."

"Who are you, Essene?" asked Abram, "Why are you here?"

"I am called Harai, here out of choice. My brothers have not abandoned Israel. They have only abandoned chaos, exactly as you have done."

"Never trust an Essene for a simple answer," raged Eleazar. "His answers only incur more questions!"

Harai smiled and bowed, deeply this time. "And you, Eleazar, have the wit to ask good ones!"

"Here out of choice!" Eleazar snapped. "What *have* you chosen, Harai?"

"Peace. For myself, for those around me, for any I can inform. As for you, Eleazar: Do you choose to die here?"

"I choose to fight."

"Enough bickering!" David said. "If we have a prophet here, let us request a prophecy." He turned to Harai. "Is Nero dead?"

"I believe so."

"Then will Vespasian be recalled to Rome?"

"It is my belief that he already has been. Are my answers direct enough?"

Despondent, Eleazar rose to his feet. Stepping to the fire, he kicked some half-burned kindling back into the flames. "Your answers are direct, but have I asked the right questions?"

Harai gazed into the flames. In Recalled Sight, two men were carrying a shrouded box between two poles—and two more, far behind, striving to catch up.

But in his mind's eye there stood a tall man in a white robe, who had not been there at the time. The man spoke: *Shalom, brother Bayt!*

Peace unto you, brother Zayin, Harai mentally replied.

"Harai!" Eleazar demanded of him. "Have we asked the right questions?"

"Questions give birth to answers," said Harai. "Then, answers bring forth learning. Which gives birth to growth and improvement, which can never be harmful. Therefore, you can never ask the wrong question! Is it not clear, the wisdom you require? Then ask—of me, or of anyone— what you need to learn!"

"Harai?" Eleazar was about to continue when Harai smiled gently.

"As you already know, my answer is yes! Is that direct enough? You have not chosen the eternal peace, which lies within. Instead, you are seeking a temporary death."

Eleazar frowned. "May I ask a different question? Will Rome seek to regain Masada?"

"So I believe."

"*Will* Rome regain Masada?"

"Rome will think so."

"What kind of answer is that?"

"I have no written history of the future! You, here on Masada, have yet to determine what will happen here . . ." Harai's eyes were perceptibly darker—". . . in concert with the Romans."

7

A Little Prestidigitation

Jerusalem

It was yet before daylight.

"Ananas!" Kadaa called into the sleeping chamber. "Wake up. They're at the gates!"

Since the day when I was appointed Captain of the Temple Guard, not once have I been able to wake that stinking old man, thought Kadaa. *Not even in an emergency, like now!*

"Kadaa! Come quickly!" someone shouted.

"Can't those incompetents do anything for themselves?" Kadaa grumbled, running toward the temple gates. "Assemble the guard!" he called to the figures on either side. *"Now!"*

Kadaa stormed off toward the guards' sleeping quarters. The Temple gate was shored up with beams to hold it secure from the mob outside. Behind it, one of the two guards leveled his gaze in Kadaa's direction, and spat.

"He has always been a blowhard," the guard said, "and I have always hated him." Kadaa was a short, almost cut-off man, with one eye half closed by a scar.

"Calm yourself, Solomon," said the other guard. "If he hears, he will punish you."

"When he comes back, let's push him out the door and let the crowd have him."

"If we did that, he couldn't punish anybody. Could he?"

At the guards' chambers, Kadaa found some two dozen men in various states of undress. "Why are you oxen not defending the main gate?" he shouted. "Are you so busy playing in bed that you can't do your jobs?"

Low grumbling began, but nothing Kadaa could hear. A knife flashed here and there, but all the blades were being sheathed, not drawn.

"By the time I get back, I want you asses on your feet and at that door or I'm going to toss you into the streets!" Characteristically, his voice rose in pitch and volume at the end. Turning his back on the troops, he hurried back toward the quarters of the old High Priest Ananas.

Darkness still cloaked the room. Ananas did not fear Kadaa, even though he knew the man wanted to kill him, and might yet find the courage to do so. Ananas had seen him many times, admiring the gold Menorah that stood before the Holy of Holies, and his gaze was not one of reverence, but of avarice.

Ananas had also seen him caressing the gold vessels of the Temple and defiling them with the covetousness in his heart. The only thing that prevented him stealing these treasures was the authority of the priests, especially the One Priest—Ananas himself.

He had seen the hatred in the guard's eyes, growing along with the duration of the siege, the unrest of the populace, and the food shortages. Hunger, of course, was the reason for the onslaught on the Temple gate. It was common knowledge that the Temple kept a store of provisions for the priests and the guards.

Ananas rolled onto his right side and stroked the empty air beside him. "Ah, my lady, I hope you are safe with your family in the south. I am so proud of our son, and cannot tell you so. Miriam, would that I could hold you again before the city falls and our people are all put on crosses."

He recalled the sight of Jonathan and Jair removing their sacred burden from its resting place in the Holy of Holies. The builders were so cunning! They foresaw that the future might bring a time of crisis, and provided for it. From generation unto generation, only the High Priest and his son knew of the door beneath the altar, and of the passage beneath the Temple leading out of the city—the passage Jonathan and Jair had taken with their sacred burden.

"Modeh Ani Lefanecha, Melech Chai Vekayam . . ." He began his morning prayers, thanking Adonai that he was still alive. Finishing, he drew his prayer shawl more tightly around his shoulders and left for the Temple's meeting room.

He sat on the top step of the chancel and waited, listening to Kadaa storming through the temple, shouting with his harsh voice: "Where are you, Ananas? Ananas!"

The old priest didn't have to wait long before the Captain of the Temple Guard burst into the room.

"There you are! Do you know the people are nearly through the door? Do you know they are nearly upon us?"

The old man gave Kadaa a well-practiced look of sadness and defeat. The dejection on his face, such a departure from his accustomed arrogance, shocked the Captain into silence. Ananas held his face up just long enough for Kadaa to get a good look at it, then slowly lowered it and began sobbing into his hands.

"What is going on here?" Kadaa asked. "What is happening?"

Rocking and wailing, Ananas waved his arm toward the Holy of Holies, where the curtain was pulled aside. Kadaa could not believe his eyes. Slowly he approached the enclosure, mouth agape, tears forming at the corners of his eyes.

"It is missing," he said in a flat voice.

The Captain's apparent calm told Ananas that Kadaa was almost hysterical. Allowing himself a very slight smile, Ananas rose slowly, continuing to wail, but gradually regaining his composure.

"How could this have happened?" Kadaa demanded. "With the crowds at the gate, at every exit, how could it have been removed?"

The old man made tears well in his eyes. "How could we have failed our ancestors in this way?" he sobbed. "Sacred objects carrying themselves out of the Temple without so much as a protest from your guards. What does the Temple treasury pay your men to do, but eat and sleep?" He let his aged voice rise in apparent anger and frustration.

"Where were you last night, Kadaa? Did you know of this?"

Kadaa fell to his knees. *He is mean and petty,* Ananas thought. *And none too clever.* In a gesture of despair, Ananas rubbed his hands over his eyes, continuing his diatribe against the temple guards. Still, he was glad that Kadaa revered the holy items he was sworn to protect.

"How could a Kohen of the Kadosh Kadashim allow this precious relic to simply vanish from the Holy of Holies?" Thoroughly enjoying his performance, Ananas let his voice peak in volume and pitch. Kadaa had progressed from shame to anger, and now was ready to be guided to his next task.

"I myself was outside this door all night," said Kadaa. "I heard you and Jonathan and Jair praying in this room. I heard you leave. No one else was here."

"You must have fallen asleep!" Ananas shouted.

Two guards slammed open the far west entrance and walked quickly into the room. "Your pardon for the interruption," one said. "The mob outside has a battering ram and is breaking down the Temple door."

"The time is come," said Ananas. "Solomon and Kalim, Kadaa, come with me."

Kadaa followed the old priest up to the altar inside the Holy of Holies. Ananas showed Kadaa where to place his hands on the altar and placed his own on either side of them. "Now, with me, push to the right."

As Solomon and Kalim watched in astonishment, the altar slowly moved aside, revealing a rectangular hole in the floor, large enough for four men to stand in together.

"This hiding place was shown to me by my father, who learned it from his father before him." said Ananas. "It has not been revealed to any other since the time of Jeroboam, after King Solomon's Temple lay in ruins. I have no fear in showing you this, because of your vows of secrecy. And before it is needed again, surely your great-grandchildren will be old and this place will be forgotten.

"You three, place these covers over the great Menorah, and these ceremonial vessels, and carry them into that passageway. Follow the tunnel as it goes, until it comes to a great rock blocking your way. Push hard on the rock, straight forward. When you move the rock aside, it will block the passage from the city to the valley floor and leave only one remaining avenue of escape from the temple—out toward the southern valley below the city. Anyone coming down the passage from the city will think the passage ends at that rock. Only one coming from the temple will be able to find the other end of the tunnel."

A great crash came from the main gate, shouting, and sounds of conflict.

"We're out of time," Ananas said. "The outer wall is breached, as is our main gate. Before moving the rock and trying to leave, wait behind the rock for three days. Or you will be caught and killed, and the Temple treasures will fall into the hands of the Romans. Go now. Pull the altar back before you leave."

The three men dropped into the hole beneath the altar and, with the priest's guidance, slid the top back into place. From his sleeve pocket, Ananas withdrew a thin piece of brass roughly as long as his forearm, lowering it into a hole in the top of the altar. He heard it slip into place and watched as the heavy stone altar gradually sank into the crypt, filling the hole it had covered and seeming to become a part of the floor.

At the Temple entrance, the commotion was growing louder. The old priest could hear a crowd approaching. With what could have passed as a sigh of relief, he turned and faced the entrance to the Hall of Worship. Still remaining within the Holy of Holies, he reached one hand to the curtain, now tied open, but normally closed to conceal the holy objects.

He waited until the crowd burst into the room.

"There's the old hypocrite! Get him!"

With a flourish, Ananas closed the curtain and allowed his memory to return to better times. *I am Dalet,* he thought, *Door to the Temple that houses the Name of God.*

And now, I am closing the door.

A woman had just entered the Hall of Worship. "Where are the provisions?" she screamed.

"Get that priest!" a man shouted. He rushed toward the Holy of Holies, with another behind him. He grabbed the curtains, pulled them apart and stood there, staring. The other pushed him aside and peered in.

"There's nothing there! I swear, I saw a priest and an altar behind this curtain."

"They never had anything in here. All a hoax from the beginning. Behind this curtain, supposedly, was the Ark of the Covenant, containing the tablets upon which God wrote the Ten Commandments in his own Hand."

"Legend," sneered the ill-tempered woman who had first entered the hall. "Priests use superstition to earn their money. That's all they're good for."

8

Concealment

Masada

The moon rode high, and Harai walked the northern lip of Masada. Behind him, the ancient summer palace of Herod lay dark and deserted.

Some of the refugees were sleeping in its vacant rooms, but most had chosen quarters above, on the main plateau. He glanced at the northwest horizon, then lowered his eyes. Hands together, each in its opposite sleeve, he walked back through the palace courtyard, into the main hall, to a passageway leading to the baths at the rear of the complex.

The warming fires had gone out long ago, and the water in the pools was cold and stagnant. Harai raised his head to listen. In complete silence, he continued onward to where bathers used to disrobe.

In his mind's eye he saw the bygone soldiers, statesmen, kings—replete with feasting or just returned from battle. Now, only silence and darkness. He continued to the far side of the room to a low door and, lowering his head, entered the complete darkness and started down to the chambers below.

****

On the plateau's main level, Eleazar could not sleep. He rolled this way and that, finally dozed, only to be awakened by his own snoring.

"Tonight's talks made you restless," said his wife, Hazar. "Go walk, and you will feel sleepy."

"Where is there to walk?" he asked. "The streets of the city?"

"Just go."

Eleazar rose from their sleeping mat and went into the night. The air was cool. He pulled his shirt closer around his shoulders and walked on. His restless feet took him around to the west rim and he paused at the guard tower. How easy it was, he thought, to take Masada. The Romans were completely fooled.

Ever since he was a boy, Jerusalem had been in turmoil. But it was the High Priest's new ruling on foreigners sacrificing in the temple that sparked the insurrection.

He kicked a stone ahead of him, listening to it skitter along the ground. At the north end of the plateau, he began climbing down the descent to the palace grounds. As though being led, he wandered in through the main gate.

Eleazar shivered slightly and turned toward the entrance to the baths. Lighting a torch he had picked up along the way, he continued toward the furnaces below.

Why was he coming here? No one had been in this place since Herod's slaves tended the fires. Entering the furnace area, he felt a cold stone floor under his feet. Above him, columns and arches supported a stone ceiling. Firewood was stacked in one corner of the room. Several raised platforms bore piles of charcoal, and he walked through the feathery ashes of many fires which had drifted and scattered across the floor.

How many slaves had carried that wood up here? He lowered the torch the better to see his footing. Ahead he saw the figure of a man, waiting at the far end of the room.

"What ghost is this?" he said aloud.

"It is I," answered Harai.

"Abbi Yashan?" asked Eleazar in amazement. "Why are you here?"

"To speak with you."

"You are the reason I couldn't sleep tonight?

"Did you have difficulty sleeping?"

"I did, Essene. What else explains why we both are here at the same time, in this awful place?"

Harai's eyes became very intense. He extended his right hand slightly. "It is a pleasure to see my friend!"

"Why are you here, Harai?"

"To discuss a problem." Harai's voice was strong and steady now. But his right hand trembled slightly, and he lowered his head, as if concentrating.

"Yes," said Eleazar. "What can I do?"

"Our provisions are not properly stored. Gather the young men, and remove seven of the building blocks in this wall. Hollow out a chamber behind there, sixteen cubits square and high enough for a tall man to stand without grazing his scalp. Tell no one else of this, since this will supply Masada, secretly, when our other foods are gone."

"I will remove seven blocks in this wall," Eleazar recited. "And, behind this wall, hollow a chamber sixteen cubits square . . ."

"The work shall begin at first light," Harai added. "None shall be told except the men doing the work. Now, return to your sleeping mat. You will not remember being here tonight. And on first waking, tomorrow, you will present this endeavor as your own idea. Your sleep will be refreshing and fulfilling. Now go."

Eleazar had lowered the torch. Now Harai took it from his hand, so that he would not burn himself.

Eleazar turned. Walking in total darkness as easily as though in direct sunlight, he made his way back out through the arches of the palace, up to the plateau.

At first light, he circled Hazar's waist with his arm. "Awake again?" she asked. "Go back to sleep!"

"I slept well all night," said Eleazar, "except when I dreamed that our food supplies on Masada were running low."

"Foolishness!" Hazar murmured. "The bins have enough to feed twice our number, for years to come."

Eleazar rose and said no more.

****

The furnace chamber was just as dark at noon as it was at midnight. To see what they were doing, the men lit torches. Eleazar had chosen David, Ashar, and Carib to do the work.

Entering the room, they did not see the Essene seated on one of the ash-covered fire platforms. A strange silence fell over them. Only Eleazar spoke occasionally, to direct the work. "Remove no more than seven stones. That will be enough for entering and leaving."

"Seven will make the entrance wider than necessary," Ashar said.

"Remove seven of the blocks," Eleazar said, "carefully, so that no one can ever know they have been replaced."

As the men began preparing the chamber, Harai remembered Simon's admonition against falsehood and wrong use of force—both of which he had committed today.

****

"Hjarai," said Simon, on that day long ago, "What is morality?"

"Giving up the material world so that our spirits are free to go home to God."

"But Hjarai, how does morality do this for us?"

"By giving away what material good comes to me, I remind myself that I am the master of that material good . . . that material things have only material value, but no real value.

"In strict truthfulness I bring myself into the Light of God and incur no spiritual debts to my fellows which I will have to repay before ascending. In sexual abstinence, the creative forces within accrue, strengthening my ability to believe, to hear and see, to heal others—and to build the power I need for the ultimate spiritual ascension."

"Hjarai, after gathering strength for the ascension, can you still become embroiled in matter and become unable to leave it?"

"I can, my Brother Simon, by falling prey to the temptation that power brings. By using that power to bend others to my will."

"Beware of that temptation," said Simon. "It is your final enemy."

9

Opening the Day

Qumran

Qumran was the Essenes' home near the Ayin Feshkha oasis. The journey from Jerusalem had taken three days. Unaccustomed to such long walks, Hjarai was utterly exhausted.

Simon led him to a building of stone where other boys, around Hjarai's own age, were preparing their sleeping mats.

"This one is yours. It was prepared for you."

The boy had never possessed anything that he could remember. Now, having his own personal sleeping mat was slightly unbelievable. "*Todah*, friend Simon. Thank you."

"I will return for you in the morning, Hjarai. For the good of all, you must learn our customs, our habits. Tomorrow will be the time for that."

Simon turned to go.

Other men in white homespun were speaking briefly with some of the other boys, then leaving one by one. Hjarai stretched out on his mat, recalling what Leah had said about the Pious Ones: *No one has ever seen them eat.*

Would they let him starve? Or did the Pious Ones never eat, just *drink*—living solely on the unclean blood drained from the throats of sheep and goats and cattle? Such hideous gossip he had heard from the children of Gehenna.

Turning his head to the right, he looked into the timid eyes of another boy, watching him with curiosity and trepidation.

Finally he overcame his fear and shyness. "My mentor told me I am Hjarai. Did they give you a name, too?"

He saw the fear leave the boy's eyes.

"I am to be called Itzchak," he said in hushed tones. "And him over there," he gestured, "that's Yashua. He's got a mother and father."

"Do you?" Hjarai asked.

"No," answered Itzchak. "I have none. Platta, the tax collector in Yaffe, says I was a worm hatched out in camel shit. But there must be something wrong with me, 'cause camel-shit worms never grow big as me."

Not long after Hjarai slept, he dreamt of Simon. Simon was watching him from the door of the room where he lay on his new mat. *Twenty-two of them*, Simon announced. *What the Council of 24 calls an Aleph-Bet—twenty-two, working together for a common goal.*

Other men in white homespun were entering the room, each taking his place beside a different sleeping boy. The dream-Simon placed his hand on Hjarai's right shoulder.

"Time to open the day. Come with me!"

Outside, the land sloped downward to the east. Simon spoke softly: "There are twelve times twelve thousand of us, each with his own duty. Gathered today are near to one thousand—some from as far as the wild lands north of Rome—to witness this dedication."

"Is this my *Aleph-Bet* which is to be dedicated today?"

Simon nodded.

Simon led Hjarai to the very end and sat him down beside Itzchak. Yashua, the one with parents, was seated next to Itzchak.

A light dew covered the ground. The air was still, the sky filled with stars. Hjarai looked over at Itzchak. Both afraid to speak, they looked to the east and saw a man who had not been standing there before.

He wore a solid white piece of cloth that hung to his ankles. His rich black hair was tied in a single braid behind his head. The light surrounding the man was brighter than any Hjarai had seen before.

Hjarai's eyes grew large and his thoughts fell silent, for there were two separate lights on either side of the man, and slightly behind him. The man between the lights was looking directly at him. Hjarai found himself sweating and his cheeks warming.

The man's gaze seemed filled with warmth and comfort. Hjarai knew he had always been a known and loved part of this company. All the other boys were crying with the same joy.

As they watched, a deep resonance filled the air—the voice of the man standing before them.

"My brother Hey, see that this gathering not be disturbed."

From behind them, they heard the response, "My brother Aleph, it shall not."

"My brother," asked the man in front, "how have you determined this?"

"Many brothers, at proper locations, will lead off the curious."

"Brother Bayt. Have all present been duly initiated into our order?"

"Yes, brother Aleph. All present except for the new *Aleph-Bet*."

"And how have you determined this?"

"By touching the hearts of each."

"My brother Gimel?" asked the man addressed as Aleph. "What is the hour?"

"Our last hour of the night, when the light touches the horizon but the sun has not yet risen."

"What is the purpose of this gathering?" Aleph asked.

"To open the day," Gimel replied, "and dedicate this new *Aleph-Bet* to its new union and ultimate function."

"The orb of day has driven away the darkness," intoned the Aleph, "and the intellectual and spiritual light we seek is upon us."

"How do we open the day?" asked Aleph.

"By welcoming the orb of enlightenment which is about to crest our horizon and praying that, like that light, the Messiah may rise out of the darkness under which mankind dwells, bringing the light and joy of a new day."

The voices of all the company joined in the chanting, prayers, and thanksgiving as the sun crested the horizon.

Morning came to Ayin Feshka. The sun was above the horizon.

There were now two rows of boys behind him, all watching the Teacher of Righteousness. The sun, rising behind him, shone through his clothing and, seemingly, through the man himself. The brilliance of the sunrise outshone the two lights on either side of him, but Hjarai could still feel their presence.

Later, Hjarai asked Simon, "Who were those who spoke this morning?"

"Those purified by suffering and sorrow, and by the intercession of the *Elohim*, known as the *Achad*, the One. The Aleph of this Aleph-Bet is the Aleph of Alephs, the reigning head of our Order, the Teacher of Righteousness."

"What were those lights flanking the Teacher of Righteousness? Can you tell me?"

"Let's suppose that you are blind, as so many are. I ask you to describe my face. What is your reply?"

Baffled, Hjarai shook his head.

"Any explanation you can give must involve words. Words can only compare what you're explaining to what you already know. If there's nothing similar in your experience, then you will have no words to describe my face.

"This is why some of our lessons here are taught in the form of stories, or represented by symbols. As for the two lights you saw, let me say—for now—that they are symbols of man's spiritual nature and of his existence in many forms at once."

"Is this the same as the lights I see around you?"

"The lights you saw around the Teacher of Righteousness are separate from him, in a different way than the lights you see around me. Do not *think* about the lights, Hjarai, *feel* about them. Look at the lights around me now, and tell me what you feel."

As Hjarai watched, Simon's light seemed to darken from near white to a color Hjarai could not name. "The light is like blue, but it has red in it too. It's beautiful."

"You are thinking," Simon admonished. "Try feeling the light."

Hjarai reached out his hand, within the limits of the light he saw around Simon. "I can feel where it is."

"Put your hand down, Hjarai. Then tell me what your heart feels."

****

The gentle western breeze blew a wisp of hair across Harai's cheek. First light elicited song from Masada's cliff-dwelling sparrows. He heard footsteps approaching. His brooding eyes brightened, but he did not turn.

"*Shalom*, Harai," said Eleazar.

"Thank you," said Harai. "My wish for you is also peace."

"Why are you always up to watch the sunrise?"

Eleazar had so many questions because his mind was restless, stressed by the conflict Harai had given him, digging without knowing why! Eleazar now knew that Nero was dead, and that Flavius had been recalled to Rome, leaving his son Titus as governor. Eleazar feared, because Titus was known to be cruel and treacherous, too proud to leave a handful of Jews in command of any scrap of Judea—especially a place like this, forcibly wrested from Rome.

"They will come to us soon," he said aloud.

"True," said Eleazar. "Is that why you watch the east?"

"I wait for the light to come, and to enjoy watching its progress."

Harai sighed deeply, and folded his hands in his lap. Eleazar was tired after digging the crypt that Harai had ordered. The calluses on

Eleazar's hands testified to his decades of work—farming, building, pulling loads, fighting for his homeland. Was it really necessary to hide from him what he had done?

Eleazar glimpsed the brief smile that crossed Harai's lips. "Are you mocking me?" he demanded.

"I am wondering how your clothing became so soiled."

"There is no stream here for washing clothes," Eleazar snapped. He gazed down with a puzzled expression and began brushing dirt from his clothes. "How *did* I get so dirty?"

He didn't remember a thing! No one would ever know!

Eleazar crawled up on the wall beside Harai who, to hide his smile, turned back to watch the eastern horizon. "You have not yet told me why you watch the east."

Harai remained silent for a moment. "Do you not find it beautiful, that the sun brings light and warmth and life where before there was none?"

"It has always been this way," Eleazar shrugged. "First the darkness, then the light."

Harai looked at Eleazar's intense, nearly angry gaze, and felt the man's sincerity.

"There are things you can learn, Eleazar, which I have no words to tell. Close your eyes. Turn your face to the sunlight."

Eleazar did so.

"Can you feel the warmth on your face?"

"Yes . . ."

"Feel it for a moment," said Harai. "Then tell me. What is the sun itself feeling this morning?"

Eleazar lifted his head and Harai saw his lips turn up in a slight smile. "I will tell you what the sun feels, Essene. It feels joy."

10

Scorpions

Flight from Jerusalem

Along the road to Jericho, Dan and Jair kept on the alert for soldiers.

"We must stop Yerod and Jonathan before they reach the Romans at the oasis," said Jair in a loud whisper.

"The soldiers may have moved on by now."

"Keep low."

"I am keeping low," said Dan.

"Don't go so fast." Jair paused and looked at the dust behind them. "Were you close enough to hear anything?"

"Yes, too close. They were from Masada, which has fallen to the Sicarii. They are in no hurry to report to Flavius."

Jair quickly hugged Dan, and kissed him on both cheeks. "So the fortress we're headed for is no longer Roman, but Jewish once again! What else did you overhear?"

"They fear being punished for losing Masada."

"Did the soldiers say anything about Jerusalem?"

"No," Dan said. "Most were asleep. "They talked of torturing scorpions over their campfire. They nearly caught me."

They walked on, more slowly, so as not to raise the dust. *What of Ananas,* Jair worried, *and the sacred objects in his care? Again the Temple will be destroyed, as it has been twice before! Good that he sent Miriam out of the city before the Romans arrived.* His brow furrowed with distress. *Provisions were exhausted, except for the cache in the Temple. That's why the crowd was so furious.*

"Did you hear Josephus, General of Galilee, exhorting the people to surrender the city gates?"

"I heard him," Dan said.

"But isn't he the son of Matatyahu? Yoseph Ben Matatyahu? Now his name, as he shouted it to the city, is Josephus Flavius. He's adopted the name of our enemy and our enemy's language as well."

In the rising heat of the day, Dan wiped the sweat from his face. "When lives are in danger or families can't be fed, traitors abound."

"They say he surrendered almost at once. And now, he's encouraging more to be traitors like him. We depended on him for protection from the north. What kind of man is he?"

"Why are you so hard on him? We were fools to rebel! Could you withstand the swords of Rome's Tenth Legion with his puny two hundred farmers with winnowing hooks? Can you imagine how Yoseph must feel, groveling before our enemy? He is trying to save lives, and has sacrificed even his family name."

"Dan, look ahead." They stared southwards, at a haze of dust rising on the morning air. "I think that must be the road."

A small stone hit Jair on the left shoulder. Looking around, he saw Jonathan crouched behind a small rise, holding one finger in front of his mouth. Jair and Dan both dropped to a crouch. Jonathan hooked his two smallest fingers together. With his palms facing outward and his fingers closed, he mimicked an eagle, the symbol of Rome, then pointed at the dust rising in the south.

All four hid themselves separately, until the dust cloud had made its way safely past, on toward Jerusalem. Jair and Dan cautiously rose. Watching carefully, they walked in a low crouch to where the other two waited.

"Dan told me about their camp at the oasis," Jair told them. "We were afraid you'd walk right into them."

"We would have," Jonathan agreed. "But as we approached, we heard them calling to each other, searching for something in these hills."

"Me," said Dan, and told them about his narrow escape.

As the discussion went on, Jair looked from face to face, assessing each man. Yerod was their weak link. He had nearly folded in the passageway, but he was physically strong. He could help carry the heavy load for a great distance, as long as nothing frightened him. *If we're caught after we're lucky enough to reach Masada, could he hold up under torture?*

Jonathan and Dan were both Kohens, sons of the high priests, descended from Moses' own family, which was what made them Kohens. They seemed strong enough, but Jair suspected they knew more than they were telling. That pig Kadaa always said they preferred each other to women, but he said that of everyone, even about Ananas, the old priest.

"Where do we go?" asked Yerod.

"I think we should continue to Masada, as the Essene suggested," said Jonathan. "Dan?"

"Masada seems to be safest right now."

"Herod's summer palace?" Jair asked. "The Romans will be very eager to get it back from us."

"Masada can't be taken by conventional means," said Jonathan. "Have you ever seen it?"

"I have never been to Masada," said Jair, "but don't you think Flavius will head there as soon as he finishes with Jerusalem?"

"He will come, and then he will leave," said Jonathan. "It's impossible to take Masada."

"If the Sicarii took it from Rome," said Yerod, "then surely Rome can take it back."

"If I know Eleazar and David," said Jonathan, "we took it by trickery. The only way Rome could win it back is by being even more clever, except they don't have the advantage we had. They were arrogant enough to think themselves invincible. We know we are weak."

"Who needs tricks when they have so many men?" asked Jair. "All they have to do is march up the hill. Even if we could stand against their numbers, our troops don't have the training, the organization, the discipline."

"Jair, when you see Masada and still feel it is not a safe place, then we will talk of other alternatives," said Jonathan.

Jair nodded his assent. *How could any fortress withstand Rome? But where else could they hide it?*

"It's agreed then," said Jonathan. "Masada it is."

Night was best for traveling. But they had slept very little the past two days and needed rest before the sun went down. "One of us should stay awake," said Jonathan, "in case someone stumbles across us."

"I'll take the first watch," said Jair. "I'll watch until the sun is at its height, and then wake Yerod."

"I will watch until the shadows are as tall as Jair, and then wake Jonathan," said Yerod.

"Wake me too, at that time," said Dan. "I will walk ahead to see what there is to be seen, then return by dark."

"May Adonai watch over us," said Jonathan, stretching out on the ground.

"Jonathan," whispered Yerod.

"Yes?"

"How much gold is in that box, do you think?"

Jonathan saw the greed in his eyes. He thought of nothing but the monetary value of this sacred treasure.

"Much gold, probably," said Jonathan. "You have felt its weight. But it would have to be melted down to gain the value of the gold. A horrible thought."

Yerod rolled the other way and turned his eyes to the blanketed box, trying to imagine the wealth beneath its protective cover. He could never get it away from these men without help; even Jair would resist its temptations. Yerod had seen the sacred item only once, when it was placed in its protective box of acacia wood.

What he could buy with that gold! A comfortable home in any city of the world, and any woman he wanted. How could he keep it from being stolen? He might hire guards, but how could he trust them?

Jair glanced around the encampment. Jonathan seemed to be falling asleep. He turned his gaze to Dan, who lay on his side, head propped on his arm, looking back at him. Yerod, too, was lying on one side, facing the sacred burden. Dan and Jonathan didn't fully trust him, Jair thought. Dan lay awake to watch. Jonathan was fearful of falling asleep, while Yerod clearly lusted after the gold of the sacred object.

Jair raised his gaze to the distant horizon, where he saw a light puffy cloud float by and at the same time listened to his memories of his father, Ananas, yelling at his poor sister. Then his smile faded as he remembered that both his father and his sister were still in Jerusalem.

Dan saw Jair frown. Was he thinking of the gold we are carrying? Why should they trust him?

Jonathan made a slight movement to catch Dan's gaze, then moved his eyes toward Yerod, who was still on his side, watching the acacia box. What was he doing? Dan wondered. It seemed that this temple guard wanted the gold for himself.

Dan returned his gaze to Jonathan, who held his stare until Dan nodded. Then Jonathan laid his head back and closed his eyes. Dan did the same, but neither slept.

Jair had been awake for what seemed a very long time. Except for the bread and wine that Itzchak had given them, they had eaten nothing for days. But many farmers and shepherds lived in the country they were traveling through, and perhaps they could beg one chicken, or even two, to roast over a fire.

If only he'd had some rest over the last few days, staying awake wouldn't seem so hard. He stood up, but the heat of the day made even this exertion strenuous. The nearby hillside promised to give the best view . . .

Dan watched Jair climb the low hill and seat himself near the top, so that only his head showed above the crest of the hill. Even exposed as he was, he would not attract attention. The Romans' dust cloud was now arching slightly to the north, where the road branched to the right, toward Jerusalem. Had they been headed for Bethlehem, they would have continued west.

The morning dragged on; the heat rose. Jair had been sitting in the wilderness without moving, so after a time the little creatures that lived on the hillside forgot that he was there. A family of *akbarim* came sniffing out of their burrow. Jair, in his weary boredom, watched the mice. They foraged across the ground, under pebbles—which to them must seem like boulders—and under the shade of brush. One surprised a scorpion and was trying to kill it without getting stung. Two others were playing together. *Like lovers,* Jair thought.

A shadow passed over them, so fast that at first Jair thought he had imagined it. The mice knew better and scattered back to their burrow. Above, Jair saw a disappointed hawk circling and then, dipping away to the east. Jair watched the scorpion hurry away, finding a hiding place under the roots of a dry bush.

When the *akbarim* did not venture out to entertain him again, Jair's mind wandered. He unsheathed his long knife and stuck it into the ground, then tried to watch closely enough to see its shadow move. He couldn't, but whenever he looked back, it had grown shorter. Soon, when the shadow was at its minimum, he would wake Yerod.

A slight movement caught his eye. Near the roots of the bush where the scorpion had disappeared, a small beetle was making its way along the ground. It stumbled over a pebble, and recovered. In a flash the scorpion was before it, performing its deadly dance of death, its tail held high. The sting came so fast that Jair did not see it.

Was the hawk nearby? To the east and the west, the sky was clear, but to the north he saw a cloud of dark smoke, as if from a mighty fire, billowing off the horizon, drifting toward the east—indisputable evidence that Jerusalem was burning.

His eyes filled with tears. "Yerushaleyim, my home," he sobbed softly. "Rome, may God damn you and curse your children!"

Just north of them, he noticed what seemed to be a thin haze of dust, so thin he wasn't sure. Had he been sitting in the sun too long?

The scorpion held the beetle with one claw and tore at it with the other. Jair checked his knife sticking in the ground and saw that the shadow remaining was about as thick as two fingers. Almost time to

wake Yerod. To the north, the huge column of smoke seemed even wider. "Yerushaleyim," he sobbed, then thought he saw that slight haze of
dust. It seemed closer.

His knife's shadow was now as thick as one finger. Should he wake
one of his companions? He looked back at the scorpion and the beetle.
*There we are, Israel and Rome, fighting in the dust. Rome wants only
power, and we want only to go our way in peace.*

Jair sat up stiffly. Had he heard a sound from the north? Yes, there
it was again. Voices. Rising, he saw the scorpion raising its claws at him.
*Maybe the scorpion is more like Israel, readying to battle a huge op-
ponent one hundred times its strength. But with such a sting!!*

Jonathan awoke with a start and pulled his knife, instantly awake
and ready for the kill. "Jair, what are you doing?"

Jair placed a finger over his lips. "Listen!"

Dan, awakened from his half doze, yawning. "What—?" he started to
say, immediately quieted by Jair's signal. Yerod slept on.

"Voices," said Jair, "to the north. And a thin haze of dust, as if raised
by someone walking."

"I will go," said Dan. He rose and kicked Yerod lightly on the shoulder. "Come, guardian of the Temple treasure. We will go and see who is
approaching."

Yerod rose to his feet and rubbed his eyes, trying to keep hold of a
dream about selling gold to Egyptian princes.

Very slowly, he and Dan moved off to the north. At the bottom of
the first rise, Dan told Yerod to wait while he climbed the low hill for a
better view. He crawled forward until his eyes were just over the top of
the hill.

His first sight was of multiple columns of smoke, rising and swirl-
ing. In his heart, he knew that Jerusalem had fallen. Tears blurred his
vision. After a moment, he was able to refocus and search for the haze
of dust that Jair had reported.

There was no dust. But then, Dan heard the sounds of digging—the
chunk of a wide metal blade breaking up the soil—then someone sobbing. He glanced behind him to see where Yerod was.

That man was a danger to them all. He coveted only the treasure
that honored the Holy, but not the Holy itself, whose safety must never
be in doubt. *Perhaps I am too harsh,* Dan considered. *Nonetheless, the
man must die.*

Sliding back down the hill, he motioned for Yerod to go first. "North.
Quietly."

Dan didn't want this fool behind him, not while Yerod had a knife,
and they were both alone in the wilderness.

The sobbing grew louder. Yerod halted, while Jonathan mounted a low hillock for a better view. On returning, he drew his knife and indicated that Yerod should do the same. They rounded the hill and confronted a lone youth seated on the ground, sobbing, facing the rising smoke to the north.

He had been plunging his knife into the ground, again and again. It now lay beside a small shallow hole.

"Shut your mouth," Jonathan told him.

Seeing the two men with drawn knives, the boy threw himself face down on the ground at their feet. "I have no money," he wailed. "I am from the city you see burning to the north. Don't hurt me," he pleaded.

"Pull your face out of the earth," said Jonathan in softer tones, "and tell us your name and family."

The boy sobbed out the last of his fear and lifted his head to look at the two men. "Are you *Shodedim*?"

"We are not robbers," replied Jonathan. "We are men of Jerusalem, just as you are, fleeing the same enemy you fear."

The boy sat up, hugging his knees. "I am Yosiah, son of Adab, the stonemason. My family is all dead, and they burn before your eyes."

"How can you be sure they are dead?" asked Yerod.

"I saw them killed. My father was at the city gates when the Romans burst through. My mother tried to defend him. They cut her down too."

Jonathan remembered the Essene's request: *Feed the hungry.* "When have you last eaten?"

"Not since Sabbath. My father had some grain hidden in our home, but that was the last of it."

Jonathan produced the bag Itzchak had given him and held it out to the boy. "Here are figs and some bread. Eat what you wish."

Yerod's eyes grew large. "No!" he shouted and lunged for the bag. Jonathan knocked him away with one swift punch, and Yerod fell to the ground. He quickly sat up, glaring at Jonathan.

"When did you last eat, Yerod?" Jonathan asked.

"Yesterday afternoon, at the Temple. But we have no other food, and you would give what we have to this beggar of the streets!"

"I am no beggar," snapped Yosia. "I am the son of a stonemason, a builder."

"Builder or beggar makes little difference now," growled Yerod, fingering the hilt of his knife.

"You'd better not do anything foolish, Temple guard," Jonathan said softly.

Yosiah glanced quickly at the two men, then hurriedly opened the bag and crammed a fig into his mouth. He ate several more, then handed the bag to Yerod. "Take," he said, "eat, feed the hungry."

Yerod snatched the bag from his hands and took the three remaining figs.

Jonathan watched in amazement. "Are you properly shamed, Yerod? This boy, whom you would have starved, has given you the last of his own food."

"I am not fond of taunting, Kohen, and I am hungry. Our travel plans do not include taverns or inns, only bearing a burden."

"Don't speak of our task," Jonathan answered angrily. "All we know of this boy is his hunger."

Yosiah listened with interest. "You are a Kohen?" he asked. "Do you know what happened to Ananas? Everyone says he has disappeared, and the Temple treasures are gone as well. Some say Ananas stole them; others say his son Jonathan took them."

"I am Jonathan. Ananas does not steal, and neither do his sons. How do you even know of this slander?"

"I was in the streets this morning when Titus's troops entered the city."

"Titus?" exclaimed Jonathan. "Flavius was at our gates, not his bastard son."

"Nero is dead, Flavius was called home. All this time we all thought it was Flavius at the gates, when he has been gone for weeks."

"How do you know this?" demanded Jonathan.

"From the traitor Josephus. He announced that Titus was in charge, but under his father's orders not to burn the city or harm anyone. But that Titus had lost patience and was going to slaughter every living thing in Jerusalem."

Yerod, seeing Jonathan off guard, slowly began to draw his sword. But Jonathan pulled his own dagger which, Yerod knew, he could throw with great accuracy. Sullenly he returned his sword to its sheath.

"Yerod," sighed Jonathan, "you are as great a fool as the Jews warring within Jerusalem's gates. If only we could have fought as one! But with the priests against the Pharisees; and the Sadducees and the Sicarii and the Christus cults all against one other, we had no chance against Rome. And now, with only four of us, all you can think of is your own avarice, your own desire for the burden we share. Have you no shame?"

Yerod leaped to his feet. "You will not live to call me fool again!" He snapped his sword out of its sheath but, eyes wide with astonishment, dropped it to the ground. Very gently, he placed one hand on the hilt of Jonathan's dagger, imbedded in his throat. He pulled the dagger out, his throat pouring blood, and drew back his hand to fling the dagger at

Jonathan. Instead, he fainted and collapsed to the ground.

Yosiah watched in shock as Yerod's blood soaked into the sand.

"He will now join his fathers," Jonathan said. "We have been concerned about him, and now we need not be."

"If you hadn't done it, I would have," Dan said, rounding the hillock behind Jonathan.

"I thought you would," Jonathan said. "You trust Jair?"

"As well as I trust any man. Sincere and honest—after all, your father chose him! Besides, no man can carry it by himself."

"Agreed." Jonathan motioned toward the boy. "What do you suggest we do with this one?"

Dan looked at Yosiah and said, "Where do you hope your journey to end?"

"My father's brother lives at En-Gedi. I hope to go there."

"And so do Titus's soldiers," said Dan. "En-Gedi is no shelter, no escape."

"Titus!" Dan exclaimed. "Did Flavius leave his bastard in charge? Titus loves death, enjoys watching men die. But he won't be marching for a few days, yet. There are too many in Jerusalem he wants to see crucified."

All were silenced by the horror of what Dan had said. Yosiah turned to watch the smoke from the burning city.

"We are headed south," Jonathan told him. "To the west of En-Gedi. If you can walk that far, you may come with us."

Dan spoke: "Only if you bring that dead man's sword."

11

The Order of Malchesidek

Jerusalem

"Terentius Rufus, this holy city stinks."

Rufus and Titus stood just inside Jerusalem's south gate. "When we were here last, when I appointed you first in command, I thought the stench was beyond description. Now, it defies belief."

"Lord," replied Rufus, "it is the smell of death. You can barely see the pavement for the blood and the corpses."

"And even those are obscured by the smoke from the Jews' temple. I ordered that it be spared, and that those taken inside be kept for questioning. What excuse do your subordinates offer for their obvious disobedience?"

"They say that rebels inside set the fire. That in defiance, some even threw themselves into the fire to die, rather than be our captives."

"Terentius Rufus." Titus narrowed his eyes. "These fanatics choose death by Jewish fire over the hope of Roman clemency?"

Terentius shrugged. "How can I know their thoughts? There are also reports of two men stabbing each other at the same time, so that they commit murder, but not the sin of suicide. In some dwellings, whole families lay dead by their own hand."

The two men stepped into the city, picking their way amid the rubble and carnage.

"The destruction of their temple annoys me," said Titus. "The Jews might have knelt down to us, had their Holy of Holies remained intact. Now their Temple is in ashes, and they are dispersed. Rome will receive no more taxes from this ravaged, useless land."

A contingent of soldiers was approaching toward the south gate. Their prisoners were bound loosely in ropes, the women and children unfettered. One man lagged behind, limping from a deep wound in his thigh. A soldier behind him struck him heavily with his shield. "Get moving, you turd." The wounded man tripped over a dead body and fell to the ground.

One of the soldiers saw Titus and Rufus standing near the south gate. Word spread among them and they stopped to salute.

"Let them remove their prisoners," Titus ordered, "except for that one who fell."

As soon as the soldiers departed, Titus walked to the fallen man. Rufus kept pace with him, his sword drawn.

"Please don't get too close to him, my Caesar. He may be dangerous," Terentius Rufus said.

Titus now stood over the fallen man. "Who are you, Jew?" he asked. His troops had come to know that low tone of voice as Titus's Death Rattle.

The fallen man turned his face, covered with dirt from his fall, toward Titus.

"He seems near death, Ceasar. I wonder, is he even able to speak?"

Titus drew back his boot and kicked the man's head. "I asked you a question, Jew. Who are you?"

With great effort, the man said, *"Shema Yisroel, Adonai Elohenu, Adonai, Echod."*

"Terentius Rufus? Every time I kill one of them, they always say that. What does it mean?"

"'The Lord our God, the Lord is One.' They always say it when killed by an enemy. It's sort of a rallying cry, a motto. They even write it on strips of parchment and hang it on their door frames, thinking it protects their homes."

Titus drew his short sword. With great care and precision, he pressed it slowly into the man's throat. As it sank into his windpipe, the man grasped the sharp edge with both hands, drawing blood. His heaving breath bubbled through the deep gash in his throat. Titus's sword sank deeper, and Rufus watched the man's back arch and his eyes bulge from their sockets. With a final thrust, Titus pressed the sword deeper, severing the man's spine, then plunged the bloodied sword into the dirt beside the dead man.

"Did you see how life faded from his eyes?"

"Yes, Caesar."

The dead man was wearing a torn shirt, gathered at the waist. With one foot against the corpse's chest, Titus cut the cloth from the man's body with several short slashes, leaving the man naked. Then with great care, he wiped the man's blood off his sword.

"I like watching them crucified also, but they take too long to die. I get bored watching. I like the sword better. Then the death happens fast enough that I can actually see it."

Titus drew back his boot and kicked the dead man's head. "Damn their defiance! What makes them so stubborn?"

"They say a free man cannot be enslaved. If we take a child of theirs before he learns their traditions, and teach him he is a slave, then that child will think himself a slave and so will all his children. But if they grow up with their heritage intact, they would rather die in combat than surrender. Even when they have no food and no hope."

"Fools," said Titus. The two continued on, into the city. There was much noise ahead—shouts, and the clash of swords.

"Some in and around the temple are still resisting," said Rufus.

****

Jerusalem

As Titus finished his evening meal, he saw Terentius Rufus and three other soldiers coming through the camp, escorting a lone prisoner. The man was tall, with wavy black hair tied in back, and wore a white frock with a purple cloak buttoned in front. The soldiers pushed him hard from behind, so that he fell to his knees at the front of Titus's tent.

Terentius Rufus approached and dropped on one knee. "Sir."

"Arise and tell me, who is this man? And why is he dressed this way?"

Rufus stood. "He says he is Simon, son of Gioras. He pretends to be a god of the earth. Only four days ago, he arose from a hole in the ground where their temple stood, and tried to walk out of the city as though he were invisible. He is the one who held the upper city against us and refused your kind offers of clemency if he surrendered. When our men entered the hole he came from, they found scores of rebels, mostly dead by their own hands. The stench was unbelievable."

Titus stood, and stepped around his dining table. "Simon, son of Gioras, speak," he said.

"Your mercy," the man said humbly.

"Your mercy will be death," said Titus. "You will be held for the victory. Meanwhile, I have been wondering. We have taken your temple, which was said to house much gold and valuable relics. We found a few candlesticks and bolts of cloth, and incense. Where are the legendary great Menorah and the famous Ark of the Covenant?"

"I have never seen them, your majesty."

Titus waited. The man said no more.

When Vespasian was recalled to Rome and appointed Titus commander of the Tenth Legion in his stead, he gave his son a swagger stick, ornately cast in bronze. Titus liked its heft and found that human bone would give way without damaging the bronze. He now lifted it from beside his plate. With a swift motion, Titus struck Simon across the cheek.

Simon fell to the floor, bleeding. Titus took two steps closer and stood over him. Simon, his cheek caved in and blood filling his right eye, stared up at Titus.

"Answer my question, Jew, or you will not live until the victory celebration."

Simon pushed himself up to a kneeling position. "Among the people, it was said that the great Menorah and the Ark were smuggled out of Jerusalem."

"Where to?" snarled Titus.

"Those who first broke into the Temple said they saw a priest, with light glowing around him, standing in the Holy of Holies. The Ark and the Menorah were already gone, and the priest vanished before their eyes, like a ghost."

"Terentius Rufus," roared Titus, "have you heard any such reports?"

"I have, my lord. Others have told the same story."

"Where do you think these objects have been taken?"

"Some secret crypt under the foundation of the temple," answered Rufus. "We have found many underground rooms and passageways. It was in such a place that Simon and his men were hiding. They had provisioned themselves for many days, but ran out before we had departed the area. We did not find any of the treasures in these caves."

"Simon, son of Gioras," Titus snarled, "where do you think these relics are hidden?"

"There are many places where they could be," said Simon, his cheek swelling. "I think Terentius Rufus is correct. If not, the most probable places are Solomon's mines, or the home of the Pious Ones, who deem themselves the protectors of holiness."

"Terentius Rufus, who are these Pious Ones he refers to?"

"They are also called Essenes. Some call them Nazerites. They are said to have descended from the Order of Malchesidek, but none has confirmed this. They live in a monastery near the Qumran Wadi. The priest seen in the temple is said to have dressed as an Essene. Later, some said of him that, like the Essenes, no one had ever seen him eat."

"What nonsense is this?" snapped Titus.

"Of the Essenes, it is true," said Simon. "They may eat in secret, but none has ever reported seeing them do so. When they enter the Order, it is said that they take vows to follow a diet even more strict than that of the ancient law. It is said that an Essene separated from his commune would soon starve, because he cannot obtain elsewhere the food he has sworn to eat."

"Do you know of this, Terentius Rufus?" asked Titus.

"I know nothing of their eating habits."

"And who, may I ask, is Malchesidek?"

"I do not know, Caesar," said Terentius Rufus. "I will send for Josephus. He may have some information."

"Do that."

Rufus whispered into the ear of another soldier, who walked briskly away.

To Simon, Titus asked, "What do you know of Malchesidek?"

"It is said that Malchesidek was the first High Priest, who named the city Jerusalem. Before it was called Salem."

"It is said you held the upper city, Simon. Where is John, who held the lower city?"

"I believe he is hiding in the labyrinth of passages under the city, as I was. There is another access to it."

Titus saw Josephus approaching with the soldier sent to get him. He was tall for a Gallilean. His coal black hair partially obscured his patrician features. His expensive tunic was topped off with a Roman-style cloak. "Josephus," said Titus. "Tell me of the Order of Malchesidek."

Simon turned in surprise. "Traitor! I thought we had killed you."

"Terentius Rufus," said Titus. "Take the prisoner away and keep him alive and under close supervision. Now, Josephus, continue."

The same soldier who had fetched Josephus led Simon away, with two others following.

"The Order of Malchesidek ruled this city for a time. When the Maccabees fell from power, the order retired from the city and now live near an oasis called Ain Feshka. They are now called Essenes, and never speak the name Malchesidek publicly. This was told to me by my father, who heard it from his father and so on, for generations.

"Some have said that they studied under the Masters at Therapeute in Egypt. It was there that they adopted some of their practices, such as healing and prophesying."

"And this nonsense about their diet?"

"My father said Malchesidek was descended from the first men placed on Earth. Only those who fell from their true spiritual nature had to eat for physical sustenance. Those who had ascended again to the spiritual plane appeared to us as men, but were really angels, subsisting on the love of God. He further said that those who were yet trying to ascend could eat only living food, nuts, vegetables, sprouted seeds . . . no flesh of any kind. This is only legend, of course, but no one I know of has ever seen them eat."

"Terentius Rufus," said Titus, "lead one hundred soldiers to the Ayin Feshka Oasis, find these Pious Ones, take them all prisoner and bring them here for questioning."

Another soldier was waiting for him to finish with Josephus. Titus now gave him the signal to approach. The man stepped in front of Titus and knelt. "My lord," he said.

"Arise and speak."

"While exploring one of the underground passageways, we heard voices arguing; they seemed to be coming from behind a rock. We could not hear what they were saying, but immediately began working to move the rock. There was yet another passage behind it. Inside we found three men, one dead, another dying. This prisoner is the only one who still lives."

As he said this, another soldier pushed forward a man in uniform, heavily bound, with fetters on his feet. The first soldier kicked the man's knees from behind, forcing him to the ground. "Kneel before our commander," he snapped.

"I am Kadaa," the man said, "captain of the Temple guard."

"My lord," the first soldier interrupted, "in the secret passage, we also found these articles." Soldiers in the rear immediately stepped forward with a small litter bearing the great Menorah and other objects.

"What are these things?" Titus demanded.

Kadaa lowered his head.

"Don't play with me, Jew," said Titus. "I have killed many men for the pleasure of watching them die. I will enjoy taking your life with my own hands."

"These are the sacred vessels of the Holy of Holies. Ananas, the High Priest ordered me and two others to hide them so that they would not fall into the hands of our enemies."

"Where did the High Priest instruct you to hide them?"

"He said to take them to Masada."

"Where is the Ark of the Covenant?"

"I don't know," replied Kadaa.

"'I don't know' is another way of saying, 'I am ready to die.' Are you ready to die now, Kadaa?"

"I believe the old priest smuggled it out earlier. When I was last in the Holy of Holies, the Ark was gone."

Titus fondled his swagger stick, feeling the cool smoothness of the bronze that had so recently broken Simon's cheekbone. "Was this Ananas an Essene?"

"He could have been. It was rumored that he was educated by the Pious Ones, but never went with them," Kadaa replied.

"Where do you think the Ark of the Covenant is?" Titus demanded.

"At Masada, I think, since that is where I was to take these vessels."

"But you weren't taking them to Masada, were you? You were going to keep them for yourself. They would have made you rich. Is that why you killed the other two?"

"I was trying to hide the vessels, as Ananas ordered."

"One more question, captain of the guard. During the time you knew Ananas, did you ever see him eat anything?"

Kadaa raised his eyes in surprise. "I never did."

12

The Ankh of Therapeute

Masada

"I am afraid that Israel will have no more kings," Eleazar said.

"But I believe there will be kings again, someday," said Harai.

The hundreds camped on Masada watched the thick column of smoke rising from beyond the northwest horizon. Many of them crowded the high wall and watched in silence, some of them crying, a few chanting old rhymes about Jerusalem.

"It must be quite a fire, to be seen from so far away," one said.

"A whole city burning at once could make such a blaze."

"Why would they burn it? It was a great city," another cried mournfully.

"It was Titus's doing. You've heard the stories about him, haven't you?"

"Don't repeat them now," Eleazar told the man. "There is enough grief today, and no little fear that he will come here next."

"Do you think so?" Eleazar asked Harai. "Do you think Titus will come?"

"He has much to do," said Harai. "He has many generals, and I think he will send one of them first."

"The sun is hot. I am going to sit in the shade." Eleazar walked away from the high wall, his back to the smoke.

He is too full of grief to watch the smoke, thought Harai. *As are all of us.* He watched as the crowd gradually dispersed. Their best hope was that Rome would leave and forget about them. The Romans had left no guard at the foot of Masada, so groups went out from time to time, raiding Roman camps and strongholds, or searching for family and friends. Some never returned.

Harai saw David and Soo-ooni, hand in hand, walk toward the northern lip and start climbing down to the palace. It was good to see joy present, even on such a day. Reaching the palace level, they strolled along its perimeter, talking, apparently oblivious to the smoke on the far horizon.

Simon, my brother, where are we really going? He heard footsteps approaching and knew that it was Adameh, Soo-ooni's mother.

"What do you see, Harai?"

"I see youth, Adameh. What do you see?"

"Fear," she said. "I see my little girl, now almost a woman, in a world which will not have her. The man she wants is a warrior. He will probably die before their first child is grown. I weep for her, and I fear for her children, if she lives to bear them."

Harai's voice rose: "Thus says the Lord: **'A voice is heard in Ramah, lamentation and bitter weeping. Rachel is weeping for her children; she refuses to be comforted for her children, because they are not.'** Thus says the Lord: **'Keep your voice from weeping, and your eyes from tears; for your work shall be rewarded,'** says the Lord. **'. . . and they shall come back from the land of the enemy. There is hope for your future,'** says the Lord. **'And your children shall come back to their own country.'"**

"Jeremiah was speaking of the exile in Babylon," said Adameh. "Why do you repeat these things now?"

"Jeremiah speaks of every exile, and this is the beginning of one greater than he knew. Rachel weeps again."

Eleazar had returned. "And does the prophet again offer hope?" he asked.

"Hope is a spring in the heart of man," said Harai. "It rises and falls with the seasons. The prophet reminds us of this."

"Hope is all we have right now," said Eleazar, "and fear. And who is the prophet this time? You?"

"I am Harai." *And Zayin,* he told himself.

****

A simple word could send his mind into the past, reminding him of how he became who he was.

He recalled standing by the wall to the garbage dump in Jerusalem.

He had gained weight since his days at Gehenna and was taller, healthier. Another change was apparent: He now wore a white robe, and his hair was in a single braid lying across one shoulder.

And HaSapas was gone. Daydreaming by the wall of Gehenna, Hjarai remembered his own time in the trash, as a discard of the city. Now other children had taken his place, digging through the filth.

"Come on, Hjarai," said his friend Itzchak. "The others have gone on into the city." The harsh sound of his earlier name rang in his ears, but Harai remembered his old name with fondness, and Simon's gift of it.

Hjarai barely heard Itzchak, for one of the children of Gehenna had struck another boy and taken away a piece of discarded food. Hjarai's eyes were watering with the sorrow he felt. The victim dodged away and tried to run. But his attacker kicked him from behind, knocking him to the ground, and jumped on his back.

Itzchak pulled at Hjarai's arm. "If you don't come now, the others will be so far ahead we'll never find them!"

They were going for a mass Bar Mitzvah in the great Temple. The studies at Qumran had included many things, as well as reading and writing the language of God.

"You must learn to use your energy,'" Simon told him. It is the light that illumines all things, and you can use it for healing yourself and others."

"Is this the same light I see around you, my brother?"

"Not exactly the same. The light you see is a manifestation of the light energy focused within me. This energy is in you, also. Hold up your hand, like this."

Simon held his hand above his face and lifted his eyes to look directly at it.

Hjarai did the same.

"Now," said Simon, "see the light around the edges of your own hand. It may seem faint at first. But as you watch, you will see that objects beyond the edge of your hand are slightly distorted by the light emanating from your hand."

"I don't see it."

"You are holding your hand so that the sky is above it. The light of the sun is brighter than your light. Turn so that your hand is in front of that building."

Hjarai stood as Simon suggested. "Yes!" he said excitedly. "I can see it. It's almost white, like yours!"

"The light can be focused," said Simon, holding out his hand palm upward, at waist height. "You see the light around my hand?"

"Yes," said Hjarai.

"Watch."

In Simon's palm, the light seemed to brighten, then rose straight up in a bright pillar, about a cubit in height. There it stopped and seemed to split into two columns that arched to meet each other once again.

"What is it doing?" Simon asked.

"It has formed into an ankh."

"Now, place your hand through the opening at the top. Do you feel anything?"

"No."

"Move your hand out through the side of the ankh."

Hjarai did so. "I can feel warmth and resistance."

"You do it now."

Hjarai held out his hand and watched, but nothing happened. "How did you do that?"

Simon smiled. "This is the first lesson on your long journey. Everyone has three inner forces that God has given us, which must combine to form creative energy. Will is the direction finder, directing the energy and steering the cart. Faith is the cart which carries the power. Desire is the ox that pulls the cart. When you align your Will, your Faith, and your Desire—or Will, Conviction and Passion, as some say—nothing is impossible. Try again."

Hjarai held out his hand.

"Decide that this is what you want to do, Hjarai. Say it."

"I will make an ankh with my aura," said Hjarai.

"I see disbelief on your face," Simon chuckled. "Practice, and when you can do this, come to me. But for now, tell me. Why did I make an ankh for you?"

"I don't know."

"To us, the ankh is an important symbol, representing this power of which I have told you. The circle on top represents the One God, the creative force. For you, it represents Faith. The crossbar represents Desire, which can thwart as well as enable; and the upright shaft represents Will. The ankh also represents the human condition, with God above, then Woman horizontal yet above Man—the upright—in power and nearness to God. While man is usually the driving Will, too often he is ruled by that which is upright! So here is a double meaning: a caution to Man not to be ruled by his passions.

"The Ankh comes to us from our teachers at Therapuete in Egypt. It is a symbol from our ancient schools of healing. It has always been used by us in this way, even when we were enslaved in Egypt, before the days of Moses."

"That is enough of lessons for today. Go and practice."

The Temple was crowded with boys who had journeyed to Jerusalem for the occasion. Each read a line or two from the Torah, then explained the meaning of the passage. There were so many that Hjarai's turn did not come until mid-afternoon. He did not stay for the festivities afterward, but returned to Gehenna, where Simon found him near sunset.

"Have you learned to make the ankh?"

Hjarai did not answer at once, but continued to watch the children, orphans of the city, rooting through the garbage, driven by hunger.

"Hjarai!"

"It is a hard time for me to think about ankhs," he replied. "Look at them."

"I see them, just as I saw you. What I see is misdirected Will . . . Faith strong, but gravely misdirected, and chaotic emotions and desires. Hjarai, what do you see?"

"Children, abandoned by their families, by the city; abandoned by the priests and the pharisees. How can they have any control over what has happened to them? They are victims, as I was, before you who saved me."

"You were never lost. You came here by your own choice. You had faith in who you were, and adamant desire to remain that—what you believed in was yourself! Had you remained with the bread merchant, his woman would have nagged him to adopt you. You didn't know that they searched for you after you left them! But you believed yourself a discard, so you came here, where the rest of the city's garbage ends up."

Hjarai was almost defiant. "So how did my Will, Faith, and Emotion summon you to save me?"

Simon only smiled. "Tell me of the ankh you have not yet made."

"Again you ask of the ankh? I don't understand the connection."

"Have you heard? Some believe in a paradise to which the dead ascend immediately. Yet many of the very same believe in an anti-paradise. A heavenly Gehenna—therefore, everlasting!—where God abandons souls as garbage, and leaves them there to burn."

"So I have heard! Is any of that true?"

"Those who believe so have hit upon a truth, but misunderstand it. In truth, we are only spirits, composed of light! Using flesh and bone—what you think of as legs and arms, hands and feet—to grapple with the lower elements of existence.

"Hjarai, your spirit is equal to mine! You exist in more ways than you can understand. Presently, your focus is only the flesh. Why? Because you worry that you can survive in no other form! Understand me so far?"

"What do you mean by focus?"

"Just now, you were not aware that I was walking up behind you. Yet my existence was just as real as the children you were watching, was it not?"

"But Simon, I didn't know you were there because I was giving my full attention elsewhere."

"That is what I mean. Your entire focus was on the suffering before you, so that your awareness did not include my presence."

"I think so," said Hjarai.

"As a spirit, you are everywhere at all times. You are in every time. Because you are an emanation from the One God, you are everything that God is. And your awareness or focus is centered on what you have chosen—which, for now, is being in flesh.

"Because of your intense focus, you have forgotten why you chose this form of awareness. You've even forgotten that you chose at all, but have come to believe that you have no control to change your focus."

"Do you mean that when I lived here, that I had come to think that I was a part of it?"

"That's right," said Simon. "The light you see around your body is a reminder that you are more than what you have focused on. That light is what you really are, but you are only vaguely aware of it because you focus on your flesh and the suffering around you. This is why you must learn to control the light that comes from you. It will help you remember that you are the Light emanating from the One God. You exist in a realm of spirit, not one of dust and dirt, flesh and corruption.

"You have chosen to focus on flesh and material surroundings for a reason that you selected before you were born, before you began this apparent existence. When your awareness finally includes your true nature, you will be able to make the ankh easily."

"This doesn't explain how my Desire, Faith, and Emotion summoned you," said Hjarai.

"Your decision to be a part of your present *Aleph-Bet* was made long ago. Before entering your present existence, you also decided to learn for only a short time at the school of Gehenna."

"This seems too simple an answer. What about these children who are here now? Must they have chosen, before birth, to leave this place to be able to leave it? If they haven't made this choice, do they have to stay until they die?"

"They have the freedom of choice and of Will," said Simon, "but don't understand how to use it."

"I suppose that all they have to do is change their focus."

"That's right."

"They are where they are and they are who they are. How can they change this?"

"By first believing they can."

****

The walls of Masada were growing warm in the sun. Harai moved his hand slowly over the coarse rock, and considered its immense age. He could almost feel the sounds the workmen made 100 or more years before, under the pitiless supervision of Herod's soldiers. Why must people believe in cruelty? he wondered. *Why couldn't they not feel the joy of God, Who created them?*

Harai closed his eyes and felt the sunlight's warmth on his face. He filtered out the suffering and sorrow around him, and centered in on his being: his Source.

Adameh and Eleazar, standing beside him at the north wall, were thinking of their deaths, and of the end of their world, their nation.

"Why do you smile, Essene?" asked Eleazar, with annoyance. "I see the smoke of the Holy City on our horizon and beyond it, Rome glutting itself on the wealth of our Temple. I see nothing but pain and sorrow, yet you smile. Are you a secret Roman?"

"Do you not feel the sunlight, Eleazar?" asked Harai.

"Today's tragedy overshadows any sunlight," Eleazar grumbled.

"It has not overshadowed the sunlight for David and Soo-ooni, below us. Look."

"Youth thinks only of its loins," said Eleazar.

"Youth remembers the joy of its Source," said Harai. "You remember it too, Eleazar, and would smile in its brilliance if only you could turn from this suffering which you choose instead."

"I have led this people to safety in Masada. Here they can live in peace in the face of Rome's might."

"Lead them now to Egypt, before Titus sends his generals to kill you. Your hatred summons Rome."

"If this is a place to die," said Adameh, "why have you chosen to come here?"

"I have my part to play," said Harai. "When it is over, I will leave."

"Where will you go?" asked Eleazar. "To Egypt?"

"My brothers have gone to Damascus to continue their work. My work will soon be done here at Masada, then I will return to my Source."

"He means he will die," Eleazar said to Adameh. "He, too, chooses death."

"There is no death," said Harai. "There is only God.

"Your choosing death results from your belief that there is only death and nothing beyond. After you have followed your faith in death, your faith in hopelessness, you will find the truth in my words."

Eleazar walked away. Over his shoulder, he shot back, "The God of Israel has forsaken His people, but at Masada, He will defend us."

Harai turned his face back to the sunlight and closed his eyes.

"What you say is confusing," Adameh said. "Do you mean that you will return to Abraham, our Father, without dying?"

"Death is an illusion, Adameh. Those who believe in illusions make the illusions real for themselves. Those who focus on the illusion make what they have chosen into everything there is. Eleazar has chosen illusion for all who are here."

13

Six

Flight from Jerusalem

Still choosing to travel at night only, the two men picked their way down the ravine, which had been cut into the valley by centuries of flash floods.

"Why couldn't we have chosen an easier path?" grumbled Dan, struggling down the steep slope to the wadi floor below. "These poles are hard to handle on unsteady ground, and our footing harder to see in the darkness."

Small stones, loosened by their footsteps, rolled down the hillside. Rivulets of sweat ran down Jonathan's face, and his frock was soaked. "This is the last wadi before Masada. After we climb the other side and clear that hill beyond, we should be able to see it."

"I hope there is plenty of water there. We smell worse than a caravan fresh from the desert." said Dan.

Jonathan laughed but his foot slipped and he sat down on his buttocks, hard. He dropped his end of the poles. Dan dug in his heels and held on. The heavy box between them hit the ground. Jair, at the bottom of the wadi, watched them both grunting with the effort of stopping their burden from sliding down the hill.

"I told you it was slick as eel snot," he chuckled, and started back up the slope to help. Moments later, safely at the bottom, the three seated themselves on the ground, puffing from the exertion of the climb down.

"Could we follow the wadi down to the road from En-Gedi?" asked Jair. "Surely the Romans have not yet come this far south."

"There is a garrison at En-Gedi," said Jonathan.

Dan nodded. "During my watch in yesterday's sunlight, I saw several runners heading south along the road, and a small troop coming north. We must assume they are everywhere; we can't risk this falling into their hands."

"I agree," said Jonathan. "The Ark is the most sacred item in Israel. The extra effort of carrying it through these ravines is nothing compared to the cost of losing it."

"But Israel is lost," said Jair. "We will never be free again. Rome has seen to that."

Jonathan stood and faced up the valley. "Never is a very long time. It may take much time, but someday Rome will fall to its own vices, just as Greece did, just as Babylon did. We will always be the children of Abraham, the people of the Book. We will never forget, and the Ark of the Covenant between God and our people must always be safe, awaiting our return."

After recovering their breath, they took up their and crossed the bottom of the dry wadi. The south side of the ravine was even steeper. On this climb, Jonathan and Dan each took the lower end of one pole, with Jair tugging at the upper ends. With the heat of the day almost upon them, they struggled upwards until they gained the level, where they faced yet another hill to climb.

At the top of the hill, Jair stopped. "Look there! In the distance to the west. Is that a farm?"

"There is a small hut," said Dan. "Maybe someone is there who will give us food, and perhaps there is a well."

With the sun just cresting the horizon, they approached the hut. Dan, who was carrying the lead end of the poles, called back to Jonathan, "There is someone sitting out in front!"

"Yes, I see him," said Jair.

Jonathan wiped his face on his sleeve and looked again. "Whoever it is," he said, "he's been watching and knows we're coming."

As they drew closer, they saw a man seated on the ground, legs crossed, wearing a white cloth. He seemed to take little notice of their approach, even when they lowered their burden to the ground and stood directly in front of him.

"An Essene," said Jonathan.

I am Vav, Six, thought the silent one, aware of their presence, but reluctant to come out of his meditation.

"Wake up, Pious One," said Dan, loudly.

"Ask if he has food," Jair said to Dan.

"Let him sleep," said Jonathan. "We can look around and see for ourselves."

Eyes still closed, the Essene raised his head and took a deep, gasping breath. His eyes opened imperceptibly, and he rose to his feet without touching the ground with his hands.

"Your progress has been slow," he said.

"You have been expecting us?" asked Jonathan suspiciously.

"It was kind of you to allow Yosiah to return to his family at En-Gedi," said the Essene. "Lesser men would not have done so."

"Who is this man?" demanded Dan.

"How do you know so much?" asked Jonathan. "Did Yosiah talk about us?"

"Yosiah did not betray you. I have never been far from you, since you left Jerusalem."

"It was dark in the city," said Jonathan. "Are you Itzchak?"

"You remember well," said the Essene. "I am appointed to oversee your safety as you carry the holy burden to Masada."

Jair and Jonathan again exchanged glances. Dan started laughing. "You don't look like a warrior," he chuckled. "Where is your sword?"

"I am not a warrior," said Itzchak. "But I have my abilities, and so far, they have seemed adequate."

"What abilities," demanded Dan, "but to pray meekly, and sleep in direct sunlight until your skin is burned black?"

"Does my skin appear burned to you?" asked Itzchak with a smile.

"No," said Dan. "You must not have been sleeping for long."

"I was not sleeping, but overseeing your journey."

"Have you overseen that we have no food?" snapped Dan. "Have you brought us provisions to give us strength to carry this box to Masada, or do you prattle stupidly?"

"One should be kind to strangers," said the Essene. "The Greeks believed that the gods sometimes appeared to humans in the form of a stranger, and that to anger a god could create . . . inconvenience."

Dan began laughing. "You, a god?"

"The writings of the ancients tell us to forgive fools because they know not that they do evil. Yes, I have brought you food."

Dan stopped laughing.

"It is inside this hovel," said Itzchak. "Eat what you can and carry the rest with you. Remember the rule. Take. Eat. Give to the hungry."

All three entered the hut. Resting on a small table were two loaves of coarse brown bread and a cloth sack full of dried figs. Hanging on a hook beside the door was a skin of water, treated with thin wine.

"He didn't lie," said Dan, tearing a loaf in half. "Who is he?"

"I never saw him before the night we left Jerusalem. He gave us food then too," said Jonathan.

"How did he know where we are, that he can bring food again?" asked Jair.

"The Essenes are a strange group. It is said that Malchesidek was their founder," said Jonathan.

"Who is Malchesidek?" asked Dan, through a mouthful of bread.

"In Ha Cheder, I was taught that he was a very holy man, the first High Priest of the Temple."

"Then he must have lived at the time of King Solomon," said Dan.

"I don't know," said Jonathan. "My Rabbi taught that Malchesidek was like Aleph is to our letters—the first, the founder, the ox. My teacher once referred to him as the founder of the Great White Brotherhood of Light the 'first Aleph,' but he didn't explain what that meant. Ask Itzchak. He probably knows."

"I remember something like that from my lessons too," said Dan. He took a couple of figs and walked out the door.

Jonathan and Jair continued eating silently, each with his own thoughts. They heard Dan's footsteps as he walked around the small shelter. "Itzchak!" he called out, "Itzchak!"

Having rounded the hut, Dan came back in, figs in hand, but he had stopped eating. "He's gone," said Dan.

Jair looked up in surprise, then went outside to look for himself.

"Jonathan, I walked around the hut and looked in every direction. He couldn't have walked out of sight in that short a time."

Outside, Jonathan found Jair sitting on the ground, his mouth still full. The Ark, in its box of acacia wood, was right where they had set it down, and the Essene was nowhere to be found. "Where is he?" asked Jonathan.

"I don't know," said Jair. "Maybe the ground swallowed him up." A few seconds later, Jair pointed to a small speck far to the east and said, "Look. Is that him walking there?"

But it was too far to tell for sure.

Later that evening, as the moon was rising in the east, they crested the last hill. On the horizon was a high plateau, rising out of the plain. "Is that it?" asked Dan.

"It must be," said Jair.

"That's it," said Jonathan. "I can see the smoke from their cooking fires."

"How many are there, do you think?" asked Dan.

"Hundreds," said Jair. "It seemed that everyone who left Jerusalem said they were going to either Damascus, Ethiopia, or Masada."

"There seems to be a ledge on the northern end, just below the top. Can you see it?" asked Dan.

"That's where Herod built his summer palace in the days of the Maccabees. Do you know the story?" asked Jonathan.

"Yes," said Dan. "It seems that summer is too hot for the puppet kings. They have to get up high to keep cool. If it's really cool up there, as they say, what a pleasant change for us!"

"Do you think we can make it from here in one night?" asked Jair.

"Yes, if we don't have more valleys to crawl through," said Jonathan. "What do you think, Dan?"

"I think so, too," Dan said. "Speaking of cooking fires—look there at the foot of the mountain, on the west side. See the smoke there?"

"Probably that Essene," said Dan. "Look, there's the road to En-Gedi, leading off to the east."

"Yes," said Jonathan. "And there seems to be smoke there too. Who would be camping on the lower level when they could go up to where it's more comfortable?"

"I hope we aren't too late. There may be Romans here already."

"When we get closer we can sneak in and find out whose fire that is."

"I think we better stay low," said Jonathan. "We are right on top of this hill and easily seen."

Hurriedly they carried the burden between the two poles down the face of the slope and into the shadows of the low hills. Out of sight. "I will go ahead," Dan said, "and come back by first light." With that, he walked off into the darkness.

"It's getting too dark to continue. I don't want to stumble and drop this box again," said Jonathan.

"Neither do I," said Jair. "I hope up there they have something to sleep on that's softer than the ground. The earth has been my bed for too long."

Suddenly they heard footsteps approaching. Both fell silent, drew their long Sicarii knives and stood, waiting. "Maybe it's Dan, coming back already," whispered Jair.

"Dan walks more quickly," Jonathan whispered back.

Both men faded back from the Ark to give more room for any confrontation. The footsteps drew closer. Jonathan thought he saw a shadow. If whoever it was came just a little closer . . . Then he saw that the approaching intruder was clad in white, gently illuminating the shadows around him.

"It's the Essene again," said Jonathan.

Itzchak smiled at their drawn knives. "Greetings, my friends. I can see you did not recognize me."

"Where have you been?" asked Jonathan, not too kindly.

"Looking ahead," said the Essene.

"How did you find us?" asked Jair.

"By looking behind," said the Essene smiling. "Anything else you'd like to ask?"

"What did you see ahead?" asked Jonathan.

"A small troop of Roman soldiers, camped at both paths to the plateau. Titus sent them to take the tableland away from what he thought were a loose band of simpletons. When they return to him, he will learn that retaking Masada will not be as easy as he thought."

Very tired from their long journey, Jonathan and Jair edged back and seated themselves on the ground near the Ark. The Essene sat beside them.

"They tried to march up the cart path and impress the Sicarii with their boldness. They forgot about the rock slides that they themselves had prepared against just such an attack. Those on top let loose the slide and stopped the advance without a single defender being hurt, but some of the soldiers were killed."

"How did you learn all this, Essene?" asked Jonathan.

"By watching," said Itzchak. "Then the Romans retreated down the cart path and deliberated. In a few hours the troop split up. Half went around to the serpentine path and, at a prearranged time, they tried to climb both paths at once. The serpentine path was guarded from above by men with slings and bows. Where the path turns, exposing itself to the cliff beyond, they cut down the soldiers like shooting rats. On the cart path there were still more slides, and two of the ones used earlier had been replenished."

"Just as Ananas said, it is the safest place. Masada can't be taken," said Jonathan.

"That remains to be seen," said Itzchak. "I believe they are too proud to leave this one spot unbloodied and will return with a larger army."

Jonathan and Jair asked no more questions. Both turned their gaze to the plateau, watching smoke rise from the cooking fires. Soon they lay back on the ground and slept. Itzchak remained seated, watching Masada.

The sun was already high in the sky when Jonathan awoke. Either Itzchak was sitting in the exact place as before, or he had not budged all night.

Now he turned and gave Jonathan a warm smile. "Are you ready for one more day of carrying? This coming night, you will sleep atop Masada."

"But the Romans—"

"Look! What do you *not* see?"

Jonathan looked. He could see none of the smoke from the cooking fires of the evening before.

"You need not fear the Romans, now. Their platoon departed this morning, at first light."

14

Reinventing the Wheel

Jerusalem

The lamp over Titus's table was burning low. He strained his eyes to continue reading the letter from his father, brought by courier that day. "Guard!" he shouted.

A soldier entered his tent immediately.

"Fix this cursed lamp!"

Titus stood and paced while the guard pulled a small pick from his pocket and bent over the lamp. The smell of his sweat filled the cavernous cloth house where Titus spent his nights, and sometimes his days.

At the rear of the tent, a sleeping area was divided by a hanging cloth—light tan, and nearly sheer. Inside could be seen the outline of a bed, with thick quilted blankets forming the playground, as the soldiers called it, where Titus "entertained" from time to time.

"I've sampled some local wine in there," he liked to say with a wry smile to his captains. His favorite reminiscence was of the daughter of a local merchant, a Sadducee. She had been delightfully full of fight. She had called him a pig, then went on to explain that pigs weren't kosher, so that he would understand that he had been insulted. His eyes now turned to the middle room of the tent, where his clothes and weapons were stored. He'd been in this pigsty of a country so long he had nothing decent to wear for the homecoming.

Julius, the soldier working on the lamp turned. "It needs more oil, sir. I will get some."

"Hurry." said Titus. "I'd like to finish reading."

The soldier saluted and left the tent quickly. Titus liked Julius. A big man, and a good soldier.

Titus had ordered a second chair beside the table, for the rare occasions when he desired to talk with someone—usually Julius, who had pulled duty tonight guarding the tent. The other soldiers didn't like that duty much, because Titus hated waiting and liked to be attended to immediately.

His thoughts turned to Adrianus. That fool had returned very humbly, knelt as was expected, and laid his sword on the ground at Titus' feet, in a gesture of failure which everyone recognized.

Titus had known something was very wrong. Through gritted teeth, he said in his most threatening voice, "Sheath your sword and come inside."

After Adrianus privately explained what had happened at Masada, Titus had him arrested and confined to the prisoners' quarters, separate from the Jewish prisoners. Two days later, Titus called for him, demoted him to the lowest rank, and placed him as one of his personal guards. If Adrianus hadn't made Titus wait for his wine, he would be alive today.

The soldier returned with the lamp oil. "Permission to enter your tent with the oil, sir."

"Come in," ordered Titus.

Julius went directly to the lamp and began pouring oil into its bowl. Titus's gaze fell upon a small Galilean shield—coarse leather over a rough wood frame, one the soldier had taken as a battle souvenir. Beside it, resting on the floor near the entrance to his bed chamber, lay a heavy club which, the soldier reported, was the Jews' only weapon.

Swords and spears and chariots—Rome's best fighting men, against leather shields and wooden clubs! Titus eyed the Star of David painted on the leather. "Julius, how did these primitives arrive at such a complex sign for their shields? What does this sign mean?"

"I don't know, Caesar," said Julius. "It seems that they wear it or paint it on their shields to signify that they are Jews, just as our Eagle denotes that we are Rome."

"Continue."

The soldier leaned back over the lamp and continued pouring the fresh oil.

Titus was weary. The troops he had sent to Qumran had returned with their message that the place was deserted. No Essenes! Nearby, they'd found one terrified farmer who told them that a few weeks before, the monastery's inhabitants had packed up and moved away, leaving not so much as a pot behind. Knowing their leader all too well, his soldiers returned with the farmer for questioning.

"Your name, Jew?" Titus demanded.

"Obidiah."

"The Essenes left, and they told you nothing?" asked Titus.

"They told me 'Farewell!' They said, 'Our work in Israel is finished; time to move on to new tasks.' They did not say what those tasks might be, nor where they were headed."

"But where did they go?"

"They took the road toward Jericho, which only goes a short way east before it meets another road, leading south toward Egypt or north toward Damascus. They could have met other roads leading farther east."

Titus nodded, then ordered the farmer to join the other prisoners to be taken to Rome for the Triumph. "He looks healthy," he told Julius. "Perhaps you can get a good price for him at the slave market."

But privately, he was crestfallen. Where had the Essenes gone? How could he capture the Ark, as his father Vespasian had commanded, if he couldn't even find those who had spirited it away?

Julius rose from his task. "The lamp will burn well for a time, Caesar."

"You may go." The soldier saluted and left, to stand guard until Titus's next demand.

Again Titus sat at the table. He did not continue reading, but stared straight ahead, seeing nothing before his eyes. His thoughts were far away, across the sea, in Rome.

Vespasian had been proclaimed the new Emperor! Titus had thought he would be. He visualized his father, seated at the head of the Senate—in an elegant white toga so difficult to put on, scepter in hand, a handsome figure. Titus's mother, Elena, would be proud of him. Traditionally, an Emperor had the right to name his heir. But his successor could not reign secure until he won approval from the Roman army. Claudius, and now Vespasian, had been elevated to the purple by military acclaim. And "Little Boots" Caligula was assassinated by his own Praetorian Guard . . .

Soldiers had tired of having living gods on the Imperial throne. They worshiped Mithras, whose shrines depicted him killing a full-grown bull with a frighteningly puny knife.

Courage, cunning, victory! For their emperor, soldiers wanted the sort of leader they all aspired to be: a triumphant general like Julius Caesar. Though never an emperor himself, his name now meant *Emper-*

or on every Mediterranean shore and throughout the civilized world!

Titus's gaze reverted to the leather shield. "Guard!" he called out. The centurion Julius was back in a trice.

"Sit down."

"Yes, Caesar."

"These zealot Jews show such determination! What soldiers they might become, if they could only be trained—but first, of course, won over.

"I remember a battle where my men attacked Judeans. Our armor, swords, and chariots, against barefoot shepherds with knives and clubs. Such courage! They may have been slaughtered to a man, but never did they retreat or surrender."

"Julius," idly, Titus wiped his left hand over his mouth, down over his chin, exploring his beard's fresh stubble, "have any other priests of Herod's temple been captured?"

"Most were killed."

"Why? When I specifically asked they be taken alive?"

"We were not expecting them to fight just as hard as the rabble, and with greater cunning. Some had concealed short sharp knives in their silken pockets, and they surprised those soldiers who seized them. They killed no small number of their guards before we cut them down."

"Question every Jewish prisoner. Are any priests among them? Were any temple guards taken alive? If so, I want to question them all. Go!"

Alone again, Titus heard Julius' voice passing on the orders. Titus had seen an Essene years ago, when he first visited the Romans stationed in Judea. The occasion was the announcement of Nero's coronation. The troops received the news with bored indifference, but it was violently unpopular among the native Judeans.

With Titus's chariot behind a team of four, he led a troop of twenty-five soldiers on horseback. They were headed east from Joppa. The road was wretched, progress was slow.

At an oasis, Titus ordered them to stop for the night. At the spring, they encountered a man clothed in white, carrying a rod like a shepherd's staff, but topped by a symbol that Titus had never seen.

"What is that, atop your staff?" Titus asked.

"The symbol of our Order."

"And what order is that?"

"The people of this land call us Watchers, though others call us the Pious Ones. Not seeking piety, however, we do not prefer that name."

Titus interpreted the Essene's smile as a sign of submission, so he did not punish the man. "What do you call yourselves?"

"We do not ascribe to any appellation. We represent the spirits of man and the Spirit of God, co-joined. A name or definition tries to make a thing specific, finite. Since the Essence we represent is infinite, so we do not insult it with definitions. Some call us a name that we prefer over the many others: *Ha Bonayim*, meaning the Builders."

"Why that name?" asked Titus.

"Because it is central to our teachings. By trimming our hearts of the superfluous vices of life, we fit ourselves as living building blocks to that House not made with hands: The eternal Temple of El Shadai—God Almighty."

Only later that night did Titus realize that the man had conversed with him in perfect Latin!—albeit with an accent he could not place. On his return to Rome, when Titus related the encounter to his father, Vespasian asked, "What was the Essene's name?"

"When I asked him this, he said, 'I am called by my brothers the First Aleph.'"

"When I visited Palestine for the first time, I also met an Essene on the road to Jerusalem who said the same things and also told me he was called the First Aleph. Do you know what this means?"

"No, father. I have learned very little of their customs and language."

"Was this truly coincidence?" asked Vespasian. "Aleph is also the first letter of the Hebrew alphabet. If he called himself Aleph, he meant he is number one, because aleph also means one. Their bayt, or bet, means two. I think they never advanced much because of this awkward numbering system. Did you know that when we first took Judea, they didn't even have the wheel?"

****

Titus' father's letter lay on his table unread, and his lamp flickered slightly from the breeze wafting through the tent. The entire Tenth Legion lay camped around him, preparing for the night's rest. Now that Jerusalem was finally subdued, he must turn his attention to the rest of this backward land.

He could hear several feet approaching his tent and a voice whimpering, "I have done no wrong. Where are you taking me?"

"Quiet, old fool," one of the soldiers barked.

"My lord?" called Julius's voice at the tent's entrance,

"Enter," said Titus.

"We found a priest of the Temple among the prisoners. He awaits your pleasure."

"Bring him before me."

Two other soldiers half dragged an old man into the tent. His clothing was ragged. Several bruises were visible on his face, and a partly healed gash on his cheek was newly broken open and bleeding.

"What are you called?"

"I am called Caleb, sir," said the old man.

"You will address me as 'my Lord,'" said Titus.

"There is only one Lord," said the priest, "and only Him may I address with that name."

Titus caught Julius's eye, lifted his right fist beside his neck, and made a twisting motion. Julius nodded, stepped outside, and returned in a moment with a cloth sash which he wrapped loosely around the old man's neck.

"Tell me again," said Titus. "What is your name?"

"I am still called Caleb, sir," said the old priest, hatred flaring in his eyes.

Titus nodded to Julius, who tied the ends of the sash and put a heavy stick through the knot. He turned the stick once, tightening the sash slightly.

"If you are to survive this interview," said Titus, "you must cooperate, or you will die, slowly. Do you understand?" He nodded again to Julius, who tightened the sash by another half turn.

The old man's face began to turn red. "I am already dead," he gasped and began to recite: "Shema . . ."

Titus rose quickly to his feet, picked up a small riding crop and slapped the priest across the face. He nodded to Julius to loosen the sash. The angry welt in the old man's face was beginning to ooze blood.

"You will say only that which I order you to say, and nothing more, Jew! Understand?"

"I understand."

"I order you now, to say, 'Yes, my Lord.'"

"Shema Yisroel . . ." the priest began again.

Titus struck him another sharp blow with the riding crop. The old man screamed and went limp.

"Get a pail of water," Titus said to Julius.

As he waited for the water, his mind again turned to the Ark of the Covenant. He dared not return to Rome without it.

He recalled his last meeting with Vespasian, just before the news of Nero's death reached Jerusalem, and his father's departure for Rome. "Subduing these people," Vespasian said, "is impossible, as long as they have that box with the tablets in it. It keeps them inspired, and they will defend it at any cost."

"What is it, exactly?" Titus had asked.

"They call it the Ark of the Covenant, and here is the myth behind it. One of their ancient leaders was Mo-eesh, and his god burdened him

with tablets of stone, on which were engraved the tenets of their religion. They are said to be kept in a richly decorated box, deep in the
temple. Of course no one living has ever seen this box, much less the
tablets it supposedly contains. Only their high priest has access to it,
and this privilege is passed on from father to son. Or perhaps, only the
duty of propagating the legend is passed on. Who knows?"

"So," Titus sighed. "To take this box, we first must take Jerusalem?"

"Yes."

Julius arrived with the water. Titus pointed to the old man lying on
the floor of the tent. "Drag him outside and pour the water in his face to
wake him up. Then bring him back in here."

Old fool! If only he would cooperate, he could die easily.

A few minutes later, "My Lord?"

"Enter."

"He's awake," said Julius, "but soaking wet. Do you still wish that we
bring him back inside?"

"Yes, but keep him away from the hangings and furniture."

Some of the blood had washed off the old man's face, revealing that
his left eye was missing. Two soldiers were holding him up, one on either side.

"I will ask you questions," said Titus, "and the manner in which you
answer will determine your fate." The old man raised his good eye to
Titus. Weariness and pain were reflected in his look, but the defiance
was still present.

"Your city is in ruins," said Titus. "Your people are destroyed. Your
temple is being torn down. Do you know why?"

The old man hung silently between the two soldiers. The sash was
still around his neck, but the stick was gone. Blood and water dripped
from his beard.

"I will tell you why. We are searching for the temple's treasure. You
could save us much time—and yourself much pain—by telling where
you hid it." Titus waited, but the old priest made no move to answer.
Then he saw Titus pick up the riding crop, and fear replaced the defiance in his face.

"It might save the lives of dozens of your people if you help. It would
also save what remains of your temple."

The old man took a deep breath, trying to gather enough strength
to stand on his own. "The treasures are gone," he said. "You can never
have them."

"Where have they gone?" asked Titus mildly.

"To where you Roman swine can never have them."

Titus drew closer, flicking his crop back and forth. With his other hand, he placed his dagger at the man's throat. Titus nodded to the two soldiers supporting the old man. They knew what Titus was about to do, and both grasped the man under his armpits to support him.

"Where?" demanded Titus, glaring into the old man's good eye.

"They are safe from you, you whore's son, Titus. They are at Masada."

With a wild gleam in his eyes, Titus slowly pressed the blade into the man's throat. "Pray to me now, old man," he said. "I am not yet a god, but I intend to be deified! For now, I rule Judea, and you can pray to me for life."

"*Shema Yisroel, Adonai, Elohenu, Adonai . . .*"

Titus plunged the knife into the old man's throat and watched as the right eye went dim and rolled upwards. He then wiped the knife carefully on the dead man's clothing. "I hate it when a good blade rusts," he told Julius. "Take the Jew out of here and throw his body beyond the camp for the wild dogs' supper. Then send for Flavius Silva."

A look of fear crossed Julius' face. "My Lord?"

"Speak."

"Silva is in Jericho, or possibly En-Gedi. It will take several days to recall him."

"Do it," ordered Titus, and sat back in his chair to finish the letter from his father.

Masada, he thought to himself, over and over, *Masada*.

15

The Ark

The Plain below Masada

"My Brother Harai awaits you above," said Itzchak. "Can you see him?"

The three looked up at the towering heights, fingers shielding their eyes against the midday sun. "I see someone dressed in white, like yourself," said Jonathan.

"That is Harai. He will help you conceal your sacred burden."

They were nearing the foot of the mountain from the north. Far above, along the north lip, several people were watching their approach. The heat of noon shimmered the air, and Jair and Dan, carrying the pole-ends, were sweating profusely. Jonathan walked behind with Itzchak, who spoke only when directly addressed.

"If there were a breeze, this heat would be bearable," said Dan, puffing slightly.

"No point in complaining," said Jair, wiping his face on his sleeve. "We haven't much farther to go. You know," he said to Itzchak over his shoulder, "when you told us to take this to Masada, we obeyed as innocent children. We had no idea how far it would be, carrying this heavy thing. Can you explain to us, now, why you couldn't select some closer hiding place?"

"Yes, Itzchak," said Jonathan, "why Masada? Surely there are other places equally safe."

They walked quietly for a few more steps before Itzchak answered. "Did you know that in ages past, Masada was called Musudu?"

Jonathan looked down for a moment, picking his steps in the rough terrain. "What does that mean?"

"According to ancient legend, Musudu is the cornerstone of the earth, upon which Adonai piled a great mountain to cover up the abyss."

Dan said, "What does this have to do with this Holy Relic?"

"In all great buildings, the first stone laid is known as the cornerstone, at the building's northeast corner. Hidden in, or beneath, the cornerstone are objects that the builders want to keep safe for future generations to discover and learn from. What more appropriate place than the cornerstone of the Earth?"

"I have never heard this story before," said Dan.

"Neither have I," Jair agreed.

"I have heard of it," Jonathan smiled. "I thank you for reminding me of it."

As they approached the serpentine path, they saw a party of men descending. "When we meet with that group," said Itzchak, "it would be unwise to let them know what you are carrying."

"How can we keep it from them?" asked Jonathan.

"Say, 'It is something to nourish the future.' Use those exact words. I believe Harai has prepared them for this. In this way, you can mislead them, but you need not lie."

At the foot of the serpentine path, Itzchak stopped. "I need not go any farther. My work is now completed, and I will rejoin my brothers."

Jonathan and Jair, who were now carrying the poles, came to a halt. "Are you going to go back to Qumran?" asked Dan.

"The Brotherhood has abandoned Qumran, and Rome has defiled it. I am told that my brothers have moved to a place near Damascus, but my destination is elsewhere. Goodbye."

The party descending from the plateau could now be heard on the path above, around the first turn. The first man who came into sight was young, darkly complected even for a Semite, and wore the long knife of the Sicarii.

"I am David," he called down. "Who are you?"

****

From above, in the palace grounds, Eleazar and Harai watched the plain below. "Do you think the Romans will return?" asked Eleazar.

"I believe so," said Harai. "You must lead these people away, if you want them to survive."

"If this place is so dangerous, why do you remain?"

"My work here is nearly finished," said Harai. "Then I will leave."

"What is this work you speak of?" asked Eleazar. "Before, I believe, the word you used was *choice*, but you did not tell what it was, nor why you made it."

"My choice might be to convince you to leave this place while you still can. More than nine hundred are here on Masada, thinking they are safe because you, Eleazar, told them so. Think of the children and the young, like David and Soo-ooni, who will soon wed."

"I don't understand your fear for us, Harai."

"Isn't it clear enough? The Romans will be back."

"And we will drive them away, as we did before. They knew they could not take this mountain."

"We did not drive them away. They left of their own accord."

The two men fell silent for a moment. Then Eleazar asked, "Who, do you think, are the men we saw approaching from the north?"

"More from Jerusalem, seeking asylum on this mountain."

"One was clothed in white, like you. Another Pious One?"

"He might be. It would be good to see a Brother again before this is over, but I doubt he will join us." Harai stood up and headed back through the palace grounds. "I may be needed at the top of the path. If you're curious about the newcomers, Eleazar, come with me."

Others were waiting by the wall at the top of the serpentine path. Harai knew the women were talking about him, and giggling. Of course they were curious, since no woman they knew had ever lain with a member of his Brotherhood.

"I hear they have no tools for the purpose," said one.

"Nor the desire," said another. Then their gossip drifted to the coming betrothal of David and Soo-ooni. And when should the earth be turned for the next crop?

Harai remembered another trip to Jerusalem with his Aleph-Bet, twenty-two boys, plus their teachers. They had waited on the Temple steps, their white clothes dazzling in the direct rays of the hot sun.

He had felt some one's gaze on him. Turning, he saw a young girl of about his age. Her black hair reflected the light on her cheeks. Never before had a girl's lips looked so soft.

Only two months before, Simon had spoken to him: "You are becoming a man. The hair on your chin and upper lip tell me this."

"I have hair growing other places too, Simon. It itches."

"Yes, I remember. It will not be long before you become curious about women."

"I already am."

"Have you seen any you find particularly appealing?"

Hjarai waved his hand at the monastery. "There are not many to be seen!"

"True," said Simon. "But farmers who live around us have daughters. What of them?"

Feeling his cheeks warming, Hjarai averted his eyes from his teacher as he thought of the daughter of the shepherd Hezekiah. He liked to watch the rise of her breasts under her loose clothing, especially when she bent to pick up a lamb or draw water from the well. He would go nearer so he could watch, and wondered what her body looked like, underneath.

"In the life of every man," laughed Simon, "there comes a time when he believes that the most wondrous thing that Adonai created in all the Earth was women, and he did not make enough of them."

Hjarai blushed even more deeply and turned to look at his teacher.

"Then there will come a time—perhaps several times—when a man thinks that the most wondrous thing that Adonai made was one woman. Sometimes, the man is lucky enough to marry her, but usually not."

"But members of our Order do not marry," Hjarai said.

"No, but some have chosen a woman and left our Order. You have not yet taken your vows. I remind you, Hjarai, you are still free to choose."

"But my Aleph-Bet has already been dedicated."

"But not initiated! As yet, you do not know its purpose. Nor the task you have chosen to undertake."

"How can I make a fair decision without that knowledge?"

"You are equally ignorant of both choices, Hjarai. Either way, you'll learn a very great deal. Neither choice may be the best one. Make your best decision, in accord with the wisdom you have now."

On the steps to the Temple, Hjarai felt his cheeks burning, and the girl with the soft lips smiled at him, with mischief in her eyes. Hjarai felt a growing warmth elsewhere, and quickly averted his gaze. When he looked back, the girl was gone.

"Incredible," he told Simon later. "Overwhelming."

"Are you still overwhelmed?"

"The memory remains warm in my heart, but no, I am no longer overwhelmed."

"This desire is man's strongest drive, and can be harnessed for good. Have you made the ankh yet?"

"Yes," said Hjarai. "Would you like to see?"

"Show me."

"Watch."

The light gathered around Hjarai's hand, slowly becoming brighter. Slowly, the column rose. It split to form two arches, joining in a circle, while the crosspiece below slowly extended to complete the ankh.

"What does it teach you?" asked Simon.

"To govern my passions." Hjarai closed his hand, and the ankh quickly faded.

"Can you?" asked Simon.

"I think so," he said, trying to conceal the sadness in his voice.

****

Harai and Eleazar heard the men puffing up the snake path. "You must have stones in this box," David grumbled.

"Not stones," said Dan.

The men rounded the last turn and came into sight. Jair was carrying the poles in front, with David behind. "Not far to go now," David grunted.

"My name is Eleazar. What's in your box?"

Harai, at Eleazar's elbow, replied, "Nourishment for the future. Bring it over here." He indicated the northern wall. "Leave it there, and I will watch over it while you rest."

Dan and David set their burden on the ground. Eleazar, immediately behind them, was followed by a curious throng.

"Harai, what are you doing?"

"Everything is as it should be. I would like to speak with these men, alone."

"Harai, you forget."

"No, Eleazar! Come back later; I will explain." He turned to Dan, Jonathan, and Jair. "Come!"

Eleazar herded the crowd back onto the plateau. Harai waited until all but the three carriers were out of earshot. "You have done well," he said.

Jonathan gazed down at the plain below. The view was spectacular, the air definitely cooler. But what was this growing warmth? He placed his hand in his pocket and felt the ankh that Itzchak had given him that fearful night in Jerusalem. It was the last time he had seen his father and his wife . . . "You are Harai?" he asked.

"I am he."

"Then this must be given to you," he said, handing him the ankh.

Harai stretched out his hand and received it. "The baton," he said softly, then raised his voice again. "Thank you, Jonathan." He tied a leather strip through the circle at the top and hung it around his neck. As the ankh hung against the old man's chest, it seemed to glow faintly. Then the glow spread, and the ankh seemed to fade right into his chest.

"Where did it go?" asked Jonathan.

"It is here," said Harai, placing his hand over his breast. "There is one task left," he continued. "We must carry your burden to the palace grounds below. For the time being, your task is done. Eleazar and David will see to burying it. Go. Rest."

****

Harai recalled the first time he had seen the Ark of the Covenant. Hjarai and his Aleph-Bet had gained access to the Temple. Its doors seemed huge to him, overlaid with gold. "The mosaic pavement of black and white," Simon told him, "represents good and evil, spirit and matter interspersed in everyone's life." The hanging cloth concealing the Holy of Holies completely hid what lay behind it.

The others present, who were not Essenes, were politely ushered out of the room. On the raised dias, the High Priest stood waiting with a smile. "This is our Brother, Dalet," said Simon. "His son is Dalet in your Aleph-Bet. He will be High Priest when the time comes."

The priest saw that none was present except Essenes. "I will now show you that which you will protect." He pulled the cloth aside, revealing the inside of the Holy of Holies. Entering the small space, he picked up a highly decorated scroll. "This," he said, "is Torah."

Respectfully he placed the scroll back on its stand and motioned with his hand to a large box overlaid with gold, with two figures standing on its lid. "This is the Holy Ark, made in the time of Moses, and still contains the tablets. They, with the Torah, are the most sacred items to our people."

"But they are only objects," said Hjarai to Simon, later.

"True, but they represent spiritual truths which man must never forget. Copies have been made of the law written on the tablets, but the carving on the stone tablets was written by the very hand of Adonai, on the mountain."

Now old Harai watched over the box, resting in the evening light, on the plateau; and he remembered the girl. Such a beauty! He wondered what her name was.

16

The Hammer

Jerusalem

"Cooking! Bah," muttered Belius, the cook's helper. He was a soldier, not a carrier of burdens. Walking down the long path to the well, he carried a wooden bucket swinging loosely in each hand. His father had raised him to be a fighter of battles, not to carry water for the cursed cook.

"My son will be a general," he used to say. "My son, the general." When Belius said they'd made him a cook's helper, his father only laughed: "Wait till they get to know you. They'll give you a legion to command." But for six years now, he'd been a cook's helper.

His foot slipped on a loose stone. He dropped the empty bucket, stumbling against the wall beside the path. "Ha!" laughed Dolofus from behind. "If you stop grumbling and watch your feet, maybe you can carry the water in only two or three trips. Instead you slop out half of it, making my job harder."

Belius shot a fierce glance over his shoulder. Dolofus was also a cook's helper. Later this morning they would fetch more flour and other supplies; then maybe they could serve the troops. "Carry your own load, and I'll carry mine. If your tongue weren't so quick, you wouldn't be the brunt of so many jokes."

"Pick up your bucket and get moving," said Dolofus. "If we take as long as we did yesterday, we will be punished." Belius scooped up the wooden bucket and continued on. If Tabach made good his threat, he would not have leave to go to the women, or drink the wine in their camps. With this fear in mind, he quickened his pace. To his anger, he saw there were women crowded around the well, filling pots for their own cooking. This could only cause them to be further delayed.

"Aside!" he shouted at them. "Aside!"

"Move away!" shouted Dolofus.

The women moved away and waited while Belius and Dolofus filled their buckets. "You pigs," one muttered. Belius stood suddenly, nearly spilling the water from his bucket. "Who said that?" he demanded.

None of the women spoke.

"I asked you Jews a question. Who said that!"

"Let it go," said Dolofus. "We have to get this water back to Tabach or lose our two-day liberty."

As Belius dipped his other bucket, another woman said, "Ha Pateesh is coming. He will have you carry much water," she snickered, "for he has many men with him."

Dolofus saw which woman it was, and Belius straightened up in surprise at the name. "Ha Pateesh?" he said slowly. His difficulty in pronouncing anything Hebrew was a great joke among the few Jewish servants who served in the kitchen. "Ha Pateesh is what you call the general Flavius Silva?"

"Yes, that is his name."

"How do you know he's coming, and we do not?" asked Dolofus.

"I have heard his name much today, and it is still only the first hour."

Belius exchanged a glance with Dolofus and, with a great effort, lifted his two buckets and followed him back up the hill to the cooking tent in Titus's camp. When safely out of the women's hearing, Belius spoke: "Do you think he is really coming?"

"Who knows? These peasants always seem to learn of such things before you and me."

"Have you seen Flavius Silva?"

"No. But I've heard he's a big man."

"He's big, all right," Belius nodded. "Wait till you see him!"

"There are lots of big men," said Dolofus.

"This one is different. The look in his eye scares me. I think poison runs in his veins instead of blood. At his camp in Briton, after the last battle there was a big celebration. All the soldiers drank too much and were playing with the local women. Silva stayed in his tent and drank alone. Late in the evening, he came out and pulled one of the soldiers off a woman he wanted. The soldier was drunk and struck Silva before he recognized him."

Belius fell silent, and they could hear the sounds of morning in the camp ahead of them.

"What did Silva do?" puffed Dolofus.

Belius told the story through heaves of breath. "Grinning, he had poor Anias held down by five men. He took Anias's dagger out of its sheath and put it in Anias's one nostril. Anias begged forgiveness, telling Silva he didn't know it was him. Silva just pushed, a little at a time, till the whole side of his nose was slit open."

Dolofus looked back at Belius. "Sounds like someone Titus would admire."

"When he finished with the one side then he did the other, quick. Anias bled all night. You should see his face now!"

As the path swerved to the right, the cooking tent came into view. Smoke rose from a large fire in the rear, and other assistants were hurrying around to Tabach's bidding. A tall African man was stirring a huge pot suspended over the fire. Sweat poured down his bare chest and back.

"Is it boiling yet?" Tabach shouted.

"Not yet!" the black man called.

Belius and Dolofus climbed a short ladder beside the pot and, in turn, emptied their buckets into the pot. As Belius started back down to the well, he whispered to the black man, "Patah Hotep! I hear Flavius Silva is coming."

"Ha Pateesh, is it," said Patah Hotep with his Egyptian accent, "I wonder what Titus wants with him?"

On the path, Dolofus said, "Flavius Silva is the one Titus sent to En-Gedi. And wasn't it he who led the battle against Josephus at Nazareth?" asked Dolofus.

"Yes. Josephus, that old Jew who hangs around Titus. He's been ordered to write a history of the Jewish people. Do you see how he hangs his head when anyone looks at him? Like a kicked dog, with its tail between its legs."

"Those who were there say that Josephus was a good general for Galilee. I have heard the women speaking well of him. Now they call him a traitor."

"I too have heard them say this," said Belius, holding his empty buckets away from his legs.

"When Josephus saw Silva coming across the plain, and saw he was outnumbered more than ten to one, still he was willing to fight and ordered his men to advance. Then he saw Flavius Silva, an enormous man on horseback. He ordered his men to stop, rode forward alone, and waited. Silva rode out to meet him. They talked for only a moment, before Josephus dismounted and lay down his sword."

They rounded the last curve to the well and again found it surround-ed by women. "Silva is that frightening to look at. Why do you think these Jews call him *Ha Pateesh,* the Hammer?"

****

"My lord?" Julius called into Titus's tent.

Titus was lying on his face in the playground dreaming of Shiela, the daughter of the Sadducee. It was good to have a woman; he would have to find another soon.

A low moan told Julius that Titus was awake. Experience had taught him not to press, for Titus was especially mean-tempered in the morn-ing. He could hear Titus pulling on some clothing before giving the command, "Enter."

Julius pulled aside the cloth that covered the tent's entrance and stepped into the relative darkness. As his eyes adjusted, he saw Titus seated at the table, waiting for Julius's excuse for awakening him.

"Sir, a soldier has just ridden into camp to announce that Flavius Silva will arrive within the hour."

"Silva," muttered Titus, and his eyes fell again to the letter from his father, written on parchment. Wax tablets were preferred for letters de-livered in Rome, but not here, in the hot Judean climate. "That will be all."

Julius exited the tent, and Titus waited quietly. *Ha Pateesh,* they called him—what a good name! Given a task, he never abandoned it till the nail was driven home.

As a boy, Silva had lived in the southern Alps, which explained his sandy hair and blue eyes, which very few Romans possessed. And be-cause of them, many men had made the fatal mistake of questioning Silva's ancestry.

Even at 17 years old, he was a sizable man. As the story went, a ram-paging bear killed Silva's mother. Silva chose a heavy long-handled, wooden hammer that his father used for splitting wood. He left for the mountains, following the bear's tracks in such a hurry that at first his father didn't realize where he was headed.

By the time he caught up with his son, he had found the bear. They were performing a dance of death around each other. Each time the bear swiped at Silva, its huge paw suffered a heavy swing of the mallet. Finally, when the bear lunged for him, Silva swung the hammer down on its skull with such force, the bear fell, stunned. After a short time, it stood up again, and snapped at him. Silva hit the bear from the side, breaking its jaw. The bear reared up, roaring with pain and went for him again, leaving deep scars on Silva's arms and chest. Fortunately for Silva, his father had arrived in time.

Vespasion believed that Silva was the man to finish the fight in Judea. Titus agreed, and called for his guard.

Julius appeared in the entry.

"Breakfast."

Silva's exploits in the Judean conflict confirmed his nickname. Given an order to take a city or capture a rebel, he was unrelenting. He was the most determined man Titus had known, and Titus wondered why Silva hadn't sent a troop to Damascus to capture an Essene.

When the meal came, Titus toyed with it. "These trail rations are getting tiresome," he complained to Julius.

"Sir, there was no food left in Jerusalem. We had thought they were hoarding, but truly, there was nothing to eat, not even in their temple."

"Send scouts to the local villages for sheep, or some other decent meat."

Titus was picking the food from his teeth with a short knife when cheering and shouting was heard throughout the camp. *Silva always has to make a grand entrance, doesn't he?*

His popularity with the men derives from fear, Titus thought. *Why else are they so eager to gain his approval?*

"You may go." Julius saluted and backed out of the tent.

Titus, in full armor, and weapons, emerged from the tent. He squinted against the brightness of the Judean sun. As his eyes became accustomed to the glare, he surveyed his encampment. Some men were dozing on their bedding on the ground, or polishing weapons, or gambling in the shade of blankets spread between pikes.

But most had cupped their hands over eyes, gazing to the south, where long columns of soldiers stretched back toward the horizon. At its head, was a figure on horseback, with a red tunic over his armor. *Silva!*

****

His entourage moved slowly up through the camp. All the soldiers except the four immediately behind Silva dismounted and allowed their horses to be led away. The long lines of footsoldiers broke ranks and began mingling with the other soldiers.

Silva reined in his horse far from Titus's tent. On an unseen signal, all five dismounted and handed their horses' reins to waiting grooms. Advancing closer to Titus, they knelt, bowing their heads.

"Commander!" said Silva in a deep, clear voice.

"Arise, my friend," said Titus. "Dismiss your guards as you see fit."

Silva arose. Soldiers nearby drew back a step. Titus stepped forward, and Silva grasped his right hand in greeting.

Inside the tent, Titus motioned Silva to the visitors' chair beside his table. As they sat, Titus smelled the odor of a man who had been many days on the road. "You will want a bath," said Titus. "I'm sure your men are preparing one for you even now."

"I gave them the order a week ago," laughed Silva.

"I received your courier from Qumran. Shame you found no Essenes there. Anything else of interest?"

Silva shook his head. "From Qumran we continued to En-Gedi. The sun was hot. The trail back, dusty and long."

"And at En-Gedi, what did you find?"

"A sleepy village. There had been a stronghold of Sicarii, but all had joined the rebels at Masada."

Titus frowned. "You did not go to Masada?"

"I sent a few hundred to report back. Given Masada's strength, I did not turn my attention to taking it—at that time."

"What did your men learn?"

Silva leaned his chair back from the table and crossed his legs. "There are about nine hundred up there, mostly men. They have enhanced the fortifications, and maintain the rock slides above both paths to the top. I lost fifteen men to the rocks, and a few to arrows, shot from higher up.

"My men couldn't make it half way up. Given the nature of those paths, they can't march up in force. On the cart path, the climb is so difficult that the exertion weakens them, leaving them unable to fight effectively. The threat of arrows and rock slides quite disheartened them."

"Silva," said Titus, "I am curious. The farmer said the Essenes had decamped. Damascus being so far, I would never order you there. But taking such an initiative would be in your character. Why did you not send men to Damascus to fetch me a few?"

"I will tell you why." Silva knew that Titus was chronically bored and loved a good story. "First, allow me to tell you more of Qumran. After the men had made sure the buildings were empty, I entered the main hall alone. I was greeted by brown stone corridors. In the solemn dining hall, the locals told me no one spoke during meals."

"So, they do eat!" Titus laughed.

"There, I found long tables. I could almost feel the reverence of these men. At one end of the hall was a corridor that led to a place of ritual bathing. When my eyes became adjusted to the dim light, I seemed to see a white-robed man, standing some ten paces away, watching me. He was of about forty years, his hair beginning to gray and gathered in one single braid over his shoulder. 'Who are you?' he asked me. I answered,

'Flavius Silva, General of Titus, son of the Emperor.' 'I asked not for your name,' said the Essene sarcastically, 'but for a definition of who you are. Tell me. Who are you?'

"Taken aback at this boldness, I said, 'I am a warrior, a leader of men.' 'No,' said the Essene. 'I am the warrior. I defend that which is righteous—against you, the destroyer of peace, a catastrophe to all things that are good, an abomination. You are merely a man, so entrenched in his world that he thinks the only power is physical. You are in error, Flavius Silva.'

"The smile I gave him would have chilled any soldier in my command. But the Essene did not know me. I slowly approached the Essene, removing my dagger from its sheath. 'Where have your people gone to, Jew?' 'To Damascus,' he replied.

"I was ready to stain the waters with his arrogant blood. 'And what will they do there?' I asked. 'There,' the Jew replied, 'they will continue shaping men into building blocks for the new Temple of our God, to replace the physical one your people destroyed. There, they will vanish into anonymity, just as they did here in Qumran, after the reign of Solomon.'

"The Essene and I were nearly nose to nose. 'Now, Jew, I will prove to you that power is physical.' And I sheathed my dagger in his stomach, with such force that the point broke off on the stone wall behind him. But there was no resistance to the blade and no blood! I pulled back the blade and struck again, but it was as though the Essene was not present. 'Who are you?' I asked him. 'I am Hjet,' he answered, 'the number eight, the fence that divides good from evil. I protect the good and keep out those who would destroy the sacred. I keep you out, Flavius Silva.'

"As he spoke to me, the Essene raised his right hand, then said, 'You may not follow to Damascus, Evil One, or there you will find an early death. Instead, you will expend your efforts on that which is useless.'

"I sheathed my knife and, when I raised my eyes again, the Essene was nowhere to be seen. I had my men search the building carefully for secret passageways through which he might have escaped. I refused to believe there was no one in the building, and saw the look in their eyes—they wondered if I was thinking clearly. Later, I overheard one speaking of the day Silva saw a ghost. And perhaps I did!

"To answer your question," he said to Titus, "I feared that sending a contingent after the Essenes would be fruitless. Damascus is a region, more than a city. It would be no quick task to track them down and root them out of there. Also, they may have lied to the farmer—or he to us. I think it more likely that the Essenes returned to Egypt where, legend has it, they first appeared."

Titus was not sure how to reply. Silva must have been feverish, in delirium, for he was the last man on earth to entertain fantasies. "I'm sorry you failed to bring me an Essene," Titus said finally. "Perhaps others, of flesh and blood, will yet be found around Qumran."

"I'd rather look elsewhere. The men who returned from Masada said they saw a figure seated on the high north wall, watching them. There may be at least one Essene at Masada!"

Vespasian's letter to Titus instructed him to capture the Ark of the Covenant —without which Rome could never completely subdue the Jews. If the Essenes had anything to do with spiriting it away, then Titus must find an Essene of flesh and blood.

"Can your men be sure they saw an Essene?"

"At such a distance?" Silva shook his head. "But the man they saw was dressed in pure white. They said his cloak was bright in the sunlight and that at night, it was still visible, even in the dark. Members of that sect have a distinct preference for whiteness. He could well have been Essene."

"Do you think that the whole Qumran community is at Masada?"

"No. My men spoke of only that single one."

"Might there still be some Essenes around Jerusalem?"

"The men are on notice to look for them," said Silva, "but no such reports have reached my ears."

"Vespasian believes that to crush the Jews once and for all, we must first crush their religion—based on a handful of laws that their god wrote on rocks! These stones, supposedly, were stored in the Ark of the Covenant, in the center room of the temple. Everything I've learned suggests the Essenes had something to do with hiding them."

Silva was quiet for a moment. "What covenant does this allude to?"

"Their god told his wandering hero, Moses, that he would protect Moses' people if they obeyed his laws. That was the agreement."

Silva laughed. "It would seem that the Jews have broken it!"

Titus remained grim. "An Essene on Masada . . . Is that where they've hidden the ark?"

"That is possible."

"It is my order that you take your men, together with half the men I have here. That you take Masada by whatever means necessary. That you capture this Essene and make him help you search Masada until you find this so-called Ark of the Covenant."

17

The Divine Spark

Masada

Their trip to the western village of Harad, to gather more people to Masada, had been in vain. The people accused Jonathan and Eleazar of drawing down the anger of Titus. "Soon, because of you, we will beggar ourselves to feed their hungry soldiers. Rome will take our sheep and meager crops. Unless you leave Masada."

"At Masada you will be safe from Rome forever. There's food enough for many."

"If you could take Masada, then Rome can take it back."

****

After his climb up the steep path, Eleazar was puffing. "The air is certainly cooler up here!"

Jonathan nodded. "I wonder why."

Eleazar wiped sweat from his face and looked out over the plain below. He set down his bundle—a thin sleeping mat and what little food was left from the journey.

"I need to rest," he said.

"We're almost to the top," said Jair. "Every time I climb this mountain, it seems steeper and higher." He and Jonathan both dropped their sleeping mats and sat on the ground.

Where Jonathan sat, the path was narrower, and as he sat, his legs dangled over the edge. He drank from a skin of water and passed it to Jair.

"Perhaps Harad was right. We may not be as safe as we think."

"Safe enough," said Eleazar. "When those from En-Gedi came to fight us, you saw their feeble efforts?"

"They were few, and unprepared."

"Unprepared? There were hundreds of them! They had their weapons, they had courage. What else could they bring against us?"

"They weren't determined," Jonathan put in. "They came, they looked us over, and they left. If they want Masada, they'll be back with far more men, and try far harder."

"And as before," said Eleazar, "they will fail."

"The Essene thinks we are in danger," said Jonathan.

"Essenes are children, with childish ideas. Harai is no warrior and has no grasp of the concepts of war."

"Aren't the Essenes said to be prophets?" asked Jonathan. "He may know something he hasn't told us."

"Anyone can prophesy." Eleazer shook his head. "I prophesy that the sun will disappear in a few hours, and the world will be in darkness. See if my prophecy does not come true! They foresee war, and there come wars; they foresee peace, and there is peace. How could they be wrong when their prophecies are so vague?"

"Many have faith in their words," said Jonathan.

"There are many fools!"

Eleazar gave Jonathan an angry glance. "Ancient writings say that a fool is known by his many words."

Jonathan laughed. "Let there at least be peace among us."

"The ancient writings also say that the words of a wise man are always gracious," said Eleazar, "and the words of Harai are always gracious."

Eleazar drank from the water skin, then passed it back to Jonathan. "Only a fool would try to take Masada."

"Or an angry general," said Jair. "I think Harai is right."

"You know the story," said Eleazar. "An Essene told a little boy that someday he would be king. When the boy, Herod, became King of Israel, he summoned the Essene again and asked how long he would live. The Essene answered, 'Until the end of your reign.' 'How long will I reign?' asked Herod. 'Until you die,' the Essene said."

"When I was a boy," Eleazar continued. "I knew an Essene. He was more direct than others I've known since. He used to preach in the streets, and in the Temple, and drew great crowds. Not a warrior, but he had courage."

"You mean the one called Yashua?" asked Jonathan.

"Yes," said Eleazar. "He was from Galilee, very prominent for an Essene. Around him he gathered a group who were not Essenes. He said that if he could teach only twelve, the truth would spread in time and there might be peace in the world. For his trouble, he drove Rome to such a fury that they nailed him to a tree to die."

"The Romans feared he would change things," said Jonathan. "My father said they didn't understand him."

"He started a new sect. *They* think they understand him," said Eleazar.

"According to my father, they don't understand him, either."

"What can your father know of him?" asked Eleazar. "As a priest of the temple, Ananas could have angered Rome against him."

"Yeshua was my father's friend. Ananas often praised him as a teacher, but lamented that his followers listened only to what they wanted to hear."

"Yeshua is dead," said Eleazar. "What good to us are a dead man's words?"

"Ananas said that Yashua came back from the land of shadows," said Jonathan. "I did not see him, but my father did. He said Yashua wanted to return with his body to Adonai, as all devoted Essenes do. Ananas said that Yashua did this; and his teaching was that anyone can do the same: A man who can leave this material world in peace is free to leave it, to return to Adonai."

"I hate Rome too much to leave it in peace, even if I could," said Eleazar.

"So do I," said Jonathan. "We must stay at Masada."

The men rose and continued their climb. "I have heard his followers preaching," said Eleazar. "They talk of nothing but his defeating death."

"They have lost interest in Israel," Jair put in. "They even took a name, from a Greek word for enlightenment: *Christos*. They refuse to fight Rome and die like fools; instead, they're saying that Adonai will protect them."

At the top of the climb, the three met Harai sitting on the wall. They threw themselves on the ground to rest.

Jonathan drank from the nearly empty skin on his shoulder, then passed it to Eleazar. "Ask him about Yashua," he said.

Eleazar drank, handed the skin to Jair, and looked up at Harai.

"Peace to you, Silent One. We have been talking of the brother you called Gimel. I said he is dead. Jonathan says he is not."

"What you think of as death," said Harai, "is only a change. Departure from this physical body."

"Did Gimel take his body back to Adonai? What do you say?"

"Ascension is the spiritual right of all that lives."

Jonathan began laughing. "Then why does everyone die?"

"I have already told you, there is no death. Ask instead, why does everyone choose physical death, instead of returning to Adonai?"

"You play with words, Harai," said Eleazar, "but this time, I will play with you. Since you have asked the question, tell me the answer!"

"Why have you chosen physical death?" asked Harai. "If you understand why you do this, you may understand why others do so."

"I have not chosen death," said Eleazar.

"You have chosen to fight, you have chosen to hate. In each moment of your life, when you choose hatred instead of love, you choose death instead of life. Every moment you spend hating, you add death to your body. Each moment that you choose love, you add life to your body. More important, hatred is the death of the spirit that gives life to your body, and love is the life of it. When you fail to love, you cannot live."

"Love and hatred are not something we choose," said Eleazar, "but a response inside us."

"You say within you are two emotions, over which you have no control. I tell you there is only one, and within us lies the choice of which way to direct it."

"Look at what Rome has done to us! How can the Romans be loved?"

****

Harai remembered the question he put to Simon, his teacher. "How can I love HaSapas? Look at the scar he left. Look at how he took my food. He tried to kill me."

"Hjarai, have you considered this question in your meditation?"

"No, my Brother Simon, I have not."

"In your next meditation, when you have reached the depths of your thinking, visualize HaSapas. Consider each detail of his face, so that you see him as well as if he were sitting before you. Look deeply into his eyes, until you can see exactly what he is, who he is. Then come and tell me what you have seen."

On their next meeting, Simon asked, "Did you do the meditation I suggested?"

"I did, Simon my brother."

"When you looked into the eyes of the one you think is your enemy, what did you see?"

"I saw myself," said Hjarai, and began to cry.

"Do you still hate him?"

"No," said Hjarai, "but I feel great sorrow for him."

****

Harai raised his eyes to meet Eleazar's. "Romans are only men, like you and me. Even as you and me, they do what they think they should, and follow orders. Their leaders follow the orders of their emperor, who does what he thinks he must, to keep his followers' loyalty. None of them understands his choices. None recognizes the freedom he has, nor does he recognize the results of his choices. All are trapped in ignorance."

"They are the enemy," said Eleazar. "To be hated and killed."

"You, too, are trapped in ignorance. I have tried to free you, even as Yashua tried, by telling you the truth. I understand his frustration."

"Jonathan?" David, who had overheared their conversation, joined them. "While you were gone, more refugees from Jerusalem have come to us. They say that Titus has followed his father back to Rome, but has ordered Ha Pateesh to take Masada by whatever means. They say his soldiers scour the countryside for Essenes. They want to capture a Pious One for questioning. They even sent searchers to Qumran."

Eleazar rose and brushed off his clothes in angry determination. "Silva will have no more chance than the first who came to us."

"Harai?" said David. "I am concerned. Ha Pateesh is known as a stubborn, implacable, terrible man. Titus's order to capture an Essene makes me think that he knows you are here."

"He suspects," laughed Harai. "His men looked up at me, while I looked down on them!"

"If Ha Pateesh comes to us, I fear he will stay a long time," said David.

Harai nodded. "I agree with you."

To the north, dust was rising in the distance. They could see the occasional flash of sunlight reflected on armor. Others stopped and began assembling along the north wall, watching in silence. "They're coming," an old woman muttered.

Her words seemed to echo in whispers around the gathering crowd. "They're coming." Several of the women began crying. The men grew stern; many turned away to prepare weapons.

"Make sure the rock slides are ready," Eleazar's voice called. "Make sure your knives are sharp. Let the children ready their slings. Masada will never fall!"

"Eleazar," Harai called out. "This is the last moment! You must go now, or stay for the end."

"They can't touch us up here!" shouted Eleazar. "I will never leave Masada."

"Your body never will," Harai retorted.

"Why don't you leave, if you're so afraid?"

"I will leave, but not out of fear, and by a path you do not know. If you are a leader to these people, now is your last chance to lead them to safety."

"I already have!"

"You have led them to a pit in the sky from which they can't escape. Lead them to Egypt, to Greece, but do not leave them here!"

"Here our children will not have to learn a foreign tongue. Here our religion will not be polluted with false gods, and our daughters will not marry strangers."

"True. Because here they will all be dead. Choose hatred for yourself, if you must, but not for the multitude."

"The multitude agrees with me."

"The multitude follows its leaders blindly, as do all multitudes. Lead them to life, to where they can think and choose for themselves."

"They have chosen Masada."

"They have chosen you, and *you* have chosen Masada! You have chosen death!"

"Begone, you peaceful Essene. We must prepare for war!"

****

Again Hjarai remembered his teacher and his Aleph-Bet, on a hot day on the road south from Jerusalem. Qumran was a great distance, it seemed. Hjarai watched his feet as he placed each one ahead of the other, contemplating how they bore his weight, footstep by footstep, along the road. How many steps to Qumran? Many! Some of his Aleph-Bet were singing.

They had not gone far when Hjarai saw a shadow ahead of him. He stopped and looked up. A thick beam of wood arose from the ground. Near its top was a horizontal beam, lashed to it with massive ropes, forming a shape like the letter the Greeks called *Tau*. A cross. A man was hanging from it, wrists bound to the crossbeam, and his feet to the upright. Hjarai stopped in his tracks.

"Why is he doing that, my brother Simon?"

"Others have put him there. He has chosen to submit."

"But he is in great pain! He may even die."

"He has chosen this, Hjarai. He has forgotten that he can choose otherwise."

"Why doesn't he remember?"

"He can choose to remember," said Simon.

"Why doesn't he?"

"He has so much faith in his own death that he cannot be swayed, even by his own remembrance."

"Why does Adonai permit the man to suffer so much?"

"Adonai does not, Hjarai; man permits it. Adonai never interferes with man's most important gift of all, the freedom to choose."

"Can't we take him down and save him?"

"We cannot interfere. If we took him down, he would only keep making the same choices, and he would be led back to the same place. He must choose for himself."

The crucified man hung quietly, fighting for breath. He opened his eyes and looked at Simon.

"Is there nothing we can do to ease his pain?" asked Hjarai.

"He must choose," said Simon, looking into the man's eyes.

Through parted lips, the man's teeth were tightly clenched. "Help me," he whispered.

"The man has chosen." Simon touched the man's foot. "I give you the peace of sleep," said Simon. And the man went limp. Into sleep? Into death? Hjarai wasn't sure.

****

Now Harai watched Eleazar shouting and shaking his fists. Others were running about the compound, preparing spears, gathering loose rocks, sharpening knives. He could not help them. Turning, he walked to the north wall to watch the approaching army of Ha Pateesh, The Hammer, Flavius Silva.

18

First Blood

The 10th Legion at Masada

Dust. Sweat. The clump of many boots, the rattle of armor, and heavy breathing of horses and burdened mules all rose from the Judean plain. In a low rumble, the men had been complaining for better food, more water, and complaining about the infernal heat.

Silva rode in front so that he wouldn't have to breathe the dust his troops kicked up.

His first glimpse of Masada, across the plain, had been from the top of a low rise. Because of its immensity, he assumed it was closer, and was dismayed to find it still distant by two days' march. Now that it stood before him, he was still amazed, but did not reveal that to any around him. No wonder his men had not taken it back from the Sicarii!

Now he sat under the door-canopy of his tent, watching his men prepare for a long siege: preparing a cooking area and at least three stations along the route for guarding the supply lines. He studied the walls of the mountain, nearly sheer granite. There were occasional ledges with varying degrees of slope, but it seemed too steep for a straight climb.

His body servant, Pavus, stood a few steps away, unobtrusive, but close enough to answer immediately. He too, was studying the mountain. "Pavus," called Silva.

"My General."

"How long do you think it will take?"

Pavus knew his master's conversational habits, but was wary of his unpredictable temper. Silva didn't like to kill unruly soldiers, but he did like to mutilate them, as an example to the other men.

"I think it will take a long time," Pavus answered.

"We may be able to build a shield that more than one man can carry on their shoulders. Something like an inverted trough. Then, when the rocks come, they will roll off the shield instead of injuring the soldiers. Have Carpathius send for wood. And have the cook send me one of his helpers."

The inside of Silva's tent was sparse. A chest rested on the floor beside a sleeping mat. There was a low table with one chair, and the presence of Flavius Silva seemed to fill the whole room.

"I have a task for you," he told Belius.

Finally, the General had recognized his abilities as a soldier!

"Yes, sir. How can I be of service?"

"It will take a man of courage. Are you such a one?"

"I have great courage, sir," said Belius, standing as straight as he could. Would Silva send him back to Rome with a message? Was he to have him demand provisions from nearby villages?

"If you succeed, there is a possible promotion for you."

"A promotion, sir? Tell me what you wish for me to do, my Caesar, and I will carry it out immediately."

"You have seen the rebels watching us from above, have you not?"

"Sir, I have."

"They watch us continually. Go to the foot of the cart path at the base of the mountain and there, in plain sight, discard all your weapons. Let them see you do this. Then walk up the path alone, carrying a message from me. Having seen you drop your weapons before the climb, they will not harm you."

"What is your message, sir?"

"'Flavius Silva says this to you: Lay down your arms and descend from this mountain. We will receive you at the bottom in peace, and allow you to proceed to whatever destination you desire. If you do not do so, I will lay siege to this mountain. And when I conquer it, I will execute everyone who has resisted me, and transport your women and children to Rome as slaves.' Then bring back their reply."

Approaching the bottom of the cart path, Belius's courage deserted him. *They will kill me before I get halfway up!* he thought. *They will dump stones on my head and shoot me with arrows. Why did I ever join the army?*

Silva had stepped out of his tent to watch.

At the foot of the path, Belius stopped. He unbuckled his belt, waved it before him, then tossed it aside and began his climb to the top.

****

Masada

"What do you think he's doing?" David asked Eleazar.

"Bringing a surrender demand. That's how they always begin."

"Ha Pateesh is standing in front of his tent, watching us."

"He will be watching for a long time!" said Eleazar.

"Shall we kill the soldier now, or wait till he gets to the top?"

"Why not wait and see how arrogant the message is?"

"But he will see our fortifications," said David.

"The Romans already know what we have here. They had it before us!"

"But they don't know how organized we are. This soldier will tell Silva."

"If they think we are well organized," said Eleazar, "they'll be discouraged all the sooner. And leave."

"The Essene says they will not."

After only a few dozen steps, Belius was puffing with the exertion of the climb. The cart path was steeper than it looked, and the edge was a sheer cliff. If he grew even slightly dizzy, he might plunge over the side, like that loose pebble he had just dislodged.

Silva, watching from below, realized how long it would take Belius to ascend the mountain's face, and retreated inside his tent to escape the hot sun. "Pavus!"

"Sir!"

"Watch that cook's helper. Tell me when he nears the top, or if anything happens to him before he reaches it."

****

Belius was getting thirsty. *For all the water I carried for the cook, why didn't I think to bring a water skin?*

The path curved into a small break in the face of the mountain. He could see men up there holding rocks, and his fear grew. They would try to kill him before he reached the top. But how could he climb the uneven ground with his eyes turned toward the heights? Maybe he would hear the rocks coming.

Growing impatient, Silva stepped back out into the sun and studied the mountain. "Pavus, I don't see him. Where is he?"

"Sir, do you see the break in the side of the mountain, there, about halfway up? He just disappeared into that. He should be appearing again in a moment, on the other side."

"I see him now. How long before he reaches the top, do you think, if they don't kill him first?"

"It is said that a man in good condition needs nearly half a day," said Pavus. "Belius has carried many burdens in the camp of Titus."

"Strong enough in body," said Silva, "but not in determination. Do you think he will continue to the top?"

"I think he fears disobeying you, more than he fears the Sicarii."

"Discipline is important in any army," snapped Silva, and Pavus immediately regretted the remark.

Nearing the top, Belius wiped his forehead with the back of his hand. Never before had he been so high, and he was developing a touch of vertigo. Much higher, and he would be able to see the ocean. *At the top, might I see all the way to Rome?* Down below, the ground of the plain seemed to be pulling at him, tempting him to fall.

He was growing increasingly fearful. *Silva knew they would kill me; that's why he picked a lowly cook's helper to deliver his demand.* Looking toward the top, trying to see any rocks coming, he stumbled again. Belius watched another small stone roll off the edge of the path, spinning and bouncing down the sides of the mountain. *I must watch my step, or that will be me! How did Herod climb this horrible path? Did he let them carry him up? What if one of the bearers slipped?*

Watching Belius' progress, David said to Eleazar, "He hasn't even stopped to rest."

"See how fearful he is? Look how he hugs the mountain."

"I think he'll be here in another hour."

"Yes. Gather some of the men; tell them to bring their knives, so he has a proper welcome. If he's that strong, we may require some help."

Seeing the path curving out of sight, Belius did not realize that he was nearing the top of the long climb. He was shocked to see the end of the path suddenly before him, with scores of men, women, and children gathered around the top of the hill.

One of the men approached him. "I am Eleazar," he said. "And you?"

"I am Belius. Flavius Silva has ordered me to bring you a message. . ."

Silva and Pavus stood in front of the tent, watching, when Belius vanished over the lip of the mountain. Neither man took his eyes off the top of the path.

Soldiers were lounging around the encampment. After a two-day rest from their long march from Jerusalem, they were eager for their commander's next order.

"Silva can afford to waste a cook's helper," said one to another.

"But who will replace Belius, when they kill him?"

"I don't want to be a bearer of burdens like him," said the first.

"Neither do I."

They turned their eyes to the cliff in time to see a man hoisted onto the wall, with many around him. As they watched, a long pole appeared behind him, pushing him off the edge. Belius fell, gathering speed.

The camp of Flavius Silva became very quiet.

Pavus counted the number of times the body bounced off the mountain's steep slopes, before landing on a ledge near the bottom.

"That was the answer I expected," said Silva. "But the offer to surrender had to be made. Has Carpathius left for wood for the shields?"

Carpathius had gone. Taking four carts and ten soldiers, he was gone more than a month. But once he returned with the lumber, the work didn't take long.

Finished, the wooden devices were as long as a tall man, and as wide as the distance between a man's elbow and his outstretched fingers. Smooth handles were affixed to their undersides, making it easy for soldiers to hold them steady while walking underneath. Their crests were steeply angled to deflect falling rocks and send them harmlessly down the mountain.

When enough shields were finished to protect two hundred men, Silva gave the order to move. At first light, soldiers started up both the mountains' paths. Each shield, held low over their heads, sheltered three men.

They met their first challenge where the snake path doubled back on itself. The shields were suddenly too long, and the soldiers had to round the curves very slowly. The first or last of the three had to hold his end out over the cliff, while the middle soldier hugged the rock walls. Meanwhile, at least one of them was exposed to whatever might fall from above.

Watching his men climb, Silva secretly feared that the plan would not work. The day was growing hot, and the shields were heavy. The lines were moving too slowly.

Atop Masada, they were now gathered to watch the soldiers.

Two nights before, under Eleazar's orders, the Sicarii had crept down both paths. At the narrower spots, they'd scattered bags of small round pebbles, easy to slip on and make walking treacherous.

More rock slides had been prepared. Knives were as sharp as the grinding stones could make them.

"See there?" asked David. "We spread more pebbles there than anywhere else."

"When they reach that curve," said Eleazar, "release the lower slide."

"I will," said David, and started down the path.

When the first three soldiers paused to maneuver their shield around in the curve, Eleazar signaled to David. The first slide came down on their heads, knocking the first two over the side of the cliff. The third man rolled back into the three behind him, throwing them off balance. Losing their shield off the edge of the cliff, they were bombarded with rocks, falling and tripping those behind them.

Eleazar danced in glee, then dashed to see what was happening on the other side of the mountain.

For the curve on the cart path, four more slides had been prepared, with three more above. If the Romans were courageous—or foolhardy—enough, they would be bombarded all the way up. And in places, the cart path was narrow enough that a soldier, unsteady on his feet, could fall to his death.

Silva, seated outside his tent, had not seen the death of his men on the snake path, on the far side of the mountain. All morning, he had watched his men climb the cart path. They had yet to attain the halfway point, and were going ever more slowly. The heavy shields, the heat of the sun and the steep climb all worked against them. And Silva did not remember seeing Belius slipping that frequently.

At that rate, they would not reach the top until after nightfall. The first of the troops had now reached the sharp curve on the cart path, below the first slide. The soldiers leading the upward advance did not have to slow to round the path's bends and curves as did those on the serpentine path because the cart path was wider than the other way, but they still had to slow their pace a little. In doing so, they strayed too far from the inside of the path, leaving a large gap between the mountainside and the shields exposing their legs to the rocks raining down on them.

Silva stood silently, watching his men die. After each rockfall, the soldiers pressed on. But above each slide was another, waiting to punish their overconfidence.

Soldiers climbed over the bodies of the injured who had not fallen off the path. Each slide left more rocks and injured in the way, making the soldiers' progress ever more difficult and precarious.

As the first sets of rock slides were used up, the Sicarii reloaded them and, when they were full, released them again. Farther back down the line, soldiers who thought themselves safe were newly bombarded.

"Pavus, call them back. Send a runner to the other side and send me word of what's happening there."

Carpathius, seated some distance off and watching with the rest of the soldiers, felt uneasy, since he had directed the building of the shields. Looking over at Silva, he saw the commander motioning him to approach.

"Carpathius, how might the shields be improved?"

"Hinges would let them fit around rock walls more easily, but that would weaken them. We could extend the handles into uprights, so that when rocks hit, the soldiers could rest the shield on the ground and they needn't bear the weight of the impact. But still, rocks can catch the sides of a shield, as they did just now, knocking it out of their grasp."

"Shields probably won't work. Is that what you mean?"

"Yes, sir," said Carpathius, carefully.

"What else can we do? You're a builder. Do you have any ideas?"

"The north wall is the lowest. We could build a scaffold."

"They could easily burn it down," said Silva. "If you think of anything else, come to me."

As twilight began to darken the sky, Silva heard singing in the distance. From time to time, he saw flickers of firelight reflecting off the walls at the top of the mountain. The rebels were celebrating what they thought was a victory!

He had walked through the encampment, listening to the talk of the soldiers, trying to encourage them after the day's failure. Now he stood, carefully studying the top of the mountain, watching the fires illumine the stone watchtower atop the cart path. There had to be a way to take this place!

Suddenly he became aware of a lone figure seated upon the wall—clothed in brilliant white. It was him, the Essene!

"Pavus!" Silva shouted. "Where are you?"

"Here!" Pavus came running.

"Fetch my bow and a few of the very lightest arrows."

Silva stood silently returning the gaze of the figure on the wall. To his surprise, his anger began to abate and a peaceful feeling seeped into his consciousness. He gritted his teeth and forced himself to hate the man on the cliff wall.

Pavus returned at a run and slid to a stop, a large bow in one hand, six long arrows in the other. Silva took them, without a word, and started for the foot of the high plateau. The figure on the top of the mountain remained, watching.

Silva stopped. Dropping the other arrows to the ground, he fitted one to his bowstring.

The arrow was light, but the bow was heavy, with a pull greater than most of his men could manage. Silva raised the bow, took careful aim at the Essene, and released the string.

The arrow hissed upward, higher and higher, forming an arc through the air. Silva saw the Essene stretch out his hand, catch the nearly spent arrow out of the air, and break it across his knee.

Silva, raging within, could barely make out the words that Eleazar shouted down: "Good shot!"

19

Bad Dreams

Roman Encampment at the foot of Masada

Whinnying and snorting filled the night air; Silva tossed restlessly in his sleep.

The length of the siege was growing, together with Silva's aversion to the Judean desert. Against the Sicarii, every strategy, every innovation, had only led to more Roman deaths, more Roman injuries. Silva feared what his men were already whispering: Masada could not be conquered.

This time, the whinny roused Silva to awareness. He covered his ear with a pillow, trying to recover his dream.

In it, he had stood at the foot of Masada, surrounded by soldiers. All was quiet; not a whisper could be heard. High above Masada, floating in the sky above them, was a huge rectangular box. Its edges were fretted in ornate gold. It rested on two carrying poles, extended through bronze hoops on either side. Its sides were overlaid with gold, and on top were two winged figures who looked like gods. They stood on the extreme ends of the box, each bending toward each other, as though bowing to the box's contents. Their wings nearly touched.

"They were celestial," Silva told Julius later.

Holding the ends of the poles were four men, each dressed in white. They wore their dark hair long, in a single braid. They were carrying the box skyward, out of Silva's reach.

At his shout, the men carrying the box paused, looked down at Silva, then briefly spoke among themselves, as if conferring on what to do.

****

"Cursed horses," muttered Dolofus. "If they wake Silva, he's liable to have my eyes for his next trophy. Calibius, go quiet them down."

Calibius heard a hoof stamp on the ground, then a swishing tail caught him in the face.

Why had they replaced Belius with a boy? Ever since the Jews threw Belius off the mountain, Dolofus had one awkward replacement after another, and now this one.

Another whinny, and another horse began pawing the ground.

"Calibius! Back to your bed! They are afraid of you in the dark. They know my smell, but not yours. I will finish the watering without your help."

"I will stay," said Calibius. "If I am to help you, they must get to know me, because I will water them every day."

Dolofus emptied his bucket into the trough and grabbed Calibius by the shirt. "Horses are stupid. If you must stay, move slowly. Too fast frightens them. A touch in the dark on their whithers could be a wildcat, for all they know. Don't pet them or touch them."

"As you say," Calibius replied.

****

Silva was still dreaming. This time, the four bearers were singing, carrying the box along the high wall at the top of the plateau. In his dream he was furious, shouting at them, shaking his fist. They paused to look down at him, exchanged glances and continued carrying the box along the wall, tantalizing him, enraging him.

He had a huge bow in his hand, much bigger than his own bow. Filled with strength, he fitted an arrow to the string, drew the bow, and let go. But the arrow vanished before it left the bow. The men carrying the box looked down at him, laughing.

****

Voices roused Silva, this time to wakefulness. He lay still, listening. The wind had shifted and now carried the faint sounds of singing and music.

He rose from his low bed and pulled on a light cloak. Outside the tent, he stopped to glare up at the heights of Masada, towering above his camp. No men were walking the high wall. He looked again to be sure, but thought he still heard their singing.

A guard stepped up to him. "Sir?"

"Again there is someone new watering the horses, I suppose."

"Yes, sir."

"Pass the word to him: If he doesn't do it more quietly, he may not live until the horses get used to him."

Groggy, Silva walked slowly through the camp, his uneven gait angering him still more. "Guard!"

"Yes, sir," said a soldier, coming immediately to his side.

"Who is singing!?"

"It seems to be coming from the mountain, sir."

Again he raised his eyes to the mountain. Under the open stars, he could see smoke, illumined by firelight, slowly rising above, with an occasional flash of flame appearing over the stone wall that rimmed the plateau. The rhythmic singing, carried down on the evening breeze, was punctuated with clapping and shouts. They were holding a dance!

Near Silva's feet, a soldier arose from his sleeping mat and saluted. "Sir!"

"What is it, soldier?"

"That song you hear. It's the same one the crowd sang at a wedding in Jerusalem, before the insurrection."

They were continuing to live, Silva thought, as though nothing was wrong. Every seventh day, Silva heard the chanting. When someone died, he could hear the funeral. And now, a wedding!

Without replying, Silva walked on.

Dolofus and Calibius had seen Silva leaving his tent. "We've awakened him," said Dolofus in a mournful whisper.

Both men froze, trying not to agitate the horses until Silva returned to bed. They saw him striding out through the camp, gazing up at the shape that towered against the stars.

"He's obsessed with that mountain."

"Why does Vespasian want it so badly?" puzzled Calibius. "We've been here for more than a year. There are only two ways down. A small party could defend both paths. They can't get away from us and eventually they will run out of food and water and have to come down."

Dolofus lowered his voice to a whisper: "Caesar is not that thrifty. He wants possession, now, and he shall have it, whatever the cost."

"There must be something up there of great value."

"Nothing but Jewish rabble. I don't understand why Vespasian wants them. When they're taken, they will only be crucified as an example."

"Who is this man, Jubalum, who has come to us? They say Titus sent him. All day, he walked back and forth at the foot of the mountain, stretching threads across sticks hammered into the ground. It looked like he was preparing to lay out a gaming field."

"Some say he is a builder of roads."

"We need no roads here," said Calibius.

"Maybe he'll build us a road to the top of Masada, wide enough that we can march right up."

"That would take a long time," said Calibius.

"And the laborers will be us," said Dolofus. "If he's going to try, we'll find out soon enough."

"One of the soldiers said he heard Jubalum is Syrian, that he killed a man there and would have been executed if he hadn't fled."

"He looks like a villain. He's getting a reputation. Don't gamble with him. They say he cheats at our games."

"If so, he may not live long enough to build that road to the heavens. The men will kill him."

The two men stopped talking to watch Silva continue down through the camp toward the foot of the mountain.

"What is he doing?" asked Calibius.

"Listen. Can't you hear them singing?"

Silent again, they listened. The music was slightly minor in key and they found themselves wishing they could hear it better, or even be there to watch. Silva was glaring at the top of the mountain at a solitary figure in white seated on the wall, watching him.

"What's he looking at? Who is he?" asked Calibius.

"The Essene," said Dolofus. "The soldier who captures that man alive will be a rich man when he goes back to Rome."

Silva lowered his eyes from the mountaintop. Someday, he would meet that man, and when he did, Silva would have satisfaction for the humiliation of the arrow.

He returned to his tent. In reply to his reports about the futile attacks on Masada, Titus's letter was explicit. If Silva couldn't take the mountain by any other means, build a road to the top. Could it be done? This man, Jubalum, seemed like a rogue, but Titus sent him and said he's the man for the job.

****

Harai had been watching the plain below Masada ever since its fall to the Sicarii two years before. The evening breeze felt cool on his back. *Meditate, remember, plan,* he thought. *And watch the moods of the Sicarii rise and fall.*

Finally the Roman camp below was going to sleep. Harai saw Dolofus and Calibius watering the horses. He saw Silva emerge from his tent and listen to the singing from the wedding party. *Such a tense man,* thought Harai, watching the reds and oranges play through Silva's aura. He was raging, even now as he went to bed.

Harai turned to listen to the singing. In the center of a ring of people, David and Soo-ooni were circling each other in a hand-clapping, foot-stomping dance handed down from ancient tradition.

Only the month before, her mother Adameh had finally said she was old enough. "Do you give this union your blessing?" David had asked him.

Harai smiled. "Do you ask if I approve of what you are doing?"

"Yes."

"David, I approve of the joy you bring to each other. I approve of a union between you, of your choice to give each other joy and to find it in the giving. I do doubt your union will enjoy the peace that you and I would wish for it. Ha Pateesh is very determined to win his little war."

"We have won many battles with the Romans. We have watched them try many ways to invade our little community up here. They always suffer losses. We never lose anyone."

Only an hour before, he and Soo-ooni had smashed the cup, emptied of the wine they had first shared as man and wife.

There was laughter and joy in her voice. She was flushed with excitement, and with the exertion of the dance; and David was sweating—and grinning.

At a wedding that Hjarai's Aleph-Bet had attended, Simon had told him, "The grin is for the joy yet to come, the fulfillment of union. The sweat is for the labor it will cost him. Such is the life he has chosen—joy and sweat."

Harai had pondered that lesson for a long time.

"Joy is our right," Simon said later, "not something earned by sweat. "Joy is what we are; it is God's joy that creates us. But many believe joy can only be earned. Too many believe they are not worthy of joy and turn their attention away from what they are."

Now Harai watched David and Soo-ooni walk, hand in hand, toward the palace for their wedding night. "We will sleep in Herod's own bed," David had boasted that afternoon. "What finer place could there be in all Judea?"

Eleazar, his head lowered in thought, turned aside from the dancing throng. He stopped at the wall overlooking the camp of Silva and wiped sweat from his face in frustration and worry.

Jonathan and Dan went to join him. Not far behind came Jair and two others. They gathered beside Eleazar, who was studying the enemy camp below.

"What were they doing down there today?" Eleazar asked. "There was a man walking back and forth, stretching thread in straight lines on the ground. What do you think they are doing?"

"Preparing a new strategy, I think," said Jonathan. "If they have the patience, this one may succeed."

"They are doing what the Romans are best at doing," Dan added. "They are building a road."

"Whatever it is, a road or ramp of some sort, it will take a long time," said Jair.

When they looked into Eleazar's eyes, they could see that he believed himself defeated. He turned again to stare down the side of the mountain at the Roman camp below.

"They can't build a road up here," said Jair. "The mountain's too high. They couldn't even build a bridge that high, or a tower."

"Yet they are laying out the plans for its foundation," said Eleazar.

The group walked along the wall, to a spot directly over where they had seen the Roman builder counting his paces. "It's nearly a sheer drop," said Eleazar.

"Watch this." Dan picked up a rock the size of his fist. Let's see how far it goes." He placed the rock on the wall and nudged it gently until it fell off the edge. After a brief plunge it grazed the side of the mountain, then leaped outward, spinning. But a moment later, it came to a halt with a solid *thunk*.

"I never saw that ledge!" said Dan.

"If it's too wide," said Eleazar, "slides we make from this level won't reach the builders of the ramp."

"Still," said Jonathan, "It will be good sport to aim rocks at them while they try to work."

"They are too far away for us to throw rocks," said Jonathan. "We need to build more slides here. That way we can slow them down and maybe, finally discourage them."

"They have taken serious losses," said Eleazar, "and still they continue. Nothing discourages Ha Pateesh."

"He must have lost as many soldiers as there are people among us up here," responded Dan. "What must he want, that he would spend the lives of his men this way?"

"The Romans are very proud," said Eleazar dejectedly.

"Tomorrow," said Jair, "let's get loose rocks down toward the road site, see where they fall. That will tell us if a slide could be built there, and how we must position the drop."

Harai could not hear their conversation, but he knew their feelings and their fears. He recognized the slow footsteps of Soo-ooni's mother, approaching in the dark.

"Tired from the dancing?" he called out softly.

"Abbi Yashan? Old Father, are you there?"

"I am here, Adameh."

"They are so happy," she laughed. "I have never seen such hope in the eyes of a bride and groom, or such joy. But I'm afraid they think only of this night. I fear for them, Harai."

"Adameh, your fear is justified."

"You do not think that Ha Pateesh will give up and go home?"

"No, Adameh. He is a very determined man."

"How could he be persuaded? Do you think there's a way?"

"He desires that which has been hidden. Were he to find it, he would go home —but he never will find it and so he will not go home!"

"What does he want?"

"He wants the end of us, the end of the Covenant. He thinks if he can find the Ark and destroy the sacred tablets, we will forget the laws written on them."

"Why does he believe he can find it here?"

"Because the Romans did not find it in the Temple."

"How do you know this?"

"There was a plan. Now that it is hidden from the Romans, it will never be lost to Israel."

"Hidden where?" asked Adameh, narrowing her eyes, her voice skeptical.

"In a safe place," said Harai. "At the proper time, it will be found. By then, Rome will be nearly forgotten."

"But it's not here! We could tell him that and maybe he would go away."

"He will not believe us," said Harai, "until his men have searched Masada for themselves."

Adameh fell silent for a moment. "I suppose we could invite him to come and see. But after we killed his messenger, he'd never trust us."

"If he came up here alone," asked Harai, "do you think that he would survive the trip back down?"

"No." The group around the fire was now singing old songs of Egypt. "If only my husband had lived to see this night, and David's father too. Such friends they were. When they knew I was listening, they could be very formal. But with me out of the room, they would joke and laugh."

She paused.

"Maybe I'm glad my husband did not live to see this night. I heard David talking, earlier. He thinks Ha Pateesh is building a road to us. Is it true?"

****

Silva's nightmare was of his return to Rome in disgrace for not having found the Ark. Titus, bigger than life, stood atop a huge column. Silva lay naked, chained to the ground, with captains and generals jeering at him. Women and children were flinging pebbles and rotten fruit, laughing at his nakedness.

Suddenly Titus, looking down in scorn, wasn't Titus any longer, but Vespasian—older than when Silva had seen him last. He wore a laurel wreath over gray hair, and a pure white toga. The scepter in his hand was a marble column, even bigger than the one he stood on. He raised it high over his head, to bring it down on Silva.

The dream changed. Silva was lying in a dungeon which, amazingly, had cloth walls and a dry desert breeze blowing through them. His throat had never felt drier. "I thirst!" he shouted in his dream.

No one came.

"I thirst!" he shouted again. His tongue seemed ready to split in half. Raising his hand to rub his eyes, he noticed a quiet figure in one corner of his dungeon, wearing a white robe. His long dark hair was gathered in a single braid. The Essene, extending a flagon of water in one hand!

Silva leaped up and lunged for the flagon. As he drank, he found himself taking another flagon of water from the Essene and drinking more, feeling the water fill his stomach. "Who are you?" he asked.

Silently, the Essene raised an arrow so Silva could see it, then broke it over his knee.

Silva was filled with rage, but found he couldn't move. "What do you want, Essene?"

"It's time for you to go home, now, Puer."

Silva was stunned. Only his father had called him that, and his father had been dead for more than 20 years! He glared at the Essene, unwillingly recalling his father's own words to him:

Time to go home, now. Working into the night, Silva's father had told his son many times, over the years: *Time for you to go home, now, Puer.*

"I can't," he said.

"What you seek, you will not find," said the Essene. "You must go home, now, Puer."

"Stop calling me that!" shouted Silva, holding his ears. "Stop imitating my father! Who are you, a god?"

"I am a messenger. My message is: *Time for you to go home, now, Puer.*"

When Pavus came in, Silva was tossing back and forth, screaming. "And sweating like a slave," Pavus whispered to a friend next morning.

20

Power's Corruption

Rome

"Father," said Titus as he reached for another morsel of pheasant, "I haven't rested on a proper dining couch for a long time."

Vespasian, a cup of sweet wine in his hand, was lounging on his left side, his elbow on the arm of the couch, gazing at his guests. Generals, captains and the highest-ranked soldiers of his armies had gathered with their women to watch the entertainment in the center of the hall.

"They dance beautifully, Father."

"They are dancing for their lives," said Vespasian. "Captured from forays in Syria. I warned them if they didn't perform well for this feast, I would sell them to my soldiers."

Titus, who liked to see people under stress, watched the half-naked girls with renewed interest, and tore into his pheasant. Grease dripped onto his toga as he gnawed the flesh from the slender bone.

Vespasian drank from his cup and turned to Titus. "I've missed you. I'm glad that fight is over, and you're home."

After Titus' failure to uncover the Ark of the Covenant, he feared that he'd be punished. The victory parade had reassured him. Cheering crowds lined the streets. Titus rode in the lead beside Julius, head of his personal guards. The armies followed him into Rome with fanfares of trumpets and drums.

Bringing up the rear of the parade were carts thronged with prisoners for the slave market—more money for his father's coffers. Titus had already chosen the young woman he wanted for himself: with smooth, dark skin and flashing angry eyes. His favorite fantasy, sparing him from boredom much of the way home, was of taming her. Once she understood the alternatives, she would come around quickly enough.

Vespasian leaned over to Titus. "Look at that one. What fine nipples!"

Titus raised his eyes from his food and looked at the Syrian's naked breasts. Reaching into his toga, he found a denarius bearing the visage of Vitellius, the previous Emperor. "I'll flip you for her!"

Vespasian shook his head, laughing. "I offered her and the others a lifetime of freedom, for one night of dancing. I dare not go back on a public promise. Nero did. No one ever trusted him after that."

"You're right, of course. But one can always dream!"

Vespasian smiled and patted his son's arm. "You've more than enough women to keep you busy." He turned to a concoction of periwinkles and flamingo tongues.

Titus watched the Syrian dancer, her teasing gyrations exciting his loins. She caught him looking at her and began dancing for him alone, laughing at him, her stare amused and confident.

"Titus?" asked Vespasian. "Is my wine warming your cheeks, or is it the Syrian?"

Titus blushed deeply. When he looked up again, he saw the Syrian had whirled away to find another fool to tease.

Vespasian leaned over again. "Will Silva find the Ark of the Covenant?"

Titus sobered quickly. "Silva is determined. Did you know that the Jews picked up his nickname, *Malleus*, and always call him that—albeit in Hebrew?"

"I'm not surprised," said Vespasian.

"If any man can find the Ark, it will be Silva."

Titus laughed. Now the Syrian girl was dancing for Parifius, a captain in Titus's own fourth cohort. From the look on Parifius' face, he was evidently the Syrian's latest victim.

"She shows no discrimination for rank," Vespasian observed.

"Amusing," Titus agreed. "Has she played with you yet?"

"She'd be foolish to do that," said Vespasian. "If she entices me too much, I may change my mind."

"Since my last report to you, Father, I have had several communications from Silva."

"Any progress?"

"Herodeum and Machaerus are fallen. Neither city held the Ark. He has arrived at Masada, and after several attacks, finds the mountain too well fortified. He's placed it under siege."

Vespasian nudged him to look. The Syrian girl, kicking and whirling, wore a long skirt with slits which revealed her well-shaped legs well up past the thigh. Now she was in front of Parifius, swinging her hips in time with the music, easing her skirt lower and lower.

Titus began laughing with Vespasian. Parifius, beginning to sweat, was licking his lips, moving in rhythm with the dancing girl, obviously forgetting he was in public, in the presence of his Emperor.

A woman near Parifius began a high-pitched giggle. Now Titus and Vespasian were laughing. Parifius, suddenly aware that he was the butt of the girl's humor, enraged by his embarrassment, lifted a knife from the table and lunged for the girl. But before he could reach her, two soldiers grabbed him from either side, and the girl ran from the room.

Now the entire company was laughing. Parifius stalked out of the hall with back straight, head held high, his neck cherry red.

Vespasian wiped tears from his eyes and took another sip of his wine. To Titus's surprise, he changed the subject:

"Flavius Silva said that by the time Masada falls by siege, he will be an old man." His father's mind had always been sharp. Since his elevation to the purple, he was using it as a weapon.

Titus cleared his throat. "The rebel Jews seem well supplied, he says. The palace of Herod has huge cisterns and in season, enough rain falls that they never want for water. There is enough land on the plateau that they can raise crops and graze sheep."

"They are outnumbered," Vespasian said.

"Yes, but how to reach them? You remember, there are two paths to the top: the snake path, wide enough for only one man, and the cart path, wide enough for three abreast. In some places, four."

"Three abreast should be enough to force back men who are poorly trained and poorly armed."

"True, father. But when Herod built the summer palace, his guard fortified the heights with rock slides. They are wide wooden platforms, restrained by ropes, groaning with heavy rocks. When our soldiers try to climb either path, Silva says he loses men to heavy rocks dropped from high above."

"Ah." Vespasian leaned back on his couch and reached for a large ripe olive. "All they must do is lie up there and throw down rocks? Is that enough to keep us from success?"

"So it seems."

"After they drop the rocks, it should take them some time to load the platforms again. Why can't they continue up the path when it's safe?"

"Silva says there are many slides. Every one that falls, wipes out whatever is beneath. The rocks are heavy enough to crush the soldiers' shields. After only one slide, the path is obstructed with rocks as well as the dead and injured—which makes climbing even harder. Then there is another slide to crush any men who have survived the first, and always another. According to Silva, the Jews reload them with surprising speed."

"Silva must have other ideas. Do you?"

"I suggested that he build a wide ramp to the top, march the soldiers up, twenty abreast; and dispatch an engineer to complete the structure."

"Masada is high, isn't it?" asked Vespasian. "To build such a structure would take years!"

"But a siege will take even longer. Silva says that he can't even shoot an arrow that high. By the time it reaches the top, it is spent."

Eating and drinking continued into the night. The dancers were replaced by jugglers and magicians. After a time, Parifius returned, more somber than before, and rejoined the feast. Honoring his word, Vespasian freed the Syrian dancers to return to their homeland as they wished.

Two soldiers assisted Titus to his rooms and laid him on his bed. Other servants removed his toga, covered him with a light cloth, and left him to sleep.

A few hours later, feeling sicker than ever from drink and overeating, Titus rose to relieve himself. He stumbled to the corner of his room, where a small door opened to an adjoining chamber. After eliminating most of what he had eaten, he rinsed the foul, acid taste from his mouth with water. Holding his head, he returned to bed and stretched out on his back, but the room seemed to be spinning and dipping. Instead of rising, he turned onto his side. This seemed to stabilize the room, so he closed his eyes again.

Sick as he was, it felt good to be home. Plush wall hangings, marble floors and carpets, were a relief from living in a dusty tent. Instead of soldiers and horses, he was surrounded by servants to answer his every need. He opened his eyes again, reassuring himself that it was all true. The familiarity of the room made the long trek through Israel seem an unreal dream; the only reality now was the comfort of soft cloth under his cheek. His bed was a womb where he could gestate for a night and come forth in the morning, newly born from the rigors of travel and war.

In the low light of the lone oil lamp, his gaze lingered on the shadowy bulk of a large chair, a gift from his mother, who had said it had belonged to her family since Rome was founded. "It came to us out of legend," she told him. "My grandfather told me a god gave it to our family in return for saving the life of Romulus in a battle with the northern barbarians."

Titus didn't believe it, of course. But as he looked at the chair now, a ghostly image seemed to be seated there, looking back at him. Was it Romulus, or the image of the god who gave the chair in the first place? He was determined to ignore the hallucination, but the image seemed to grow stronger. Titus continued to watch the chair, and as the image took form, Titus saw that it was jovial, friendly and seemed to be laughing at him. Not believing in the image, he closed his eyes and tried to sleep, but he thought he could feel its nearness. When he opened his eyes again and looked at the chair, the image was gone.

"A phantom of the wine," he chuckled to himself, eyes closed again. But he could still feel its presence. Slightly alarmed, he sat up in bed and scanned the room. Nothing. He lay back on his side and fell into an uneasy sleep.

****

Roman Encampment at the foot of Masada

In the light of the nearly full moon, Dolofus and Calibius were carrying water for the horses. They could see Silva standing before his tent, glaring at the mountain. "He's a man obsessed," Dolofus whispered.

"I don't think he's sleeping well," Calibius whispered back. "They say he's up most of the night. Either he stands there and glares at Masada, or he paces through the camp."

"Not sleeping will drive a man insane."

"His dreams are troubled," said Dolofus. "I have even heard him scream in his sleep."

"What could he be dreaming about?"

"Maybe he remembers that bear he fought with," said Dolofus.

"He hates this place."

"We all do," said Dolofus harshly. "We have to journey a full day to the nearest spring, spend another day stealing its meager water, then yet another day marching back with loaded carts. Each trip I make there, the water seems to flow more slowly. I fear the spring is drying up."

"If that happens, where will you go?"

"The nearest water is in the village of Harad, to the west," answered Dolofus.

Silva walked slowly down toward the construction site. In the moonlight, he could see Jubalum, walking around its base counting steps, estimating, planning. Why didn't he sleep? Silva wondered. Were his dreams troubled as well?

Silva looked again to the top of the mountain, directly over the ramp. Seated on the wall was the shadowy figure in white, watching him. Did he never sleep, either? He never moved from the wall, always watching!

Silva thought he could see light around the figure—white lights, playing around his body. His eyes were hidden in shadows, but Silva thought they glowed slightly. Who was this who could send him dreams, appear in his room, know things about him that no one else did? Who were these Essenes? If Silva could but talk to one for a moment, perhaps he could learn what he longed to know. *I can't go home,* Silva thought mournfully. *I am ordered to take this hill. Can't you understand that?*

There was Jubulum, climbing the dirt ramp. There were no rock slides directly under the western wall of the plateau. Since no path crossed under it, no slides had been built above it. A ledge, part way down the slope caught rocks dropped from above, so it was relatively safe.

"Hello, builder," Silva said.

"Good evening, sir," Jubulum replied formally.

"I see the ramp is nearly half complete. Yours was a good decision to build here, instead of at the first site. We are now high enough that they dare not show themselves at the top."

"Thank you, sir."

"Except for that one in white, the watcher."

"He is a strange one," said Jubulum. "I have never seen such a powerful magician."

"Or a god."

"I think he is only a man," said Jubulum. "With some trick he uses to slow your arrows."

"No one else has ever been able to do such a thing."

"Yet he does it."

"How long will it take to finish the ramp?"

Jubulum lowered his gaze, then raised his eyes again to the top of the plateau. "The higher we build, the greater the foundation needed for support. For every foot of incline, the ramp must be extended many cubits at the base. The sides must also be fortified. If we build all the way to the top, the entire job will take seven more years, perhaps eight."

Silva followed the slope of the dirt ramp from the plain to its present point of completion, about 400 feet up the side of the cliff. Again he heard the words in his mind: *It's time for you to go home now, Puer.*

"No, it's not!" shouted Silva.

Jubulum drew back in fear, fingering the dagger he had begun to carry in his belt. Over the last three years, Silva had been talking to himself more and more. The soldiers thought he was growing demented, and there had been mutterings of rebellion. Silva had personally killed six of his own men whom he suspected of such talk.

"Jubulum! Could a scaffold be constructed at this point, large enough that the men could climb to the top with a ram and breach that wall?"

"It could be, sir. Better to go higher with the ramp first, so that the scaffold is more stable. If we build from this present height, they may be able to push it over from the top."

Silva fell silent, listening. Jubulum had seen him do this before. Silva turned toward the east, then toward the west, as though trying to determine the direction of something he heard.

For some time, it seemed to Silva that he had been hearing the voice of his mother calling him. *Puer*, the voice called. *Come home, Puer.* He looked up and saw what he knew was there: the Essene seated on the wall overlooking the ramp, staring down at him with equal intensity.

Hate welled up from within Silva, from some source he couldn't find, but he thought of this as his Hatred Well. At the same time, he could feel the peacefulness of the Essene surrounding him, canceling his hate.

The Essene was trying to get him to disobey Titus. Defeat against such a paltry band of rabble was unthinkable, yet his men thought he was losing his mind. If they mutinied, he was sure to die. Yet what was death to him? It was acceptance of that peace the Essene threw at him, that millstone he was trying to place around Silva's spirit. *I will never give in!*

Jubulum could see Pavus approaching.

"Enough!" Silva shouted.

Jubulum's hand again went to his dagger, as he drew back out of Silva's reach. Silva had begun sobbing, and Pavus took his hand, saying, "There is wine and hot food for you, sir. There is also a woman awaiting your commands."

Silva allowed Pavus to lead him back to his tent.

The next morning, he slept late. His men were glad for his absence, and they talked in low, fearful tones of his odd behavior. Their routine was broken by the arrival of a courier from Titus, and Silva read the epistle over his noon meal.

> *From Titus to Flavius Silva, Greetings.*
> *The siege is taking too long. The idea of building the ramp is good, and will ultimately win success in the taking*

of Masada, but my father grows impatient. He has ordered me to send you this letter with the following directions.

You are to plan another direct assault. Order the soldiers to run up both ascents to the top. Command them to ignore the rock slides. "What kind of men are these who flee from rabble throwing stones?" were my father's words. He says to spend men, and not to let your soldiers be slowed or stopped by bodies or rubble on the paths. Order your soldiers to cast the dead and injured off the cliff face and out of the path of the oncoming soldiers. If the assault is swift and remorseless enough, he believes that your soldiers can make it to the top and end this siege.

I realize, as well as you, that this effort will cost many lives and may actually fail, but this is the order of Vespasian, Emperor of Rome. You will do as he commands.

Silva rose from his table and walked outside the tent. "Pavus!" he called out.

"Yes, sir."

"Tell the men that there will be no more work on the ramp until further notice. The men are to rest and have a holiday for three days. After that, there will be a new assignment. Send all the captains to my tent."

"Immediately, sir."

****

Masada

Darkness, stone, ashes—a good hiding place, thought Harai. The wall appeared to be untouched. There was no fresh dirt apparent on the floor of the room. Aloud, he said, "The wisdom of the Teacher of Righteousness has chosen well, my brother Simon."

The wisdom of the Master chose you, Harai, he seemed to hear Simon's answer in his head.

"I only follow the direction he selected," muttered Harai.

He is pleased with your work, came Simon's reply. *You did well to keep from these others what they hid in the wall. Normally, we are not open to directly influencing the minds of others. It interferes with their freedom of choice. Their willingness to assist in the rescue of the Ark made it possible for us to do this ethically.*

"Yes, my brother Simon."

Your part in deluding them, though, seems to have opened to you the idea that influencing others in this way is acceptable. I caution you about influencing Silva, as you are doing. Man's freedom of choice is absolute.

"Man's freedom of choice is limited, my brother Simon, unless he knows all his options. Flavius Silva is limited in this way."

All men are limited in this way, Harai, even you. We are limited by our chosen focus.

"But you helped me to choose, Simon. I am trying to help Silva the same way."

Beware of your help, Harai. You have taken a personal interest in the welfare of these others, when they have already chosen for themselves. You cannot help them any more. In your attempts, you endanger yourself. If you do not regain your disinterest, you may have trouble returning to us. Be warned: They belong to themselves, as each of us does.

"Yes, my brother. I will meditate and regain my oneness with my source."

You have even entertained the thought of influencing Titus to recall Silva. If you do this, Rome will always believe that the Ark is hidden here. You must stop this. Events are unfolding just as they should. Don't interfere.

"My brother Simon, your advice, as always, reveals the truth to me."

When it is time, my brother Harai, we will help you.

Harai emerged from the darkness of the furnace area under the baths and saw Eleazar approaching—obviously agitated, sweating and slightly out of breath.

"I've been looking for you! Where have you been?"

"Here," Harai answered.

"The watchers reported seeing a courier ride in this morning. Not long after, they stopped working on the ramp. Some think Silva is about to leave us and go back to Rome."

"Silva does what he must," said Harai, heading toward the main gate of the palace.

"Wait. We need your council. What do you think they're doing?"

"Leave me, Eleazar." Harai continued walking. "I must soon be on my way."

Eleazar hurried after him. "Harai!" he demanded, almost in the tone of an expletive.

Harai paused, turned and said to Eleazar, "My work here is done. I have done what I can, my friend. I can do no more for you." With that he turned away.

Dumbfounded, Eleazar left the palace and went to the western lip of the plateau, overlooking the ramp. It was now high enough that Roman archers from below were able to shoot at any who peered over the wall. Eleazar cautiously leaned his head out over the edge and saw only the engineer, Jubulum, near the top of the ramp. Eleazar pulled his head back, picked up a large rock, and laid it on top of the wall. He then climbed up on top, lifted the rock over his head, and heaved it with all his strength.

So intent was Jubulum on his plans that he did not see the rock gathering momentum in its fall. With a loud thump, the rock landed on the ground beside him, glanced off the steep slope, and began rolling and bouncing down the incline.

Startled, Jubulum looked up directly into Eleazar's face. Eleazar shook his fist at the builder and withdrew out of sight. Trembling at the near miss, Jubulum hurried down the ramp and back to the encampment.

Near the center of the plateau, Eleazar found Harai seated on the ground, legs crossed, hands resting on his knees, palms up, face lifted slightly toward the sky.

David and Soo-ooni were standing, hand in hand, near the northern extremity of the west wall. *Soon she will be ready to deliver,* Eleazar thought. The baby would probably be born just in time to die.

Adameh was with them. Eleazar knew that she and all the women had been crying much during these past few weeks.

For the first six months, work on the ramp had been slow. Archers from below were barely able to defend the workers from the rocks hurled from above. But as the ramp grew higher, the Sicarii were in greater danger from arrows. Now, if anyone so much as stuck his head out over the west wall, arrows would come flying with deadly accuracy. With this danger growing, most of the people of the tableland had lost heart. It was clear to all that if the Romans persisted, it was merely a matter of time before their ramp would reach the top and they could overrun Masada.

Fear of the inevitable became contagious. When a mother wept, all her children would join her. The men turned sullen and inward. From time to time there were fights, usually not serious. But one had been lost: a villager from Harad had come to persuade the Sicarii to leave Masada and was trapped when the Roman soldiers arrived. His frustration was more than he could take, and his constant complaining led to his death.

Perhaps he was fortunate to have died so early, thought Eleazar. At least his children did not have a father who would have to tend to the children of a Roman household in his capacity as a slave.

On the southern end of the plateau, a group of some fifty men, most of them in tears, had joined hands and were chanting a prayer to Adonai that the Romans would leave. Eleazar went to join David and Soo-ooni.

"Is Silva leaving?" asked David. "What does Harai say?"

Eleazar shook his head in bafflement. "The old fool says he is finished with us and is leaving. He always was a bit touched, but now I think he's lost his mind completely. Look at him over there." Eleazar gestured to the center of the plateau where Harai was meditating, sheep and goats grazing on the sparse vegetation around him.

"He's probably as heartsick as the rest of us," David said. "And he's no warrior, he's not even a rabbi. Don't be so hard on him."

"I'm not. He's the only one among us who has shown any vision. He never gave anything but encouragement, even if it was only riddles. But now he won't talk to me at all."

"What does he think they're doing down there?"

"He only said he can't help anymore."

"Look," said Soo-ooni, "how peaceful he seems. I wish I could understand him."

"It's easy to understand," said Eleazar. "There sits an old man who has given up, waiting to die."

"According to Amos, a large group rode off from the encampment," said David. "But most of the other soldiers are still down there. If they plan to leave, wouldn't they all depart? The others might be riding to Jerusalem for reinforcements. Look on the road to the north. You can still see the dust they're raising."

One hand resting on her swollen belly, Soo-ooni faced the north, and watched in silence as the dust trail moved farther away.

David placed one arm around her waist, holding her to him. "In time, they will leave us," he said. "In time, we will be free."

21

The Prophecy

Masada

"Eleazar, wake up!"

Amos stood at the door to the dwelling where Eleazar and his woman were sleeping.

Eleazar could barely make out the shadow in his doorway. The moon had set, and the stars gave little light. As yet, Eleazar could see no sign of morning. There were no other sounds—footsteps of others preparing a cooking fire, fetching water. Nothing except the voice in the doorway.

"For the love of God! Wake up!"

Eleazar's woman stirred in his arms. Annoyed with this disturbance, he motioned with his hand to dismiss the intruder. In the darkness, Amos missed it and called again, louder: "Eleazar!"

"What is it?" she whispered, half asleep.

"Nothing, Beloved. A sleepwalker."

"Tell him, go away," she murmured, and turned on her back. In a moment she was snoring gently.

"Eleazar," Amos called again, his voice betraying his frustration. "You must come at once!"

"I'm coming," he said.

Instead of rising, Eleazar rolled over and snuggled his arm around his woman. In the darkness, he could see the outline of her face, her mouth slightly open. Feeling her warmth, gently he leaned closer to her and kissed her cheek. She turned her face to him, and he kissed her again. "I'll be back."

Outside the doorway, the first thing he saw was Harai, still in the center of the plateau, legs crossed and hands, palms up, resting on his knees. It had been three days since he had budged!

Amos grabbed Eleazar's arm, "Come."

At the edge of the northeast wall they looked down at the Roman camp. "Amos, what are you trying to show me?"

"Can't you see? All those horses we saw them bring in yesterday? They are saddling them."

"Where do you think they're going?" asked Eleazar, still slightly groggy.

"I don't know," said Amos, "but they may think they are coming up here."

Realization struck Eleazar at last. "Check the slides. Wake everybody. I'll wake David. Where is he?"

"In the palace," Amos called over his shoulder as he hurried away.

Since David's wedding, many others had been sleeping in the palace, as a further act of rebellion, as well as to keep watch on the progress of the ever-rising ramp being constructed below. People were hurrying everywhere to prepare for what was to be. He heard voices calling out orders, women collecting children who had been roused by the activity. A chicken scurried out of Eleazar's way as he approached the stairs leading down to the palace.

Lines of men, women, and children were passing rocks, one to the other, refreshing the huge piles used to supply the slides. Their task was to be sure that the reserve piles never dwindled.

The attack began with an onrush of foot soldiers up the cart path. "Look how fast they're coming!" called a Sicarii.

"They're running," another called. "They'll be exhausted."

"Drop the first slide now," shouted Eleazar.

Down it went, rocks rumbling over the rock face of the cliffs. They heard the cries of the soldiers as they were struck.

"Look," shouted another Sicarii. "Some of them have made it past the first slide!"

"Drop the next!" shouted Eleazar. "And start reloading the first! Get to work!"

Down went the second, rumbling across the cart path below. More screams and cries drifted up to Eleazar's ears.

"Here comes a second wave!" shouted the watch from the first position. "Look," he shouted again. "They're kicking the wounded off the cliff."

"Some have cleared the second slide!" shouted the watch from the third position.

"Drop dalet number four, *now!*" shouted Eleazar. "How much longer till Aleph, Beth, and Gimel will be ready again?"

"Aleph is ready now," cried someone above the first slide.

"Look!" cried the watch at the first station. "They've already cleared the first slide!"

"Drop Aleph, Beth, and Gimel again!" shouted Eleazar. "Prepare to fight face to face when they get to the top."

"Beth and Gimel are not yet ready," came the reply.

"Drop them anyway!" shouted Eleazar.

Rumbles and screaming came to his ears again.

"Eleazar!" shouted the watch from the first position. "The horsemen are coming!"

"Get those slides loaded again," shouted Eleazar. "Prepare to drop Hey, Vav, and Zayin on my command."

Eleazar moved to the edge of the wall. Just before the horses reached the section of cart path guarded by the last four slides, he shouted, "Release Hey, number five!"

He listened to the familiar rumbling again and this time, a different kind of screaming. Leaning over the wall, he saw horses with broken legs, others trampling men, stumbling over the bodies of other horses. As he watched, two fell to their deaths over the cliff edge. The fifth slide had stopped the horses.

"Load the other slides, quickly!" shouted Eleazar, though he could see that this was already being done.

"More horses coming," shouted the watch from the first position.

Some of the horsemen from the first charge, Eleazar could see, had not been hit by the fifth slide. But the fallen horses and men above them had blocked their path. On the east face, there was not enough room for the horses to turn around, adding further to their distress. Soldiers below were pushing bodies off the cliffs. The fifth slide was being reloaded and would soon be ready for another drop.

"Drop dalet *four!*" shouted Eleazar.

Rumbling again; again screams, as the horsemen waiting for the path to be cleared under the fifth slide were bombarded.

"Ready on Aleph!" shouted Eleazar. "Drop it now!"

This time, Eleazar saw that none of the horsemen made it past the first slide. The path was strewn with wounded, most of them with broken bones, and blood everywhere.

"Reload the slides! Hurry!"

"They're coming on foot this time!" shouted the watch from the first position. "Running again!"

"Ready to release slide Aleph!" shouted Eleazar. "This time do it a bit sooner, so that none of them gets past!"

Down it went. This time the rumbling didn't seem as loud. Were the cries fainter, or was he getting calloused to suffering? *My ears are filled with battle thunder,* he thought.

"They're coming on the run!" shouted the watch at the first position.

"Prepare to drop Beth and Gimel!" shouted Eleazar. "In case they get past, make sure the rest are ready!"

"They're throwing the wounded off the cliff again!" shouted the watch from the second station. Cries and pleading of the soldiers below told Eleazar this was true.

"If any get by, those falling last will be us!" he shouted. "Any reports of more soldiers on the serpentine path?"

"There's none!" called David. He was running from slide to slide, offering encouragement and assistance, to ensure that the slides were continually supplied.

"They're under this slide again!" shouted the first watchman.

"Drop Aleph!" shouted Eleazar.

"Aleph is not ready!" David cried back.

"Is Beth ready?" called Eleazar.

"Beth is ready, and Aleph will be, in a moment!"

"Prepare to drop Beth as soon as they're under it!" shouted Eleazar.

"They're under it now!" David called.

Eleazar saw that some of the soldiers had cleared the path under the second slide. But instead of releasing the third slide, he ordered a dozen Sicarii down the cart path to deal with the soldiers hand-to-hand. "And stay above the slides!" he shouted after them.

"Why not drop rocks on them?" asked David.

"Those horses came too close. If we drop the last slides for two or three men, we may be disarming ourselves for the next rush of horsemen."

"More men on foot!" shouted the first watch position. "And they're running."

"Hold slide Aleph and Beth!" shouted Eleazar. "Let them think we are running out of rocks. Wait till they're under slide Gimel, then drop both Gimel and Dalet."

"They're under me now!" called the watch from the second station.

Eleazar watched and waited. "Drop Gimel and Dalet, *now!*" he shouted.

The first watchman called out again, "Another large group of horsemen!"

"Get Gimel and Dalet loaded! Fast!" shouted Eleazar. "Ready to drop Aleph! Ready? Drop Aleph now!"

The first of the horsemen vanished under a hail of rocks.

"There are foot soldiers with them!" shouted the first watchman. "They're clearing a path with staffs, levering the bodies out of the way!"

More horsemen streamed up from below, racing past the fallen bodies and clearing a path for those to follow.

"Drop Beth!" shouted Eleazar. "Prepare to drop Gimel and Dalet again!"

A cry from behind was almost lost in the noise of the battle.

"David!" shouted Eleazar. "Who's watching the snake path? Try to take them with arrows before they get to the first slide. Amos will replace you! Get Aleph and Beth reloaded, fast! More are coming! There, yes! Drop Gimel now!"

"Six horsemen have cleared Gimel," called the third watchman.

"Hold Dalet and Hay in reserve and prepare to drop Vauv and Zayin!"

"More foot soldiers are coming, leaping over the bodies of the fallen!" shouted the first watchman. "And more horses behind them!"

"Ready to drop Aleph!" shouted Eleazar. "Drop it now!"

"The horses are stumbling over the rocks and bodies!" the first watchman in the position called out. "More footmen are coming."

If Silva continues this, thought Eleazar, *we will kill his entire army!* "Prepare to drop slide Beth. Reload Aleph and Gimel. *Fast! Fast!*"

From the other side of the plateau, Eleazar heard David shouting orders and encouragement, the rumbling of slides being released, and the screams of soldiers as they fell to their deaths. "Ready on Beth!" he shouted. "Drop it now!"

"Madness!" came a voice from behind him.

Eleazar turned to see Harai, clothed in white cotton, facing him.

"Madness!" he repeated. "Stop this madness!"

"No more are coming!" shouted the first watchman. Eleazar could hear no more of the battle on the other side of the mountain. Had the onslaught stopped?

"There will be a stench around here in about two days," laughed Amos.

"Yes," said Eleazar.

Amos followed his gaze. Harai was holding his hands slightly away from his sides, palms facing them, almost in an attitude of blessing. What was that Essene up to now?

"Hear me!" Harai shouted.

All those within earshot stopped talking and turned to face him.

"Hear me!"

All were silent now, listening.

"Thus says the Lord: **'I am. God Almighty, am I named by you.'**

"Says the Lord: **'In many tongues I am named, and with many names you call Me. The Children of Itzchak name Me and in their tongue, they call Me. The Children of Ishmael name Me and in their tongue, they call Me.**

"**'All My children, separated by tongues, name Me with the same name in their own tongue, for I am One. I am not many, but One.'**

"Thus says the Lord: **'My children are as the stars in the sky, innumerable. Try to count them and you will learn this is true. My children are innumerable as the grains of sand under your feet. Try to number them, and you will believe.**

"**'My children contain the greatest beauty of all that is beautiful, and their faces are fair as is the face of their father. Behold their faces, and you will know awe. Behold their faces and you will know Me.'**

"Thus says the Lord: **'I weep for My children, for their faces are turned one from the other; for they know one another not, and dwell together in anger.'**

"Thus says the Lord: **'A gift I have given to all My children, the Children of the One. In My great love for them, I have given; in their great hate, I have taken away. My gift for them I have hidden, that they may know that I am the Lord, the One, the Echad.'**

"Thus says the Lord: **'My gift for them, my joy, I have protected from their hate. With Zayin I have protected it. From their hate I have given it succor, that they may know it not.'**

"**Therefore,** says the Lord: **'Return to Me and give up the hate which causes you pain. Turn your faces one to another and know that you are all My children. Turn your faces one to another and you will see that I am in you. You will see the face of the Father looking back. Return to Me and know that you are all My family. All peoples are of Me, and in Me are all peoples. And when you do so, I will return to you the gift of My joy. I will recall My weapon, and I will share with you that which makes you one. I will reveal that which is lost, and you will know that you are one, even as I am One, *Ha Echad.*'**"

All who heard were weeping silently. The mountaintop was quiet, but for the moaning of the wounded from below. Those watching over the paths kept their vigil.

Harai turned and started for the north end of the plateau, to the descent to Herod's palace. To Eleazar, it seemed that Harai was glowing in the early light of morning. He followed Harai, caught David's gaze, and motioned to him to come along.

The two followed Harai through the main gate to the baths, then down the stair to the room of fire, where Harai stopped and faced them.

"Where are you going?" asked Eleazar.

"I return to my Source," said Harai, "as I told you I would."

"Do you mean you are going back to your mother?" asked David, convinced that the old man had completely lost his mind.

"I return to my Source, as all of you will, eventually. Only I choose to go now."

As David and Eleazar watched, Harai's brightness seemed to increase. Only then did Eleazar realize that they had brought no torches with them and should be in complete darkness. The light in the room came from Harai, and on either side of him were two lights, still dim but gradually increasing in intensity.

"Do you see light?" chuckled Harai.

"Tell me what the light is," said Eleazar.

"If you look within, you will know."

"As always, you answer with riddles. What are you, Harai?"

"I will tell you," said Harai. "I am what you are: a man."

"But you are different. Why are you glowing?"

"Instead, you should ask, 'What are we?' Then I could tell you what I am."

"All right then," said Eleazar. "I will play this game with you. What are we?"

"We are the joy of God, continuously emanated from His overflowing joy. Just as you felt the joy of the sun, so you are also His joy. What makes me different is my accepting this fact, and the joy I return to Him in this knowledge. Where I am about to go, you can go also, if you but turn your attention to this truth and give up the hatred which fills you."

Harai closed his eyes and raised his face slightly, as though to feel the warmth of sunlight. His smile deepened as the lights on either side of him grew brighter and merged with his. Then the light began to fade, until David and Eleazar found themselves in complete darkness. Harai was gone.

22

Zayin

Jerusalem 1990 C.E.

Johnny B. Lewis was seated at an outdoor café on the Via Dolorosa in Jerusalem. He could hardly believe he was really there. Prill had insisted that he come with him. The weather was hot and dry. The street was crowded with all manner of people in clothing ranging from shorts and tee-shirts to black robes covering the wearer from head to foot. The waiter was wearing a happy medium between the two extremes, jeans, button-down collar and kippa, or prayer cap.

Dr. Prill plopped a newspaper in front of Johnny. "Read this article," he instructed, heading for the restrooms. The newspaper was *Ha Aretz,* one of the few English language papers in the Holy Land. Prill had highlighted the headline of an article near the bottom of the front page,

"*MASADA: Levi Believes Ark may be under the Baths.*" A sub-heading read, "*Excavations to Begin Today.*"

So, thought Johnny, *this is why Prill has been so agitated today. He's afraid it's going to be found.* As he waited, he read the article that explained that Dr. Jacob Levi was professor of archeology at a University in Haifa. He had headed up numerous digs in Israel, and when he did he usually found something of significance. Levi had been searching for the Ark for decades, with no luck. Now, the article said, because of certain Essene writings found at Masada, he felt he knew where to look.

"What do you think of that?" asked Prill, returning and sitting down, grinning at Johnny. "Will he find it?"

"If it's where you say it is, he may very well."

Prill's grin faded. "We need to skip the trip to Gethsemane today and go straight to Masada."

It was at the ticket station for the bus trip to Masada via Jericho where Johnny first spotted them. Prill was getting change for the tickets when Johnny tapped him on the shoulder and said, "Look over there."

"What is it?"

"Those men. Do you see them?"

"All dressed in white?" Prill asked with a look of concern.

"Yes. And the long braid over one shoulder."

"Ignore them. Let's get going. Our bus is about to pull out."

Both men boarded the bus behind them. The other passengers ranged from tourist types like Prill and Lewis, to women and children, to a pair of Israeli soldiers carrying machine guns. The two men in white took seats near the rear of the bus. Johnny had a hard time keeping his eyes off them. It seemed that he could feel them watching him.

Were they following them? Or was Johnny just a little paranoid?

"Dr. Prill, do you think the Essenes still exist?" Pulling him back from his thoughts was getting harder and harder. "Dr. Prill?" he repeated.

This time the professor heard Johnny. Looking a little startled, he asked, "What makes you ask that?"

"These guys dressed in white, with their hair braided like you described. The first time was at the Dome of the Rock. Remember, I pointed one out to you, and you said to be quiet? Then the two at the bus station? You said to try to ignore them."

"Oh, them. Are they still around?"

"Yeah, them! They're in the back of the bus watching us."

"I suppose they may still exist. Who knows? Josephus says they moved to Damascus. There's no further mention of them in all of history."

"Come on, Dr. Prill. Are you hedging? Tell me what you know."

"Okay, but there isn't much. They do still exist. I just don't think those two guys are Essenes. They're probably some kind of Arabs or something."

"Do you think the organization today is the same organization?"

"Yes."

The bus bounced and jolted on the uneven pavement. It had no air conditioning, and the day was very hot. One old lady, carrying a small cage with two chickens in it, got off at a small kibbutz. Johnny was relieved to be rid of the smell.

One of the white-clothed passengers in the rear of the bus seemed to be dozing. The other was watching out of the window as the bus jolted along.

Letting Prill wander back to his thoughts was a mistake, Johnny realized. *Now I'll have to crawl back into his mind to get his attention.*

"Dr. Prill!"

Johnny took his shoulder and shook it gently. Prill turned and looked at him. "What?"

"What do you expect to find at Masada?"

"Ruins."

"Do you think this Dr. Levi will be there?"

Prill's expression changed to one of concern at the mention of Levi's name. "I suppose he will be there. Otherwise I wouldn't feel so drawn to Masada, all of a sudden."

"You feel drawn there? Why?"

"I'm not sure, but as we get closer, I become more certain that's where I'm supposed to be right now."

The white-clothed man behind them had awakened from his doze. Both the might-be Essenes were watching them, even listening, it seemed to Johnny. It made his skin crawl to feel that they were being followed like this. Who could the men be?

"You don't think this Dr. Levi will actually find it, do you?"

"It's possible. I met Levi once in Paris, years ago. He's an adventurer out to pave his own path to glory. He's very smart but not worthy. If he's not worthy, he won't find it. He's an Athiest."

Johnny began to feel that he and Prill were becoming the center of some kind of intrigue, with Levi, a self-serving adventurer, about to discover the long-lost Ark of the Covenant; and Prill on a one-man crusade to keep it hidden—and members of some fanatic, modern-day Essene sect behind them, probably ready to snatch the Ark the moment it was discovered. "Masada has a military installation today, doesn't it?"

"Well, I wouldn't say it's a military installation, but there are definitely armed guards there. They use it for training soldiers sometimes. They often bring new recruits to Masada to point out the trouble the Jewish people have had in holding their own nation. After all, Masada is the last place where Jews stood as a free people in their own land before the Great Dispersion 2000 years ago. It's a very important place for Israelis, and it *is* guarded."

"So, if the Ark is discovered on Masada, it will at least be in Israeli hands, will it not?"

"It depends on who finds it," Prill said wryly. "You remember the Essenes had certain, err, abilities?"

"Maybe I should ask those guys in the back of the bus if they're Essenes?" Johnny suggested with a grin.

"Maybe you should just ignore them," Prill replied.

The mountain seemed enormous. Not like the Rockies or the Cascades, but standing up out of the low hills around it, it seemed bigger than it was. Tan-colored rock, with a little vegetation here and there, hanging on for dear life. There was a cable car to the top, but Dr. Prill insisted on walking up the serpentine path.

"Dr. Prill," Johnny told him, "you know I don't like heights. Look at how narrow that is!"

But Prill wouldn't consider anything less than a walk to the top. Most of the way Johnny was as fearful as Belius had been, hugging the wall, trying to keep one hand on the sheer rock face, and avoiding every loose pebble.

All at once, Prill began stopping every few steps, to tell about someone who died here or fell from there. He pointed to the place on the wall where Harai was seated when Silva shot an arrow at him. Prill wasn't to be hurried! "I've wanted to climb this route for a long time, Johnny. When I was a kid I used to dream of this path, but didn't know where it was, or what the dream meant. Bear with me, it's not much farther."

"Aren't you concerned about getting up there as quickly as possible? What about Levi? What about those characters on the bus? They took the cable car!"

The view was terrific, but every time Johnny looked, he got dizzy. Several places along the way were so narrow, he crawled on his hands and knees, the camera hanging from his neck and sometimes dragging on the ground. "If you want to walk back down, you go it alone," he panted at one point. "I'm taking the cable car when we come back."

Prill didn't seem to hear. When Johnny looked up again, the professor was almost fifty feet ahead. He was holding his face high, and didn't even seem to be looking where he stepped. Johnny stood and tried to keep up with him, but he just couldn't. By the time Johnny got to the top, Prill was completely out of sight.

There were tourists of all shapes and sizes, and many tourist buses at the base of the mountain. Some appeared to be archeology students. There was even a troop of soldiers—both men and women, since every able-bodied young person has to serve time in the Israeli armed forces. With their machine guns, the women looked just as fierce as the men.

Johnny discovered there were more white-clothed men with braids, about six altogether. They seemed to be gathered off to the right. Johnny could see Prill just ahead of them.

He could see that Prill was listening to a talk being given by a guide apparently supplied by the government. Seemingly distressed, Prill kept looking off to the left. Following his gaze, Johnny saw a rope hand-rail strung beside a flight of stairs leading downward into darkness. Above it was an electric cord, meaning that there were probably lights down below.

The white-clothed men were working their way through the crowd around the tour guide, trying to get close to Prill. Johnny started working his way closer also. As he did, the tour guide droned on: "On the last day of the siege, Silva had the tower wheeled up the ramp and mounted there. The soldiers climbed the tower with a battering ram under a rain of rocks and arrows from above. But they were now high enough that the Romans could return fire with arrows and cross bows. This kept the Zealots back from the wall somewhat.

"At the top they started battering the stone wall with the ram. It probably gave way easily, but behind the wall the Romans discovered a second wall, a wooden one. They immediately went to work on the second wall with their battering ram, but this wall was built differently.

"It was a double wall. There were two wooden walls built close together with the area in between filled with dirt. The dirt absorbed the shock from the ram. The Romans couldn't break through it.

"Silva ordered that fire be set to the wooden wall and soon they had a roaring blaze going. But then the wind changed, blowing the smoke and fire back into the Roman's faces. It drove them back down their tower like frightened rabbits. The Jews on Masada cheered and sang hymns of praise and thanksgiving. 'We are saved!' they cried.

"Then the wind returned to its earlier direction and the wall burned down. The Romans decided they had had enough for one day and that they would return in the morning and finish the job of re-taking Masada from the Sicarii.

"When they returned, they discovered that the people of Masada were all dead. They preferred death to being taken back to Rome as slaves. Josephus reports that the men killed their families and then each other. Rather than commit the sin of suicide, and rather than allow their wives and children to become slaves in Rome, they would rather commit the sin of murder.

"Seven were discovered hiding in one of the caves. There were two women and five children who hid rather than die. They told the story."

Just before Johnny reached him, Prill ducked down the stairs. Johnny tried to head him off but was waylaid by a flock of Israeli children led by a schoolteacher, all chattering in what sounded like Hebrew, with lots of *sh* sounds and glottal fricatives. Before Johnny could reach him, Prill was out of sight.

A guard tried to stop Prill. Johnny had gotten close enough to hear Prill say, "Don't worry, it'll be all right." He gave the guard's arm a friendly pat.

When Johnny got past the children and reached the top of the stair, the guard smiled at him and repeated, "Don't worry it'll be all right."

The white clothed men were right behind him. Johnny had managed to get between them and Prill. *Who are they? What do they want?*

Johnny hurried down the stairs. Stone walls were close around him. He heard voices off to his right, and continued toward them.

Johnny found Prill at the entrance to a sizable room, lit by several bare electric bulbs. In the room were four students and one man, aged around fifty. They were speaking English. The room had been divided by thin white strings with small red ribbons on them. The strings separated certain areas near the far wall, laying out where the digging was to take place.

Prill seemed stranger than ever, bigger somehow. The students had Prill's full attention. Johnny guessed that they were part of the team of archaeologists and that the older man was Dr. Levi.

Johnny gasped. As the white-clothed men gathered around him, they too showed shock. Prill stared incredulously as Levi walked through a large hole in the wall. Seven large blocks of stone had been removed and were stacked on the stone floor. As Levi stepped through the hole, he dropped what looked like a metal detector with, "Well, well. This has certainly done its job."

He withdrew a flashlight from his belt, turned it on and pointed it ahead of him. "Yep. Here it is! Ingrid—bring that camera over here."

One of the students stepped toward the hole. As she did, all the others, including Johnny, Prill and the white-clothed men stepped forward with her.

Johnny could clearly see inside the hole. Levi was standing beside a large chest-like box with ornate carving around the rim and sides. Hebrew letters were engraved into the wood in a script Johnny had not seen before. On the top of the box were two figures finely carved in gold, facing each other. As he concentrated on seeing it better, he could just make out that the figures had what looked like wings held out before them. Then Levi's flashlight caught the luster of the gold, a profanity of battery-driven electricity despoiling its ancient solitude. But in its glow, Johnny could see the fine detail of the carving. He could see the gold carved hair on the heads of the two figures. He could see how their wings almost touched, but not quite. The carrying poles were still in the loops fixed to either side of the chest, cracked and warped with age.

Levi was transfixed by its beauty. Gradually he seemed to get hold of himself and he said with gathering volume, "Now. Now it will be *my* name which will be connected with this treasure, for all time." Then he reached out to stroke the golden wings of the two figures. As he reached for it, Prill and several of those dressed in white, almost in unison said, "NO!!"

Their voices were an order, a warning, a pleading that he not despoil it with the touch of his hand. They looked and spoke as one in their determination that the Ark not be desecrated.

Levi's hand stroked the gold, as though he had not been listening. Then he unhurriedly removed his hand and turned toward the group waiting at the mouth of the opening. His face held an expression of surprise. He opened his mouth as though to express his awe, but whatever words he was about to utter, no one will ever know. Dr. Levi was dead before his body struck the floor.

All leaped backwards in shock. Then two of the students rushed to the body. The girl Dr. Levi had called Ingrid, screamed. Then, although Dr. Prill had not spoken, they all stopped and looked at him. "He was not a Kohen," said Dr. Prill, matter of factly. "He was not worthy. He should never have touched it."

"He didn't believe the stories about it," from one of the students.

The men in white were beginning to recover themselves. They were working their way toward the hole in the wall with furtive glances at the students and Prill and Lewis. It seemed to Johnny that they were confused as to what action to take, and they were trying to figure out what to do.

"Let's all get over here and start putting these rocks back in place," said Prill, starting toward the first one.

"Put the rocks back in place!?" exclaimed Ingrid and the other three students. "Certainly not!!" from Ingrid who appeared to have been some sort of assistant to Levi. "This belongs to the Jewish people and will certainly be turned over to the State of Israel."

"It certainly does belong to the people of Israel," agreed Prill, "and to Jews all over the world. But the time is not yet right for it to be revealed."

Prill had begun to glow. Johnny was shocked. He had learned to see auras as a teenager but he had never seen one this bright before. Prill continued, "There is still too much conflict in the world. Brothers still condemn brothers with violence for trivial differences in dogma, over money and land, over petty belief systems. If the Ark is revealed now, it will be nothing more than another bone of contention. It will instigate conflict rather than peace. The time is not yet right. When the time is right Adonai will return it to its people. You and I will not do it."

Prill's brightness was increasing. "Come now. Help me replace the rocks."

"I will not," stated Ingrid flatly. "I will also definitely not keep my mouth shut about it, so if you do manage to hide it again, it won't stay hidden for long."

Prill moved toward her. The white-clothed men also began coming up to her from behind and both sides. Prill stopped a few paces away and raised one hand slightly. "Be at peace. There is no need for concern. Everything is going to be all right."

Ingrid stopped objecting. A look of peace came over her face and she stepped back from the hole. The other students did the same, one of them taking a seat on one of the seven rocks.

It took all six of the white-clothed men and Johnny Lewis to lift the rocks back into place. They were large and cut longer than a cubit, each probably a little over 500 pounds. The students watched in amazement as the hole was closed again. When it was done, Prill walked slowly past each of them whispering softly to them.

The students left the room, walking quietly, single file. One of the white-clothed men approached Prill and pointed at Johnny. "Will you quiet his memories too? And what about us?"

So that's what he was doing, thought Johnny. *Quieting their memories. What an interesting expression.*

Prill's glow had not diminished. He seemed to be growing distant, not only in his tones but his appearance as well. "Are my brothers a danger to the secret place? I think not. You have done well. You who Watch for the Morning may go. Keep your Watch. *Shalom.*"

One by one they walked past him with a soft "Peace to you my friend."

Prill, absolutely glowing, stroked the wall with his hand, then walked around the room, pulling up the stakes and strings tied to them. When he had them all, he gathered them together and flung them into a far corner. Returning to the area of the wall they had opened, he patted the stones again, as though feeling the energy of the Ark behind them.

Johnny felt panic rising. "Dr. Prill, what is going on? What are you doing?"

Glowing brighter than ever, Prill turned to face Johnny, who could barely see his face. "You don't get it yet, do you?"

"Get what?" he asked, apprehensively.

"I didn't fully understand until I got here myself. I am Zayin. Seven. The Weapon. The bodies they found in this room, the ones in the slide show, were David and Soo-ooni. I am Zayin."

"You are the weapon?"

"Now you understand. But one thing you haven't yet grasped: You were not David, and Soo-ooni was not your wife. You only thought so because of the guilt you felt about your present-life divorce. You must resolve that somehow."

Prill was beginning to fade. He was still there, but his light was thinning, and Johnny could see the wall through him. It seemed as if Prill wasn't really there anymore, but Johnny could still hear his voice, and thought he could make out a little of his face.

"What else don't I grasp yet? There must be more. Why am I even here?"

"You have not yet remembered that you are Hjet, the number Eight, the Fence. Even so, I must now pass the baton to you. Come and take it from my hand."

Johnny saw Prill's hand extending from the light. Hanging from it was a leather cord, with an ankh, silver in color, on the end. "Take it now!" Prill said. "I have to leave."

Johnny took it from him. The ankh bore the figure of a bird, with its bill extending down the main stem. Clustered at the breast of the bird were four smaller birds.

When he looked up again to speak to Prill, there was no one there. Just as Johnny reached the doorway, he seemed to hear Prill's voice for one last time.

"*Shalom*, Hjet."

****

Lancaster, Pennsylvania 1995 C.E.

There was an investigation, of course. Levi's death was ruled a heart attack. His students who were present at the site of the dig verified that nothing else out of the ordinary had taken place. Prill's disappearance resulted in yet another investigation. For awhile, Johnny was even suspected of doing away with him. Marge Kauffman still accused him of foul play every time she saw him.

Johnny leaned back in his old wooden desk chair, propped his feet on his desk and smiled at the memories of Prill at Masada: long-haired, white-clothed men following them, Levi the adventurer who didn't believe in God or that the Ark could hurt him. Almost five years had passed.

And so. What does a clergyman do when he leaves the clergy, Johnny thought of the old inside joke. *He goes to work selling life insurance, of course. One sales job to another. A planned pitch substituted for a canned pitch. The certainty of death instead of hope for Pie in the Sky when ya Die. What flavor, Johnny? Apple? Strawberry? Peach? How do ya pitch Gimel, Christ, without Judaism? Impossible! Life Insurance pays a commission instead of guaranteed poverty. The work day is only five days instead of seven. And the next number? Eight. Forget that thought. It makes no sense.*

His experiences with Prill had become surreal to him, a mishmash, confused and confusing. *Why am I thinking about this again, now? It was Wainwright that did it, last night.*

Old Lloyd Wainwright had called Johnny to help him work out some settlement options on an ancient life insurance policy. An old sea captain in his eighties, Wainwright still delivered yachts and new shrimp boats as far as South America. Although his weatherbeaten face was deeply lined, his eyes were still blue and lively. His eyes danced when he greeted Johnny at the door of his home.

The house was a modest Cape Cod bungalow, with a semi-detached one-car garage that Wainwright used for a wood shop. Johnny felt chills when he saw Wainwright's gold ring, engraved with the figure of a pelican.

If Wainwright noticed Johnny's reaction, he said nothing, but invited Johnny to see his workshop in the garage. Inside were many wood sculptures and carvings in various stages of completion. The floor was covered with sawdust, the walls lined with press-drills, miter boxes, saws and every kind of carving device. On the table lay a cedar carving that was not quite finished. A bird with four fledglings clustered at its breast.

Wainwright stood there, watching Johnny's surprise. "It'll look better when the polishing is finished," he said. "It's a pelican feeding her young."

"I know," said Johnny. "I'm familiar with this symbol. Mr. Wainwright, do you belong to a certain very private organization, a sort of fraternity?"

"I do, but it's a private club. Not much I can tell you about it," Wainwright said apologetically, "except that no one is ever invited to join."

"Then it doesn't take new members?"

"Oh yes, of course," he smiled. "But it's really not too easy to join."

"Mr. Wainwright, I would like to try. What must I do?"

"How do you even know about us? Is your father a member?"

"No," said Johnny. "I've had some other experiences that got me interested."

"Well, first, do you believe in God?"

"Yes."

"Next, what you have to do is ask to join, which you have already done." Wainwright's eyes turned cool. "Now, do you have some token by which you think you should be recognized?"

Johnny untied his necktie, unbuttoned the top of his shirt, and pulled out the silver ankh that he had been wearing since Prill handed it to him on Masada.

Wainwright's eyes widened a little as he observed the image of the pelican engraved on the base of the jewel. "That'll certainly do for a token. Now, you need a word that will tell us if and where you will fit into our order."

"I am *Hjet*," Johnny said. "The number eight."

GLOSSARY OF NAMES

Abba	English transliteration of the Hebrew word meaning "Father"
Abbi	Could be a short version of nickname
Adameh	The name of the wife of Eleazar Ben Jair
Adonai	English transliteration of the Hebrew word meaning "Lord."
Adrianus	Roman Centurion initially in command at Masada
Aleph-Bet	The Hebrew lettering system, beginning Aleph, Beth, Gimel, Dalet, Hay, Vauv, Zayin, Chet . . . Etc.
Chalil	A type of flute
Claudius	Roman soldier formerly stationed at Masada.
Cleopatra	Queen of Egypt, wife of Ptolemy Dionysius, driven from her throne but re-established by Julius Caesar, 47 B.C.E. Antony was captivated by her and repudiated his wife, Octavia, to live with the fascinating Egyptian Queen. Josephus said Mark Antony was "such a slave to his lust for her . . ."

Eleazar Ben Jair	The leader of the Sicarii at Masada
Epidimo	An Iberian cork farmer who was conscripted into the Roman army in 60 C.E. along with his brother and two cousins. Roman soldier formerly stationed at Masada.
Essenes	A monastic sect or order of Jews of Palestine most powerful from the 2nd century B.C.E. to the time of the Great Diaspora when they fled to the Damascus area and faded into obscurity. Today there is a sect located in southern Iraq who use a name rendered loosely in English as "Nazarean." Josephus said of the Essenes that they were prophets and when they made a prophecy it usually came true. After the fall of the Maccabees around 50 B.C.E. the Essenes moved their headquarters from Jerusalem to Qumran. It is there where they are thought to have authored the "Dead Sea Scrolls."
	Some modern-day Freemasons claim a connection to the Essenes. The Scottish Rite of Freemasonry recognizes the contribution of Essenism in the 17th Degree of the Southern Jurisdiction. At this writing, the 17th Degree is being re-written. It remains to be seen whether the new degree will continue the tradition of its previous form in recognizing the Essenes of Palestine. This degree in its old format was written by the Illustrious Past Sovereign Grand Commander of the Southern Jurisdiction of the Scottish Rite of Freemasonry, Albert Pike. For more information on the Essenes, see Flavius Josephus, *The Antiquities of the Jews* (22 Volumes) and *The Wars of the Jews* (7 Volumes).
Flavius Silva	Named Governor or Procurator of Judea after the fall of Jerusalem, before the fall of Masada to Rome.
Gehenna	The garbage dump at the edge of the City of Jerusalem. Literally, the Valley of Hinnon [Ge-Hinnon] where sacrifices to Baal and Moloch were offered and where refuse of all sorts was cast and consumed in the constant, smoldering fire.

HaSapas	Literally, "The Greek," [Ha = The] [Sapas = Greek]
Harai	Name of an Essene monk. Also alludes to any small hill or mountain with a temple on top.
Herod	There were two Kings of Israel by this name: Herod the Great who reigned from 73 B.C.E.? to 4 C.E. (more or less), and Herod Antipater, 4 B.C.E. to 39 C.E. It was Herod the Great who ordered the slaughter of the innocents at the time of the birth of Christ. It was also Herod the Great who built the summer palace at Masada. Herod Antipater married his brother's wife, Herodias; is famed for being king at the time of the crucifixion of Christ; and, at the insistence of his step daughter Salome, ordered the death of John the Baptist.
Hjarai	The name given to a Jerusalem orphan by the Essenes of Qumran. Also alludes to the offal of the streets.
Iberia	Spain
Itzchak	A common name given to Jewish men. In modern English: Isaac
Jair	One of the Sicarii
Jericho	A city in Palestine
Josephus Matatyahu	Flavius Josephus' Hebrew name. Josephus was the author of a set of lengthy histories of Israel. Formerly the governor of Galilee, until he surrendered to Rome at the very beginning of the insurrection, 66 C.E. The histories written by Josephus are suspected of being slanted to whitewash Rome's crimes against Judea and the Jews. A possible example of that slanting is his accusation that the people of Masada raided nearby villages for food and supplies. The ample supplies laid in store at Masada by Herod Antipater and Herod the Great are well documented, oddly by Josephus himself. There was no need to raid villages in the area. Raids were more probably carried out by the occupying forces of Rome, especially during the siege of Masada.
Judea	The ancient name for modern-day Israel.

Judean	Anything in or from Judea
Kohen	Direct descendant of Aaron, the brother of Moses. According to legend and Holy Writ, only a Kohen could touch the Ark of the Covenant and not be instantly killed.
Machaerus	Another impregnable Roman fortress taken by the Sicarii during the insurrection in 66 C.E.
Maga-Maga	A vulgar Hebrew expression referring to sex. Nice Jewish Mothers probably refer to this expression as "the 'm' words." The hand sign representing this expression is a closed fist with the small finger and thumb protruding, representing two legs, spread wide, with the fist rocked back and forth from the wrist. *Caution: Making this sign in Europe or the Middle East could result in physical injury.*
Malschbach	A delightful hamlet just outside of Baden-Baden in Germany, where the ruins of the Roman baths exist even today.
Masada	A more or less oval shaped plateau with access limited by steep cliffs; located about 60 miles south of Jericho along the western shores of the Dead Sea, a.k.a The Sea of Salt.
Menehem	Leader of the Jerusalem Sicarii
Mesalla	Roman guard formerly stationed at Masada
Mithras	Pagan deity popularly worshiped by Roman Soldiers
Nero	Emperor of Rome at the beginning the Jewish insurrection

Pisidia

A mountainous region in south central Asia Minor in the Taurus Mountain Range, bounded on the south by Pamphylia; on the west by Lycia, Caria, and Phygria; on the north by Phrygia; and on the East by Isauria. Its size is about 120 by 50 miles. Pisidia was known in ancient times for its olive groves and rich pasture lands. A generally isolated region, it was never subjugated by conquerors until the Roman Emperor Caesar Augustus stabilized the area making Antioch, adjacent to Pisidia, a Roman colony and providing roads.

Prill, Paul

Professor of Ministry to the Bereaved

Remus

Brother to Romulus—See "Romulus"

Romulus

Twin brother to Remus. According to legend, Romulus and Remus were the sons of Mars and Rhea Silvia, a vestal virgin who was condemned to death, making orphans of her sons. The boys were adopted and suckled by a wolf and later founded the City of Rome. Quarreling over the plans for the city, Remus was slain by his brother. Romulus was later taken to heaven by his father and was worshiped by the Romans under the name "Quirinus."

Sadducee

A non-spiritual Jewish sect specializing in business.

Salome

The step-daughter of Herod Antipater, natural daughter of his wife Herodias who was the former wife of Herod's brother. It was at the insistence of Salome that Herod ordered the death of John the Baptist.

Sapas

Greek

Saxony

A region in modern-day southern Germany

Shadaih

Hebrew word meaning "Almighty," as in "El Shadaih," or "God Almighty."

Sicarii

Zealots. Patriotic Judeans who organized against Rome. Known for their long-bladed knives, or "Sicari," hence the name.

Svery	A Roman Soldier, conscripted from Malschbach in Saxony and formerly stationed at Masada
Therapeutae	An Egyptian village known to have had Essene activities. According to the modern day Carmelite Essenes, Therapeute was a center for the teaching of the Essenes' healing meditations.
Titus	Son of Vespasian and Vespasian's successor at the siege of Jerusalem after the death of Nero and Vespacian's ascent to the throne.
Tov	Hebrew word used to mean numerous things including "good" and "yes;" example: "Yom Tov," meaning "good day."
Tzaleket	Transliteration of Hebrew word meaning "Scar."
Vespasian	Roman Emperor chosen by his soldiers, Nero's successor. His name is immortalized by the *vespasiennes* [public toilets] in Paris.
Wadi	An arroyo or dry wash. The gutters in the ground left by rain water running off.
Wasserfall	Waterfall
Yacob	A common name given to Hebrew men—Jacob
Yashan	Hebrew word meaning "old."
Yerod	A common name given to Hebrew men. A guard from the temple in Jerusalem—Jerod
Yoseph	A common name given to Hebrew men: Joseph
Zayin	The seventh letter of the Hebrew aleph-bet, meaning "a weapon"

ABOUT THE AUTHOR

Robert G. Makin, PM, 32° was a prolific writer and researcher of ancient history. At the Lancaster Theological Seminary of the United Church of Christ, he acquired a background in what the Pennsylvania Reformed Churches call Mercersburg Theology. His fascination with Christian and Jewish mysticism led him to explore the Qumran Essenes independently and then in association with Free Masonry. Mr. Makin passed away in 2018.